Praise for Fiona Gibson's

"*Babyface* is enthralling. Gib[...] which is at once comic and accurate, exactly captures the lofty and lowly moments of being a new mum."
　　—Adele Parks, author of *Larger Than Life*

"I loved *Babyface* so much I read it twice! Gibson's deadpan style is amazing, and her novel is absolute gold."
　　—Melissa Senate, author of *See Jane Date*

"A fantastic debut. More than funny, it's true."
　　—Louise Bagshawe, author of *The Go-To Girl*

"A bittersweet take on bringing up baby in modern times and a great first book."
　　—*Heat*

"A winsome debut about first-time motherhood."
　　—*Observer*

"Original, funny and engaging."
　　—*Romantic Times*

Wonderboy

Fiona Gibson

RED
DRESS
I N K
™

First U.S. edition September 2005

WONDERBOY

A Red Dress Ink novel

ISBN 0-373-89532-1

© 2005 by Fiona Gibson.

This book is a work of fiction. The names, characters, incidents and places are the products of the author's imagination, and are not to be construed as real. While the author was inspired in part by actual events, none of the characters in the book is based on an actual person. Any resemblance to persons living or dead is entirely coincidental and unintentional.

www.RedDressInk.com

Printed in U.S.A.

ACKNOWLEDGMENTS

Big thanks to Wendy Varley, Cathy and Liam Gilligan,
Jenny Tucker, Kath Brown, Ellie Stott, Marie O'Riordan,
Stephen Amor, Cheryl Zimmerman and Deany Judd
(for being brilliant, supportive friends) and my parents,
Margery and Keith. My lovely writing group: Tania,
Pam, Vicki, Amanda and Elizabeth. Chris and Sue at
Atkinson Pryce, the perfectly formed little bookshop.

For generous help: Arlene at Castle Landcare,
Amanda Huntley, Andy Myles, Patrick Fulton,
Bobby Coulter, Jim "land artist" Buchanan.

Huge gratitude to Laura Langlie, Annette Green
and Beth Scanlon. All at Red Dress Ink, especially
Farrin Jacobs.

Love to Jimmy, for sending me away to finish this
(I worked and worked and only used room service
seventeen times, honest).

For Sam, Dex and Erin, my gang

part one

Children are better than grown-ups at negotiating mazes. They follow their instincts. Adults think they know all the answers, and find themselves hopelessly lost.

—From *The Magic of Mazes and Labyrinths,*
a book treasured by Tod, age five

chapter 1

Requiring General Upgrade

Gorby Cottage. Gordon and Betty bumped together: *Gorby*. This is how people name their houses around here. The fact that they name them at all should send the three of us tumbling back into the car and speeding away in a cloud of relief. But we don't do that. Marcus scans the facade of the house, nodding approvingly, as if he has made up his mind to buy it. Already, he belongs here. This is his concrete hedgehog on the front step. His red front door with the lion head knocker. Big, six-footer Marcus, solid as these cottage walls.

I clutch the sugary hand of Tod, our five-year-old son. He is sucking a vivid green strip that looks like something you'd use to bandage your car's exhaust. He nudges the hedgehog with the scuffed toe of his trainer. Marcus gives me a wide, "this is going to be *great*" kind of smile. It's the kind of smile a dentist offers just before yanking out your molar.

Tod jabs the white plastic button next to the door. The doorbell sounds like the old Avon ad: *ding-dong, Avon calling.* But we haven't come to enthuse over cuticle creams. We are here because this is for the best for Tod, best for all of us.

"I have such a good feeling," Marcus whispers, squeezing my hand.

I don't know why he's whispering, as no one is making any move to answer the door. Apart from us, the only other life-form in sight is an elderly woman in an immaculate garden across the road.

It's a cool, late-September afternoon. Leaves are falling from a gnarled oak at the far end of the woman's garden, playing chase-me across the vast lawn. She's trying to stuff them into a black plastic sack. It's the first time I have seen anyone tidying a lawn.

Marcus ding-dongs again. Tod slides the green strip slowly between his lips as if it's a debit card, and his mouth the cashpoint machine. "Maybe they've forgotten," I suggest, hopefully. "Or they've decided it's such a lovely house that they've taken it off the market."

"It's not lovely," retorts Tod.

"Why are you so negative?" Marcus asks. "Do you know what that means, being negative?"

"Of course he knows," I murmur. He's advanced, his teacher told us, at least in terms of knowing stuff: "That brain of his!" she exclaimed at parents' evening. "Tod's a *mine* of information." Then she moved on to shakier areas—concentration, sociability—and started tweaking her crystal choker in an agitated fashion, and my smile set like cement.

"It means seeing bad things," Tod says, grinning. He has wrapped the sweet around his top teeth, like a gum shield.

Marcus raps the door. I suspect that Gorby Cottage's owners have glimpsed Tod through the floral net curtains, with his horrible sweet and his bed-heady hair, and are lying flat on the floor, behind the sofa, waiting for us to go away. It's a trick I occasionally played when my mother showed up at my flat, awash with martini and shredded tissues, after Dad had left her.

"I'm sure someone's in," Marcus says, crouching to spy through the letterbox.

The woman across the road has put down her sack and is staring at us. I wave, but she carries on glowering.

"I want to go home," whines Tod.

"We're not going home," Marcus mutters, with his face still jammed at the letterbox. "Ro, do you have anything to wipe his hands? We don't want him making everything sticky."

"Peel that stuff off your teeth," I tell him. "Lick your hands, wipe them on your sweatshirt."

"You never have tissues," Tod complains.

I wish now that I had raked a comb through his hair, made him respectable.

A mortise lock fumble comes from inside the house. Marcus springs up. "Keep an open mind," he grits.

But my mind isn't open. It has snapped tightly shut, like a trap, and will remain so until we are safely home, within easy reach of an all-night supermarket, offering papayas, lychees and several varieties of tomato.

Betty wavers in the doorway, frail as grass. She seems to be staring at Tod's green lips. Marcus introduces us, shakes her hand too vigorously and strides right in. In the living room, Gordon is running a carpet sweeper across the violently patterned rug. He and his wife are wearing matching fawn cardigans.

"Marcus Skews," Marcus says, offering Gordon a hand. "Fantastic house. What a lovely village this is."

"It's pleasant," Gordon says carefully.

Tod clusters around my legs like more than one child. "What's that smell?" he asks loudly.

My son is the kind of child who, on the rare occasions when he is invited to another kid's house for tea, barks, "That's a horrible sausage." I give him a gentle nudge in the ribs. Gordon resumes his carpet sweeping enterprise, as if trying to erase the jangling pattern of ferns.

Marcus's voice is too big for the living room. The low-ceilinged room has too many corners, all gloomy and impenetrable. There are so many items of dark wooden furniture—dresser, sideboard, glass-fronted bookcases, all bearing crystal decanters and vases—that I feel like we've blundered into an antique shop, and that one clumsy movement would send the whole lot toppling over.

"I suppose," says Betty, "I'd better show you around."

She treads softly from room to room without speaking. Tod keeps sniffing and sliding his nose along his wrist. I can hear the back-and-forth burr of the carpet sweeper.

"This is just what we've been looking for," Marcus announces in a bedroom entirely done out in pastel pink, giving a marshmallow effect.

The whole house smells of old flowers and pastry. Tod coughs without covering his mouth, and clutches his groin with a felt-tip–stained hand.

"If you need the bathroom," Marcus says pleasantly, "why don't you ask?" My husband was brought up to say "bathroom"—not "toilet" or even "loo"—by schoolteacher parents who use engraved silver napkin rings, even on ordinary days.

In the bathroom a startled-looking doll with a lime-green crocheted skirt prevents the spare toilet roll from being embarrassingly naked.

"What do you think?" I ask Tod as he jets in the approximate direction of the loo.

"Where would I sleep?" he asks, eyeing the toilet-roll doll fearfully.

"In that bright, sunny room, the yellow one, overlooking the street." *The one you're going to love,* I add silently.

"It smells bad."

"No, it doesn't. You're imagining it." I try to give him a reassuring smile, but know that I resemble the molar dentist. I lick my finger and try to flatten his eyebrow—the left one, which flares up defiantly—and examine Betty's toiletries. Talc in a gigantic lavender-colored tin, a litter of puppy-shaped soaps. I can hear Marcus's voice bouncing off the downstairs walls. "Wash your hands," I remind Tod. He turns on the cold tap too hard, spraying the cuff of his sweatshirt.

"But it's different, of course, when you have children," Marcus is telling Betty when we join them in the rickety conservatory. "You've had enough of the city. Dirt, crime, the stress of it all. It's not good for a child to grow up in that environment. Isn't that right, Ro?"

I nod and grip Tod's damp hand. The conservatory seems like a pointless and possibly dangerous addition, built to house a macramé plant holder containing a cheap plastic pot and dead stick.

"When are we going home?" Tod asks.

"In a minute," says Marcus. "Stop asking."

"I only asked once." Tod's lip juts out, his "shelf lip."

Betty shows us the kitchen which she wiped down just before we arrived; it still smells of wet cloth. "Want to look in the shed?" she mutters.

"Is there a shed?" Tod asks, brightening.

"No, thank you," Marcus says, "I think we've seen everything—"

"Please," Tod whines. "Please, *please,* Dad, the shed."

"No, darling," I say. "We've taken up enough of their time already."

"What are sheds for?" Tod demands.

I usher him to the front door and bat his hand away from the doorbell before he can press it. I wonder why Gordon and Betty have a ding-dong bell and lion head knocker when they seem distinctly unkeen on answering the door. Tod is an obsessive button-pusher—he can't help himself. He stomps down the path to the front gate with his index finger still extended. With an absence of any more buttons, he uses the finger to excavate his right ear, and smears his findings onto the front of his trousers.

"Thanks for your time," Marcus says. "We'll be in touch."

Betty nods quickly, and bangs the door shut. Tod, I notice, has a fragment of loo roll attached to his heel. When Marcus catches up to him, he picks it off and stuffs it into his pocket.

"Well," he says, as Tod clambers into the car's back seat, "I don't think we need to look at any more houses."

"Are we staying in London?" Tod asks, as excited as when Betty mentioned the shed.

"No, I mean, this is perfect. It really has everything we could want."

As we drive away I glance at that sign again—Gorby Cottage, spindly black lettering on a varnished wood oval—and imagine Ro and Marcus combined. *Rocus.*

Is London really so awful? By the time we arrive back at Cecil Street, the horseshoe-shaped flowerbeds in the park—usually bleak and battered by feet—have been dusted with brightness. The front of our building sparkles, as if lightly glittered. Even the garbage bin looks more shiny than usual. Everything feels right, in the way that your hair looks especially pleasing on the day you're having it cut.

Tod leaps up the stone steps ahead of us, clearly relieved to be back in our shared magnolia hall with the upstairs girl yelling and banging. Odd words ping downstairs: *You. Pathetic. Out.* There's a deafening clang, like some outsized porcelain object being thrown, possibly a toilet. I shimmy Tod into our ground floor flat where you can still hear the shouting, but not as bad as in the hall.

Occasionally, I glimpse the upstairs girl in the street—she looks like she lives on thin soup—but we haven't spoken since the ceiling incident. Marcus had been working, and left his papers strewn all over the dining table, when water started dripping from our center light. I rattled the bathroom door and said, "Marcus, hurry up, something's dripping."

"You're imagining it," he shouted back. (My husband thinks it's my hobby, collecting nonexistent sounds and smells.)

The small puddle beneath the light proved that I was right this time. "It's *bulging*," I yelled, at the precise moment that the ceiling cracked and splattered downward, dowsing Marcus's papers and laptop with water and sodden plaster. We vacuumed the keyboard to suck out the water, and blasted it with a hair dryer, but it never recovered.

Marcus thundered upstairs and banged on the girl's door. Nobody answered. That night he wrote: *"We shall expect full compensation for damages incurred"* and placed the letter in her pigeonhole. Next morning someone had slipped it, unopened, under our door.

The upstairs girl is screaming now, like her fingers are trapped beneath something heavy and she can't tear them free. Tod gazes upward with his mouth lolling open. Marcus is hunched over the estate agent's details for Gorby Cottage, trying to blot out the noise.

"That house was too dark," I say, over the wailing. "Ceilings too low. I felt squashed. I'm only starting to feel normal again now."

Upstairs, it sounds like someone is bounding from a trampoline onto the floor. That girl is wrecking my carefully planned argument of why we should stay in London forever and how fantastically stimulating city living can be. Marcus looks up from the estate agent's blurb.

"Call this normal?" he asks. "You really want this for Tod?"

"He's fine," I say, weakly. "Aren't you, sweetheart?"

"I'm hungry," he says, wandering to our tiny kitchen, which is really part of the living room, separated only by a waist-high partition.

The shouting has died away. This is the usual pattern. There's the terrible noise, then it stops, as if she and whichever boyfriend it happens to be have decided to calmly make themselves cups of tea.

"You think it's fine," Marcus continues, "all the bullying he's had to put up with? That thing with his eyebrow?"

"Shush," I hiss. "Let's not bring that up again."

Tod emerges from the kitchen, chomping on something that could be loosely termed a sandwich: orange cheese boulders rammed between crusts. To avoid discussing our imminent move to the country, I stalk him to his bedroom. The room is long and narrow, painted leaf green at his request, with space only for a single bed, chest of drawers and shelves housing messy stacks of books. His toys are stored in a drawer under the bed, but he rarely plays with them.

He lies, stomach down, in the skinny space between his bed and the wall. I read once that animals squeeze into small spaces so bigger predators can't get them; it makes them feel safe. I wonder if that's why Tod spends so much time here.

"You okay, love?" I ask.

"Yuh," he mutters.

In his hiding place he has an airmail notepad and a clutch of Biros, some with their ink tubes removed. He has been drawing a maze, a diagram really. That's what Tod does, he draws mazes. They cover his bedroom walls, twisting like nightmare sewage systems.

"Dad really likes that cottage," I tell him.

He nibbles a corner of his sandwich. "Why are we moving?"

"You'll love the country, Tod, I promise." I want to tell him what a wonderful life we'll have in that unsullied village. We'll go for walks on the common, admire its primped shrubs. We will be neater. We no longer wish to live three doors down from a mini-cab office where the drivers switch off their engines when traveling downhill, to save petrol. Sometimes, though, nostalgia surges through me, and we haven't even moved yet.

Marcus and I have lived all our lives in London. It hasn't *suddenly* become terrifying and dangerous. Anyway, we never know what to do with ourselves in small places. We wind up in some quaint village on a house-hunting mission and, after viewing a dinky cottage, read the notices in the agent's window—"Suite Success: for all your upholstery needs including pelmets made to measure"—and wonder what to do next. Our park exploration usually coincides with the heavens opening, so we grab prepacked Spar sandwiches and drive home.

"We can't live in that house," Tod says now, having put down his sandwich, carefully writing "Way In" at the start of his maze.

"Why not?"

"They live there. Those old people with the carpet machine."

"They won't live there when it's ours." I've said it: "when," not "if." I decide then to tell Marcus that we're staying right here. This is *my* flat. I chose it, before Marcus was even invented. Tod has friends—he knows people at least—and we can't uproot him, not at five, when he's just started his second year of school, and has got over the bullying.

I return to the kitchen and heat his milk in the microwave. Babyish, but he still likes it warm in a cup with a spout. And he still owns a ratty stuffed dog, called Dog, which he insists on taking to school in his bag. No one needs to know about these things. Apart from Dog, his milk and his mazes, he'd pass for your regular five-year-old. London isn't harming him one bit.

Marcus is immersed in a TV program about a couple with lightly grilled noses who have swapped their semi in somewhere called Shirley for a crumbling structure on the Greek island of Santorini. The woman has tired, sagging eyelids but is trying to appear brave for the cameras.

"What about my job?" I ask. "I wouldn't be able to commute to Anna's from Chetsley. Someone has to pick up Tod from school."

Marcus keeps staring at the TV. The woman complains that the sand on Santorini is the wrong color; it's gray, volcanic. If she'd known that, they might have picked somewhere else. Sand should be golden, she says.

"Anna drives you crazy," Marcus adds. "You don't even like your job."

"I do," I snap.

"The whole point, Ro, is that you don't need to work. We can't stay in London just because of a piddling job that pays you—"

"I *want* to work. It's not about money."

"Then get yourself a little local job."

What kind of job is little and local? Pelmet making? I can't imagine being utterly dependent on Skews Property Letting. Would I have to ask Marcus for money to buy his own birthday present? Gain permission before purchasing new shoes?

On the TV the Shirley man admits that life will become easier when their house has hot water, and they've stopped missing little things like *Coronation Street* and being able to communicate with people. His wife complains that everyone has a nap after lunch; that's lazy, she says, adding, "You have to give things your best shot. If it doesn't work out, we can always go back to Shirley." Her husband throws her a sharp look when she says that.

Marcus takes my hand, pulls me on to the sofa beside him and kisses me full on the mouth. It feels like such a strange, self-conscious kiss; there are Marcus's lips, and Marcus's tongue, and the Shirley woman on the phone to her best friend in England, sniveling, "Love you, too, Deborah. Promise you'll visit soon."

"Where's my milk?" Tod yelps from his bedroom.

I pull away from Marcus and find my son pinning his maze to the sloping ceiling that looms over his bed. In the bathroom I run his bath, sloshing in thick blue gloop from a pirate-shaped bottle. Tod steps into the tub and assumes his usual flat-on-back position with his hair fanning out in the water.

"Toenails," I announce.

"Oh, *Mum*."

I growl, closing in with the dastardly pink-handled scissors. Tod cannot bear anything being done to him, especially involving scissors. That's why his hair's out of control, flapping all over his face. The back of his head looks quite matted and germy, like a dog's blanket, but dragging him to the hairdresser isn't worth the hassle and bribes of the Haribo sweet variety.

"Toenails," I repeat. He offers a foot, but screws up his eyes as if I might be planning to amputate each toe, one by one, with a rusting saw. He's still whimpering later as he pulls on pajamas and squashes next to me on his bed, breathing spearmint and clutching *The Magic of Mazes and Labyrinths.*

We read at least six pages per night. We've done the entire book countless times, but each evening, Tod flicks open a random page and that's where we start. I always pray that he won't pick the bit about the sexual imagery of Celtic maze patterns, how the curves and coils represent ovaries, wombs and vaginas. If I'd known about that part, I would have chosen a more appropriate book.

"Ready?" I ask.

Tod nods, checking that the toenail clipping has not involved blood loss. He opens the book and passes it to me.

A labyrinth is a maze with only one pathway. In the middle of the original labyrinth, built by King Minas on the island of Crete, lurked the terrible Minotaur. Half man, half bull, this ferocious creature devoured Greek prisoners. When Theseus entered the labyrinth, he unwound a golden thread as he progressed, his marker to help him find his way out.

"What's the mistake in Theseus's story?" I ask.

"There's only one way out of a labyrinth," Tod chirps. "You wouldn't need the thread."

He's right. One pathway, no difficult choices. He traps a yawn with quivering lips, and I kiss him good-night, remembering to take his cooled milk so he won't wake up and slurp from a cheesy cup.

To avoid the Gorby Cottage conversation, I sink into Tod's now-tepid bath water and think about my piddling job. My first task at Anna's Film Archives was to transfer the card index on to the computer so that, when a client wanted to rent a film, we'd stand a vague chance of locating it. Because I could work the computer, Anna seemed to think I had a brain the size of a bus. She would hover at my shoulder, putting me off with her dazzling secondhand dresses and diamanté accessories. Her hair fell in a smooth sheet, like black glass. Soon she had me running the place, with the help of a teenage assistant called Stanley, which enabled her to devote more time to scouring markets for frocks.

Anna isn't a fan of the countryside. Like computers, it brings out a rash and triggers sneezing fits. When Marcus and I started looking at houses, she said, "You'll wear wellies with everything. Hairy sweaters. There'll be no point in phoning you. You'll be out at the Women's Institute."

Now Marcus is in the bathroom with me, trimming his nasal hair with the battery-operated clippers. I pour in more hot water and lie back and wet my hair, the way Tod does. I picture the bulging calves I'll develop, the rucksack I'll have permanently attached to my back, stuffed with Ordinance Survey maps and Swiss Army knives incorporating that implement for prising pebbles from horses' hooves. Then I can't think anymore because the upstairs girl is shouting, *"Help me—get somebody, please."*

"Christ," Marcus says. He turns off the clippers and stomps to the phone. I hear him saying, "Domestic incident. Yes, sounds like it, had this sort of trouble before."

I dry myself, pull on jeans and a sweater—it's hairy, the country is seeping into my wardrobe already—and check on Tod. The noise hasn't woken him. An arm dangles over the edge of his bed, as if testing water.

Two police officers clatter up the short flight of steps, press the upstairs girl's buzzer and run up to her flat. I can hear them above our bathroom: the girl crying, her boyfriend shouting over everyone else, protesting. Marcus opens our door, catching the constable on her way down.

"I'm the one who called," he explains.

"We had lots of calls," she says. Her eyes have sunk into her face, like upholstery buttons. Marcus starts to tell her about our fallen-down plaster, as if she cares about his deceased laptop. "Look," he says, beckoning her into our living room, "it's been replastered but it's still rough as rice pudding."

The constable blinks at our ceiling. On the table lie details for Gorby Cottage, marked with a giant red tick.

"We have a little boy," Marcus continues. "We're having to move because of this trouble."

"It must be difficult," the constable says.

Tod appears like a specter with a pillow-creased cheek. His left eyebrow looks even bushier than normal. "What's that woman?" he demands.

"Go back to bed," Marcus says gently.

Tod glares at the policewoman. His face is the color of Horlicks. "Why don't you have a truncheon?" he asks.

I steer him back to bed as if sudden movements might cause him to fracture.

"Is anyone going to jail?" he shouts.

Later, I find Marcus making penciled notes in *The Commuter's Bible,* a book detailing every settlement within a seventy-mile radius of London and offering vital information about schools, transport links and the likelihood of 747s slicing the tops off your gladioli.

CHETSLEY. Pop: 1,200. Journey time: sixty-five mins. Delightful village with welcoming pub, the Poacher's Retreat, serving excellent Sunday lunches, children welcome. Village-store-cum-post-office, pharmacy, hair-dresser, bookshop-cum-tearoom. Good state primary school in village. See Lexley for commendable state secondary (fifteen-min drive).

From upstairs comes a smash and a scream. "See?" Marcus says, slamming the book shut.

I escape to the kitchen and accidentally stand on a block of Cheddar that Tod has thoughtfully left on the floor. It's now embedded in the bumpy sole of my suede slipper. Cheesy feet. Great.

Marcus's arms are around my waist, his mouth hot on the back of my neck. "Please, Ro," he says, "I can't stand living here anymore."

Even in bed I can't help wondering how I'll get the cheese off my slipper. It turns out that Marcus has been thinking about matters other than the delights of my body because the instant he's finished he says, "I'll call the estate agent on Monday, first thing. Let's put in an offer."

At least I didn't mention the slipper.

chapter 2

Treasure

Marcus was different when we met. He reminded me of a large-pawed dog that gets away with gnawing soft furnishings, due to his visual appeal. This stranger drove a curvaceous blue sports car that clearly did not belong in my street.

He had arrived at my flat because Pip, my flatmate, was moving in with her saxophone teacher. As I would no longer have to endure her endless practicing of scales and blaming the duck-honks on substandard reeds—and, presumably, she would no longer be charged for lessons—this was good news all round. I wouldn't miss her fondness for lurking behind me whenever I opened a book, ruining the funny bits by asking, "Why are you laughing?" On the plus side, at least her sax practice had drowned out the upstairs girl's racket.

Marcus showed up at eight. I pretended that I'd been expecting him, although I didn't have a Marcus on my list. His lips were full and very sexy. He was the kind of man you see sketched on the covers of romance novels, wearing a doctor's coat, pressed against a woman with tumbling hair. My hair didn't tumble. It was—and still is—roughly chopped, supposedly gamine, as in subtitled-French-film gamine. It's the kind of haircut that prompts small children to shout, "Is that a man or a lady?"

I was pretty certain that this man with such a harlotty car wouldn't be interested in renting a bleary room furnished only with a single bed and precarious pine shelving that trembled when you brushed past it.

"When will the flat be vacant?" Marcus asked, handing me a card with "Skews Property Letting—We've Already Found Your Perfect Home" printed on the front.

"It won't be," I said. "I live here. I'm just letting out a room."

He sighed and fished out a diary from the inside pocket of his jacket. "This is Cedric Street."

"No, Cecil Street. You've come to the wrong flat."

"God, I'm sorry."

We stood there looking at each other. Someone else was due at eight-thirty but I didn't want him to go. "I could show you round anyway," I said.

"I don't want to waste your time."

"You're not," I told him. In fact, I had already decided on a girl so meek and tiny that she'd barely be noticeable around the flat. Then again, she might have been into crazed orgies or owned a bassoon. You never can tell.

It was only March, but Marcus had a caramel tan. I wondered if he used one of those bronzing machines that grill you on all sides at once. To stop myself staring, I clattered around the kitchen, filling the kettle and delving into the cupboard to find acceptable biscuits. He used my name a lot—"These are lovely original sash windows, Ro"—and stared right into my eyes as I gave him his coffee, like he'd attended a course on how to look at women.

Marcus said I wouldn't believe the way prices were zooming round here. To illustrate this, he flattened his hand and made it soar, like a plane. I was sitting on a gold mine, he said. The view over the park—where men smacked their pit bulls and couples lay on top of each other, rummaging up T-shirts—were real assets. He glanced at my chest. Men think you don't notice them doing that.

He wandered along the hall to the bathroom, which he virtually filled all by himself. I squeezed in there with him. Sweat tweaked my upper lip. I wished that he'd vacate the bathroom so I could snatch a piece of loo roll and blot myself.

His gaze rested upon a small heap of pubic hair trimmings that Pip must have left on the side of the bath. A gingery nest, like Golden Virginia tobacco. Everyone I'd shown around must have seen them. No wonder only one person had expressed a keenness to move in. I considered making excuses (I'd trimmed my fringe, it was head hair) but my own hair is virtually black, with no hint of ginger, so he'd have known I was lying. Marcus blinked at the trimmings and gave me an amused look. I clung to the grubby light pull.

"Well," Marcus said finally, "if you ever want to let this place out, you know where I am. Call me, Ro, anytime." He smiled, showing brilliant, sharp-edged teeth.

Minutes later I watched from the window as his car streaked away down the street. We both knew I'd call, and not to have him let out my flat. I gathered up Pip's trimmings with a paper-covered hand, and was still laughing as they swilled down the loo.

Until Marcus, I had slept with two types of men: those so delighted to find themselves in bed with me—or, for that matter, with anyone—that it would all be over in a flurry of knickers and youthful panting before they sprang off and called for a mini-cab. Or the tedious lays, when you'd find yourself drifting off, wondering why the central heating system was making that juddering noise and whether you should have "bled" your radiators, whatever that means.

For a while I'd had a purely practical arrangement with Seth, a jeweler I'd met on the night bus who sliced Perspex into crescent shapes to make clumsy earrings. He presented these to me as thank-you gifts. Sex with Seth was pleasant but predictable, like a Meg Ryan movie. At least it ensured a good night's sleep, and was less hassle than getting up to make hot chocolate.

Anna liked to hear about the men who snuck in and out of my life. Some nights—before Tod, before Marcus—we'd find ourselves so bogged down by the card index system that we'd lose the will to go home. Stanley the assistant, a mushroom-colored boy who shunned daylight, would croak a weary good-night. At the slam of the door, Anna sloshed mescal into chipped mugs bearing the slogan "Call Savage Office Supplies for your stationery needs."

Mescal made her frisky and tactile. One evening, she gave me a hug, supposedly for eating the worm from the mescal bottle—she'd bet me a tenner to do it, fibbed that it tasted like fudge—and for rescuing her from chaos, because finally we had transferred the entire index on to the PC. Or rather, I had. Anna had swished about in fuchsia silk, rubbing orange-scented oil into her bony shoulders. She was doing that, slathering this stuff into her freckled skin. Then her lips were on mine. I don't know how it started. A thing went on then with her tongue, and my brain filled with a flurry of helplines and tense conversations with my parents, and I stumbled away to refill our mugs. I had yet to form a meaningful relationship with a man. Bringing women into the equation would make everything doubly complicated.

That's what I liked about Marcus. We slipped into a boy-friend–girlfriend arrangement so smoothly that I didn't need to debate whether we were having a proper relationship or just sex. He phoned when he said he would. We held hands in the street, and talked about how we might spend Christmas. He was well-practiced in bed and maneuvered my legs like joysticks, finding out how I worked.

When we were out, I'd see people glancing from Marcus to me, wondering why such a photogenic male was clutching the hand of a woman who looked as if her hair had been attacked by blunt pinking shears. I could tell they were thinking, *She must be stinking rich or have a great personality,* but I didn't care. I felt sparkly and light, as if I'd been turned into tinsel.

We'd been seeing each other for a couple of weeks when a bouquet arrived at Anna's Archives. The showy combination of scarlet and orange looked like Anna's dresses, in plant form. The card read, "?&%! Love, Marcus," which I assumed was a reference to the indescribable nature of his feelings for me.

Anna found me stuffing the flowers into a glass vase with dirt in its cracks and said, "Darling, you shouldn't have."

My hot cheeks coordinated nicely with the tulips. "Can I go early today?" I asked.

Her eyebrows shot up. They were penciled fir-tree green; Anna had a habit of applying her makeup in the dark. I didn't tell her that Marcus and I had arranged to meet in Green Park at four-thirty. That mescal kissing thing, it was nothing—but I still felt kind of disloyal.

I found him lounging on a bench, eating ice cream from a tub with a wooden spatula. His vanilla kiss landed on my ear.

"I've hidden some eggs," he announced.

"Eggs? What for?"

"Easter treasure hunt. There's half a dozen. Find them all and I'll buy you dinner."

Flowers and eggs. I had never been given so much in one day, not even by Seth, the earring man. But I didn't want to look for eggs. The idea was cute—I valued originality in a man—but I didn't fancy all that bending down and him copping a full view of my backside while I scrabbled in bushes.

"Start looking," he said, scraping the last of the ice cream from the tub.

I started pacing around halfheartedly. "Can't find any," I said.

"You're warm. Getting warmer." I spotted one, its purple wrapper glinting in a patch of bleary primroses. A couple more were stashed behind litter bins. One had been stamped on, so we abandoned that. I found another partially concealed by a prickly shrub that caused my wrist to itch, and searched for the last egg until an Irish setter bounded past, chomping foil. Couldn't chocolate make a dog sick, or even kill it?

Marcus warned me that at his favorite Chinatown restaurant the waiters were incredibly rude and prone to throwing your food at you. All the intimate tables were taken, so we were shown to a vast, glass-topped oval, like an ice rink. The waiter carried away superfluous chairs, leaving just two, several hundred miles apart.

I didn't feel like eating, not after all that chocolate. My noodles had set in a jellied pile. I worried that my seaweed starter had glued itself to my teeth. I watched Marcus, a speck in the distance, fascinated by his succulent mouth as he gnawed prawns.

He talked about work, about his talent for matching tenant and flat. I couldn't take my eyes off that mouth. He could have sold me a lean-to shed, reeking of cat wee, under the Westway. After dinner we squeezed into a chaotic pub dominated by heavily sweating girls on a hen night. A drunk woman with mascara-smeared cheeks kissed Marcus on the mouth. He laughed and wiped off the kiss with his hand.

"Sorry," the girl said to me, "I couldn't help myself."

I wanted to take him home. I was trying to be normal but my libido had taken on a life of its own, simmering over the hen party screeches. The bride-to-be, a pale stem of a girl, was dancing furiously on the worn carpet. She swung her pink sequined bag and motioned for Marcus to join her, doing a "come here" thing with her arms. He smiled and edged closer to me. We were jammed on to a PVC chair with yellow foam spilling out of its arms. I wondered, with all the attention Marcus was getting from the hens, whether I should cool off a bit, be aloof. We had only been out four or five times, yet had spent around sixty hours in bed. Maybe we should start doing other things, like visit art galleries, or go shopping.

I examined myself and examined my reflection in the pub loo. A fresh wrinkle ran from my nostril to my mouth. It was a serious wrinkle, almost a crack. It hadn't been there that morning. The stress of the egg hunt or a buildup of sleep deprivation must have brought it on. I tried to erase it by stretching my mouth as wide as it would go. I looked like Munch's *The Scream*. "Need a paracetamol?" the bride-to-be asked, tumbling out of a stall. She delved into her sequined bag.

"I'm fine, thanks," I said, trying to make my face normal and rearrange my hair in the mirror. The wax I'd smeared on had made it look oily, like crow's feathers. My new flatmate was a hairdresser. The tiny, meek girl had told me to rub in the wax, saying it would give better texture. Only after

I'd rubbed it in did she add that you had to shampoo your hair three times to get the stuff out.

I glided out of the loo and gave Marcus an aloof smile, hoping it didn't emphasize the wrinkle.

He stood up and said, "Let's go home."

My insides swirled with Easter eggs, seaweed and wine. I had to cool off, make him realize he couldn't have me whenever he wanted. I had to make it clear that, while I found him amusing and undeniably easy on the eye, I didn't *need* him.

"Okay," I said, "let's go."

And that summer, everything changed. Marcus filled my flat and my life with surprises. I'd come home from work to find a love note pushed through my letterbox. He would show up at Anna's, and we'd take so long over lunch that I'd pull down my sleeve to cover my watch, and stop worrying.

One evening, as we lay in my bed, Marcus said, "Go look in your wardrobe."

I found a suit comprising charcoal trousers and nipped-in jacket, like something you might wear to create a good impression during a court appearance. I didn't need a suit to work at Anna's—I could show up in what the hell I liked— but tried it on anyway, and wore it to work the next day. Anna gave me a confused look and said, "You look like a different person."

Then Charlotte, my small, timid flatmate, disappeared. I came home from work to find her things gone. She'd left the hair wax but no note or forwarding address.

"Why don't I move in?" Marcus suggested as I spilled my woes down the phone.

"You really want to do that?"

"Of course I do."

Did I want him around all the time? It was the sensible thing. His place was rented; he'd invested everything in Skews Property Letting and that swishy car. "It would help me out," I said.

"Ro, I'm not moving in to help you out. I'm moving in because I—"

My heart lurched.

"Because I want to," he said.

I had never lived with a boyfriend, and wondered how the introduction of grocery shopping and the cleansing of bathroom fittings might affect our relationship. That night he came over, climbed into the bath with me and announced that he had called his landlord to give notice on his flat.

Just after eleven, the door buzzer sounded. A woman babbled unintelligibly into the intercom. I peered out and saw my mother, huddled in pastel-pink rayon, being battered by rain. It had to be bad. She didn't just show up like this, without a coat.

We dressed in a hurry and I let her in. Up close I registered bloodshot eyes and a slack mouth. "He's gone," she announced. She lowered herself onto the sofa, giving Marcus a brief nod. He shook her hand, then disappeared to the bedroom so we'd have privacy.

"What do you mean?" I asked. "Gone for good?"

Her mouth was too shapeless to form proper words, but later, over the weakest tea possible—"just *briefly* introduce the bag to the water, Rowena"—I learned that my father's departure had required a passport and his favorite no-factor coconut oil.

"Majorca," Mum said, trembling. "Of all the places."

"But Majorca's yours. Yours and Dad's."

"Don't I know that? He's gone, Ro. Said I should have spotted the signs."

"What are the signs that someone's about to bugger off to Majorca?"

"There weren't any. Nothing had changed. I told him, we've never got on, never liked each other. Why leave me now?"

Mum started crying again into a tissue. Bits fell off, landing on her lap in damp flakes.

Marcus emerged from the bedroom and offered my mother more tea. "Here," he said, handing her a proper cloth hankie with navy blue *MS* initials.

"Thank you, dear," she said. She looked up at him and managed a feeble smile. "I've heard lots about you, Marcus."

She hadn't really heard lots, but she approved of the fragments I'd told her. Convertible car. Property letting. A man who buys smart, grown-up clothes for his girlfriend when it's not even her birthday.

"Majorca was our place, Marcus," she explained. "We had a favorite restaurant, right by the sea. He's probably there now, having the mixed fish special."

"*Your* mixed fish special," Marcus said softly. He patted her arm, squeezing more tears out of her.

Marcus drove home to his own flat that night. I made up a bed in the little room, placed a full box of tissues within easy reach, and spread out Mum's pink dress on the radiator.

"There's one good thing," she whispered. "You've met a decent man at last."

chapter 3

Being New

Tod was right. Gorby Cottage smells. There's a sickly whiff left by Gordon and Betty, along with a pair of medical-looking beige knickers draped over the bath. Marcus thinks I'm making it up. Soon, he says, I won't notice anything because you can never smell your own house.

I can't think of this place as really belonging to us. Gorby Cottage feels like a holiday house, somewhere you've rented for the week. In its current state, you'd be registering complaints with the letting company, taking photos as evidence: close-ups of puddles under radiators and staggering cracks in walls. You might even abandon the cottage and transfer your family to a hotel and fire off a furious letter using words like *furthermore* and mention a solicitor you don't have. Marcus enjoys writing that sort of letter. He keeps copies in his filing cabinet.

And the smell's there, all right. I worry that there's something in the locked cupboard under the window in Tod's room, which we don't have a key for. I called Betty to ask about the key but she just said, "It'll be where we left it." And she banged down the phone as if expecting the announcement that we'd changed our minds, had mistaken the country for somewhere we wanted to live.

"Think you'll like it here, Tod?" I ask.

He is lying flat on his bed on a fuddle of dirty laundry, designing a maze with an island section in the center to make it more complex. "You have to get the queen bee back to her hive," he murmurs. The queen bee has fuzzy black hair, not unlike mine, and is wearing an elaborate crown. At his last school, some of Tod's drawings were laminated and displayed in the entrance hall. They were different views of some kind of castle, built in a tree, encrusted with emeralds to create a kind of glittery pebbledash. His teacher, Emily—they used first names at his old school—grabbed my arm after school and said, "You must come and see Tod's pictures." She led me into the hall, and beamed at the drawings. "Tod calls it a tree palace," she said. "They're incredibly detailed for a five-year-old." On his last day, Emily presented Tod with a pack of glitter pens. I meant to ask for the tree palace drawings, but with the chaos of moving straight after Christmas, I forgot.

Tod is gnawing his pen end, biting off fragments of clear plastic. "Last one I did," he says, "you'd find your way out by keeping one hand on a wall. You'd get stuck at dead ends but you would escape, in the end."

"This one looks difficult," I say, studying the crumpled sheet of A4.

"Yeah. You could get really lost." He flashes an excited smile. "You might never get out. You could *die* in here."

Marcus thinks Tod takes the maze thing too far. "Can't we encourage other interests?" he asked once. "Are those stabilizers off his bike yet? Has he swum a width?" Marcus knows that balancing on two wheels is beyond our son's capabilities, and that my attempts to teach him the breast stroke resulted in Tod demanding to sit on the poolside, where he fiddled with a discarded plaster.

Tod attaches tape to each corner and sticks the maze on the yellow wall above his bed. He stands on the laundry, following the path with a finger, making a buzzing noise, being the bee.

"Don't you think you have the nicest room, sweetheart?" I ask.

"Bzzzzz," Tod says.

"It'll be lovely in summer, so sunny and cheerful. You'll be *so* happy here."

"Did it!" Tod says, arriving at the hive.

"Remember how gloomy and *miserable* your old room was?"

"No, it wasn't," he says firmly.

In fact, none of the rooms here are what you'd call cheerful. The estate agent's blurb acknowledged that Gorby Cottage would "benefit from a general upgrade." Now that it's ours, it has become apparent that "upgrade" does not mean choosing fancy paint colors or a new bathroom mirror, but extensive joinery work, rewiring and damp-proofing.

"It'll feel better," I tell Tod, "when we've put up some shelves. You'll be able to arrange all the stuff you got for Christmas. It'll be just like your old room, but bigger."

Tod flicks dirty socks on to the floor with his toes. The washing machine hasn't been plumbed in yet. When I called the plumber to enquire when he might show up and get the thing working, he said, "Well, not today," and bit into something crunchy.

In the country everything happens in slow motion if it happens at all. Dogs raise hind legs in a can't-be-fagged manner, dribbling rather than creating an arc. Across the road, a spindly ginger cat sneaks through the wrought-iron gate. The leaf collector is out there again, unpegging a sweater from the washing line. It has frozen solid. She carries it into the house by a rigid sleeve.

Tod joins me at the window, twisting the single russet curtain, which hangs by one plastic hook. His hair is the color of rained-on sand, with cradle cap underneath. I have tried olive oil and special lotions but can't budge it. Cradle cap is for babies, like the spout cup and Dog.

He breathes on the window and draws spirals on the steamed-up patch with a finger. His nails need cutting again. Can't have him showing up at his new school with grubby claws. On his bed, next to *The Magic of Mazes and Labyrinths,* is the Chetsley Primary School Handbook detailing uniform—gray trousers, burgundy sweatshirt with oak tree emblem—plus an introductory letter from the head teacher: "I sincerely hope that, with the support of parents, we can maintain an environment in which children can achieve their full potential."

Tod picks at a streak of cream-colored paint on the window. "Why did we move?" he asks.

I open my mouth to tell him: because of what happened at your old school. And the upstairs girl, the fighting. *Because it's better for you, Tod. We've done this for you.* Why can't children be grateful for big things? They greet major gifts— a new scooter, a bike, a picturesque country cottage—with bored indifference. Then they're ridiculously pleased with a sticky rubber lizard to fling at the wall, which cost fifty pence. No wonder their parents can't figure out how to please them.

"Because we'll have a better life here," I say, scooping an armful of laundry from his bed so he can't see my face.

The day that Jill, the head teacher, called me, I took a taxi to school and found Tod hunched in a chair in the office. Jill explained that two older boys had pushed him to the ground during afternoon playtime and tried to do something to his face—cut his eyebrow—with scissors they had stolen from the classroom.

There was a cut on his forehead and scrapes on his knees and shins from where he'd hit the ground. He was sitting by the photocopier, with his shoulders pulled down and his arms tightly folded across his stomach, like he was trying to burrow into himself. His class teacher, Emily, was dabbing the cut on his face with a cotton wool pad. The office smelled of antiseptic.

Jill said, "I can't tell you how sorry we are. It's the worst incident of bullying I've ever seen in this school."

When Marcus came home that night he took one look at Tod and insisted it was time for us to leave. To leave London and make a home in the country.

"It's for the best," he whispered to me after I'd tucked Tod in and read him to sleep.

Gorby Cottage has a box off the kitchen, grandly entitled The Breakfast Room. There's a utility room, which houses our dormant washing machine, and the rotting conservatory, which must have been tacked on to the back of the house when you could do what you liked to old properties. Now you have to contact several stern-sounding organizations to gain permission to remove a concrete hedgehog from your front step.

Upstairs, in the eaves, is our bedroom, Tod's room and a spare room to which Marcus optimistically refers as The

Study. This is where Tod found a block of green sponge, like my mother uses for flower arrangements. Tod places the block in the center of the breakfast table. "That maze I did," he says, pulling up a chair with a scrape, "it's not right. I don't want it flat."

"Right," I say. "You want it 3-D." He nods, stroking the green stuff. "Like hedges," I suggest. I wonder what to offer. Pipe cleaners? Miniature hedging used for toy railway settings? Of course we don't have these things. "We'll get the stuff when we're in town," I say, although we have yet to discover what town has to offer. Lexley is where Marcus will catch the 7:45 to Charing Cross. The *Lexley Gazette,* which we trawled through when looking for a suitable house with the right kind of odor, announces "Man Steals Drill Bit From Garage" and "Oldest Cat In Village Dies," but gives no indication of the availability of miniature hedging.

Tod is unimpressed by his fried breakfast. He has a habit of rejecting meals, then declaring that he's starving, clutching his belly in mock agony, the minute the last fork has been washed up. His neck, I notice, is filthy. My brisk flannel rubs are proving ineffective. He hasn't had a bath since we moved in, as there's no plug. I jammed the plughole with Marcus's black monogrammed sock—sporting an ornate *MS,* like on his hankies—but the water still seeped away.

"Eat up," Marcus instructs. "We're going exploring today. You'll need energy for that."

"Aren't I going to school?" Tod asks.

"You start tomorrow," I remind him.

We looked around the school before Christmas. I had pictured a cottagey building, like a family house, with a garden. But Chetsley Primary is a stark yellow block, like a slab of butter, with a tarmacked yard bordered by chipped blue railings.

"Stop playing with your food," Marcus scolds him. "It's not a toy."

Tod gnaws his bacon, pulling rind from his mouth. "Don't like this egg," he mumbles. Anything Tod does not wish to eat must be removed from his line of vision immediately. If the offending foodstuff has left a slimy trail on his plate, this, too, must be erased. For a child forever marred with felt tip and food particles, he is incredibly fastidious.

Marcus has cleared his own plate and is now wiping out wall-mounted cupboards with a wet tea towel. He takes wineglasses from a cardboard box and tears off their newspaper wrappings.

Sometimes I try to pinpoint precisely when he changed, when he started to step back, away from me. But of course it wasn't marked by one incident, or even a day; he crept away while I was too wrapped up in our new baby to pay proper attention. Tod refused to acquaint himself with his rocking crib and would only sleep in the adult bed. Even when splayed between us, he would wake several times during the night, thrashing and wailing and sometimes spurting milk-sick all over our pillows.

Marcus started to spend the occasional night at Will's, a friend from his octopush team. To get away from the screaming and the sick. "It's important," he said, his face chalk white. "I've still got a business to run, clients to take out. I still have to *function*."

I pointed out that Will's wife had just had a baby, too.

Yes, but Max slept in his own bedroom. You'd hardly know he was there.

As I curled around our baby, I'd tell myself that everyone found it hard at first, and that this was normal. Tod would soon sleep through the night, in a room of his own, and there would be flowers and eggs again.

★ ★ ★

The fan heater whirs lazily but it's still cold enough for our breaths to come out in pale puffs. Gordon and Betty omitted to mention that we'd need oil for the heating to work. They left the knickers and block of green sponge, but no oil. I suspect that Gordon stuck a pipe in the tank to siphon out the final drops. When I called the oil company, a woman said that someone would show up in the next two or three days. She couldn't be more specific, not with the backlog of deliveries after Christmas and New Year. "Most people," she added, "make sure they have plenty of oil to get them through the festive season."

Ding-dong, Avon calling. Being the only one properly dressed, Marcus answers the door. I snatch his brown sweater from an open bin liner of clothes and pull it on over my pajamas. Two strangers follow him into our kitchen: a woman who, despite it being January, has a bright, sunny look about her, with blond hair piled up on her head, secured by an enormous tortoiseshell gripper. She looks like a holiday rep. In Marcus's sweater, I feel like a root vegetable.

A man with a sharp, pecky nose, significantly shorter than the woman, says, "Hope you don't mind us just dropping in. Carl Griffin," he adds. "My wife, Lucille. We saw you move in. Thursday, wasn't it?"

"I think so," I say. Was it Thursday? With no job and no school routine, the days all fuzz together.

Carl eyes the packing boxes and heap of discarded newspaper. "You've got your work cut out," he says, shooting air out through his nostrils.

I wonder why they're here. I have never had dealings with neighbors, at least not in a friendly way. Perhaps they want to borrow sugar or are expecting hot drinks.

"Thought we'd say hi," Lucille says. "Wondered if we could help."

I glance at the bin liners and packing boxes and wonder if she means rummaging through our private things.

"Hard, isn't it, settling into a new place?" she continues. "Don't worry, there's plenty going on around here. You wouldn't believe it, for such a small place. So many groups you can join."

She parks her dainty rear on a vacant chair. Is this how people behave around here? Barging in at ten-thirty on a Sunday morning? We could have been doing *anything*. London might have its downsides but at least friends let you know several months in advance if they're planning to drop by. You know by September if anyone's thinking of popping round for pre-Christmas drinks.

"That would be great," I say, wondering what kind of groups she means. I have never belonged to anything, apart from a mother-and-baby gang that strolled through the park every Thursday, among hostile-looking dogs and their surly owners.

Marcus makes tea in a pot. Tod stares at Lucille's head, clearly fascinated by her tortoiseshell gripper. Carl tells us about the superior course at Lexley Golf Club and asks, "Do you play, Marcus? Not that you'll have time at the moment. Complete renovation job, isn't it? Old Gordon and Betty, it got too much for them in the end. I helped out with the garden but there's only so much you can do."

"That was good of you," Marcus says.

"You don't want the place going to rack and ruin," Carl continues. "We're a Best-Kept Village, five years running. You'll have seen the plaque in the High Street." He tries to make eye contact with Tod, who is stretching bacon rind like elastic. "Very brave," he adds, "taking this on. Our place, we bought it new. First owners. Carpeted, everything. You get great deals on a new build."

"We wanted a challenge, didn't we, Ro," Marcus says.

"Yes, that's right."

Lucille spots Tod's slab of green foam on the table. "You like flower arranging, Ro?"

"God, no. Tod's planning to cut it into strips to make little hedges."

"That's very creative," Lucille says. "I can see you're artistic, Tod. You've got pen on your cheek." Tod leans back, as if scared that she'll try to wipe off the ink.

As she gets up to leave, Lucille says, "We're in Briar Avenue, number seven, right on the corner. You must pop round for coffee."

I thank her and wonder if I might just do that: how else do adults make friends in new places? Stalk likely candidates in the street? Place an ad in the *Lexley Gazette*: "Wanted urgently—friends. All applicants considered"? Women use their babies to help them befriend other mothers, but Tod is past the baby stage. He slurps his drink noisily—the spout cup's only allowed at bedtime—and wipes a milky moustache on his pajama sleeve.

Lucille delves into her cream leather shoulder bag and hands me a card that reads, Fab-U-Look. Lexley's Premiere Pampering Experience. "I'm in the beauty business," she explains. "Massage, eyelash tinting, waxing—we're doing a special on bikini wax if you team it with the half leg. After moving house, you'll need a treat. Give yourself an overhaul."

I must look like Gorby Cottage, requiring general upgrade. Our survey mentioned rising damp and woodworm boring through sub-floor timbers. I wonder if Lucille can do anything about that.

When they've gone, the house sinks into stillness. Then I

notice other noises above the fan heater's whir: creaks and the occasional rattle, which Gorby Cottage seems to be making all by itself.

I thought the countryside was supposed to be quiet.

Marcus's journey to work will take one hour and twenty-five minutes door to door. He has treble-checked train times, driven to Lexley to study the layout of the station car park, and bought a new laptop to use on the train. The trip to Chetsley Primary School is simpler—a five-minute walk—yet I have been up since six-thirty to ensure that Tod is ink-free and respectable. I wet his hair to flatten the fuzz at the back, then blow-dry it to create an eerie, helmet-like effect. He looks like a mannequin in a 1960s children's clothing store. I could muss it up—rub that waxy stuff through it—but don't want to risk botching his do even further, not on his first day.

He stands stiffly before me, as if his school uniform is made from cast iron. I wrap my arms around him and say, "You're going to be fine."

"Yuh," he mutters.

A few minutes later I take his hand as we cross the road. We pass the perfect white cottage where the old lady chases runaway leaves. The oak's thinnest branches wave lazily. Tod still hasn't spoken as we reach the Best-Kept Village plaque, which announces Chetsley's winning years in elegantly carved script, with space underneath for future triumphs.

We pass the Poacher's Retreat, which offers Sunday lunches (children eat free), real ales and famous warm baguettes. Clusters of hanging baskets smatter the white walls, awaiting spring flowers and praise. It's the kind of welcoming country pub to which my parents would occasionally take me and my sister, Natalie. Whatever the weather, we would eat in the beer garden. Dad, a Yorkshireman with a passion for cheese, would always order a ploughman's. Natalie and I would be allowed shandy, and try to act normally as our heads turned light and fluffy as pompoms. Then my parents would squabble over whether we should or shouldn't leave a tip on the outside table—"Anyone could pinch it," my mother would snap—and we'd rattle back to London in the Morris Traveller.

Tod glances into the bookshop where homecraft manuals are arranged on a floral patchwork quilt. Outside the grocer's, a teenage girl is counting change in her palm. No one else is in sight. Where is everyone? With a jolt, I panic that I've scrambled my days and it's really Sunday. It's only when we turn the corner, and the yellow school is in view, that we see children and adults ambling toward its gates.

Tod grips my hand harder. Sometimes I'm fooled into thinking that pretty soon he'll be mature enough to play out on his own without tumbling face-first into a fast-moving river or electrocuting himself on overhead wires. His small, rather sweaty hand suggests that he'll still be clutching my legs, and unable to aim accurately while peeing, for some decades to come.

A bald janitor in a fluorescent yellow coat bats children in through the door. Tod's schoolbag slumps too low on his back; I didn't adjust the straps properly. I wish I'd taken more care over assembling his lunchbox: plain egg sandwiches, Penguin biscuit, flattened packet of Quavers. Don't children judge each other on the contents of their lunchboxes? These are rural kids. Country people like their grub; Anna warned me that her sister had gained a stone within two months of leaving London. Even her hands looked pudgier, Anna said. She had become addicted to steaming pies and slabs of cow, served in pubs like the Poacher's Retreat.

Tod's new teacher, Miss Cruickshank, stands in the playground with her arms firmly folded across a shimmery red blouse. I wonder what she and Tod will make of each other. After the eyebrow incident, when things had settled down, Emily at his old school called me in for a meeting. She plucked at her crystal choker and said, "Tod's fine, academically, but developing social skills—interacting with classmates—is just as important as learning. Perhaps you could help him at home." She had a pained look, as if she were swallowing pins. I wanted to ask, How do you make a child interact? Maybe I didn't talk to him enough. That day, after school, I fired questions at Tod and suggested fun things we could do, like make a lime-jelly pond with sweets dropped in, until he escaped to his bedroom and feigned sleep.

Miss Cruickshank waves from the main entrance. Tod's feet are nailed to the pavement. "It'll be okay, sweetheart," I whisper. "Look, here comes your teacher. Doesn't she look nice?"

Her flat brown shoes smack firmly on the tarmac. Tod presses himself into my hip. I wish Marcus were here, that he'd gone to work later just to do this bit with me. Nettie, his business partner, could have manned the office until lunchtime. But Marcus is frightened of Nettie. She is his mother's age, his mother's friend, and stumped up most of the cash to set up Skews Property Letting on the condition that she could bag the best desk, the one facing the window, and scare clients with her deep-frozen phone manner.

Miss Cruickshank's blouse is right in my face now, billowing like a windsock. She smiles briskly and says, "Hello, Tod. We met when you looked round the school, remember?"

He stares up at me, blinking rapidly. I kiss his cold, clammy cheek, and she guides him into school, this woman swathed in flammable fabric and lavender scent who I know nothing about, who could be *anyone.* That's the trouble with school:

one hundred thirty kids, controlled by six adults. What kind of ratio is that? Teachers have neither the time nor the inclination to discuss your child's progress at the end of every school day. You're not allowed to creep into the playground with a stepladder and press your face against your child's classroom window. Twice-yearly reports, and parents' evenings are your lot. Anything could go on in that building.

I should go home now and tackle the list of tasks necessary to transform Gorby Cottage into a wonderful home to wow my London friends. The school door closes. A latecomer clatters across the playground, princess hair flowing behind her like mist.

Some mothers blub at anything. Seeing their child with a tea towel on his head in a nativity play is enough to have them gulping and mopping their faces on sleeves. I'm not that sort of mum. It's school, that's all. Part of being a kid. And Tod, I remind myself, as tears spill down my cheeks, is just an ordinary kid.

chapter 4

Livestock Nightmares

Suzie lives with her three children. She also lives with Peter, who has barely registered that they have produced these infants of varying sizes, each requiring care and attention or at least the occasional whale-shaped foodstuff flung onto a plate.

Their second-floor flat is in an unloved terrace off Bethnal Green Road, across from a small playground where all the play equipment was deemed unsafe and taken away by the council. When Tod was a baby, I knew I could show up at Suzie's anytime I liked, with my son in a deeply unhygienic state, and she wouldn't start sniffing or telling me off. The chaotic nature of Suzie's existence would make me feel instantly in control and sorted, a person qualified to write authoritative tomes on the correct way to raise children.

In truth, though, it was Suzie who knew how to do things.

During our early weeks of buggy pushing, I would gobble up her childcare tips, such as placing an open bin bag in the middle of the living room, into which your sick child's soiled nappies could be lobbed. She thought nothing of strapping her youngest into a bouncy contraption that hung on the door, and leaving him there for a whole afternoon. Suzie didn't make me feel neglectful for not taking Tod to baby massage classes. "Who needs the massage?" she would retort. "The baby or the mother?" I needed Suzie then, and I need her now, to reassure me that Tod will not be irreparably damaged by being forced into an unfamiliar school, in the care of a teacher in a gigantic red blouse.

"Yes?" Suzie pants into the phone. She sounds like she has a wardrobe strapped to her back.

"Is this a bad time?" I ask.

"Ro, God, I miss— No, you can't have a biscuit, Laura. What am I, a bloody café?"

"Just wondered if you'd like to—" I start, but Suzie can't hear me because a child—presumably Barney, her toddler—is yapping for attention.

"No," Suzie says. "I haven't found the racing car key. If you left it on the floor, I'll have vacuumed it up. Now go away. I'm on the phone to Auntie Ro."

"Want to talk," Barney demands. "Want Ro."

Suzie's voice is replaced by ragged breathing. "Hello, Barney," I say. I like Barney—his nasal emissions fascinate me, those pearly rivulets descending toward his upper lip—but I don't want to talk to him now.

"Just say hello," Suzie prompts him.

A three-year-old doesn't just say hello. He sniffs into the phone and parps the first verse of Postman Pat. "Black and white cat," Barney warbles. "Got apple."

"Have you? That's nice."

"Don't like Ham," he continues. Ham is Sam, Barney's five-year-old brother. "Ham boof me," he adds.

Barney is now trilling the popular French ditty: *"Frere-ah Jack-ah, Frere-ah Jack-ah, Tommy-voo?"*

"Please put Mummy back on the phone," I plead. "Suzie?" I shout, hoping she'll hear me. She has probably collapsed from exhaustion. Suzie has devised intricate games to enable herself to lie down. She plays hospital and has the three of them wiping her forehead with moist J-Cloths and pressing plastic stethoscopes to her thudding chest. Suzie was not one of those mothers who blubbed at the gate. When Sam started reception class, she had to force herself to think about sad things—starving children in poor countries—in order to look suitably grief-stricken.

"Am in bedroom," reports Barney.

"Barney," I say sternly, "I need Mummy." I can't shout at him; he's only a kid, and not even mine. Only when there's a clonk—he must have dropped the phone—can I safely assume that he's wandered away to tip jigsaws out of their boxes.

"Ro, you still there?" Suzie says.

I phoned to confess that Marcus and I have made a dreadful mistake; that we had no right to thrust our son into the care of Miss Cruickshank when he had formed a fragile attachment to Emily with her crystal choker. But Suzie is telling me, "Weird thing happened yesterday. Sam gets himself stuck at the top of the helter-skelter in the park—you know how I am with heights? How I get nauseous just looking down from our balcony? He won't come down the steps or the slide. He's screaming his head off. Everyone's staring at me—bad mother—thinking, why isn't she up there, rescuing him?"

Why do women do this? Mothers are meant to support each other, offer mutual stroking and comments like "You're

right, there's no point in changing his nappy two hours before bathtime, it's a waste of Pampers." Secretly, though, we're
thinking: *How tight is that?*

"This woman sees Sam," Suzie continues. "She's pregnant,
massive, but hares up the helter-skelter and carries him down
under one arm."

"That was kind of her."

"You know the strangest thing? It turns out she bought
your flat."

I wonder if she complained to Suzie about the banging
upstairs, or has been flooded out.

"And she said it's perfect," Suzie adds.

Putting my flat on the market felt like preparing to have
some bodily part amputated. Marcus, however, could barely
conceal his delight. For a man who had marched into my life,
zooming his hand like a plane, saying, "I have clients desperate for places around here," he was remarkably keen to move
on. I'd suggest buying home accessories to spruce up the flat,
like a magazine rack or wastepaper bin. "It's not worth getting anything new," he'd insist, soon after he'd moved in. "We
won't be here much longer. We'll buy somewhere that really feels like ours."

I had no intention of moving, and told him so. Our one
trip to IKEA resulted in Marcus deliberately losing himself
in the warehouse section, and becoming so incensed with
the buffeting checkout queues that he stormed off, saying
he wasn't wasting another minute of his life to pay for some
pistachio-colored candles and a shower curtain patterned
with fish.

Our excursion to a bathroom showroom was equally
fruitless. I only wanted a new loo. The seat had parted company from the main toilet bit and could send you pinging

off to the left if you didn't have your wits about you. Marcus stared mournfully at a loo that possessed a removable ring for easy cleaning. I sat on it to demonstrate its elegant lines, but felt stupid, worse than lying on a mattress in a bed shop. I regretted bringing him to the bathroom place. I'd been right to worry about living together; one minute you're kissing in the backs of taxis. Next thing you're staring at bidets. There's no in-between bit. Couples should be warned about that.

Marcus wanted to move soon after the wedding, then during my pregnancy, before I became too unwieldy. Then I *was* too unwieldy and we decided to wait until after the birth. Tod started crawling, then walking, and then demanding sets of one hundred felt tips, never to have their lids replaced, and we were still there. Whenever something went wrong with the flat, like the fighting upstairs or wasps taking up residence in the bathroom extractor fan, Marcus would give me a look that said: *see?* And he would point out that the proceeds from selling my place would convert neatly into a stately home in the country, or at least a traditional cottage with garden. It might be ten thousand miles from a Pret a Manger, but at least we'd have *space.*

Colette and Jamie looked round the flat on a mellow autumn afternoon. I envied Colette because she was French, rather than resorting to having her hair violently chopped in order to look French, and pregnant. She also had the good fortune to be with a man who caressed her neck in front of strangers, and might soon be living in my flat.

Jamie was handsome in a stubble-jawed way and enthused over the rooms' generous proportions. Colette nibbled a ginger biscuit she had fished from her pocket. "I'm in property myself," Marcus said. "This area's going to boom."

I prayed that the upstairs girl would start yelling or let her bath overflow and destroy our ceiling again, but all that trick-led down to our flat was polite applause from her TV.

"You're so lucky, overlooking the park," Colette said.

"Park?" I scoffed. "I'd hardly call it that. Full of crazies and vicious dogs. You can't move for broken glass. Last weekend someone spat at you, didn't they, Marcus?"

"Not *badly,*" he said.

"We're leaving London," I rattled on, "mainly for Tod, our son. He had a bad time at school last year. The schools," I added, eyeing her belly, "are the worst in the country."

I was acting like a salesperson in reverse. Jamie glanced out of the window, possibly looking for evidence of vicious dogs and spitting, or even vicious dogs spitting. Marcus looked as if he could have gladly stamped on my foot.

"For a baby, though, it's ideal," he said. "Huge living room for playing in. You could leave the pram in the hall. It's safe around here, and everyone's friendly."

Colette stroked her bump. "The baby's kicking so much," she announced. "He's excited. He wants this to be his home."

Marcus has left me a list of people to call: builder (to assess risky-looking back wall), plumber (to rectify foul laundry situation), electrician (quote for rewiring and replacement of circuit board), damp-proof specialist (builder to give quote also) and oil man. We still have no heating. We do have hot water, due to an antiquated instant heater, but you can't spend all your time flat out in the bath. Already, it has become apparent that my city attire is inappropriate for life in an outsize, stone-built fridge. Anna was right about the country dictating one's wardrobe. I must invest in more knitwear, heavy-duty socks, and possibly a balaclava.

To put off all that phoning, I mooch in the garden that skirts all sides of the cottage. As I know nothing about gardening, I'm not sure if everything's dead or just sleeping. All I can identify are standard roses jutting defiantly from frost-hardened soil.

Round the back is an expanse of pink gravel, the oil tank and a damp wooden shed. We could convert it into a den for Tod, or maybe Marcus will use it, turn into a shed man. From the front garden I watch the woman who tidies her lawn. She is clipping a bush, despite this being January and, presumably, little growth going on. I know that much about plants. The woman stops pruning and stares, blatantly, the way children do just before they say something awful like "That man's fat." I give her a friendly wave. I'm expecting a little wave back—maybe she'll show up later with some of those old-fashioned cakes, the kind with millions of currants hiding beneath a pastry roof—but she turns away and violently scissors the bush.

Lunchtime, and I'm back at school. Not *at* it exactly, not in the building, but resting gently against a privet hedge, a vantage point from which I can view most of the playground and hopefully merge with the greenery in Marcus's mossy sweater.

In the playground, children mill around in sweatshirted clumps. I try to relax and look casual, but everything about me feels shifty. My fingers are coiled. My toes feel moist in my new lace-up boots. I am gripping a village store carrier bag, to create the impression that I have just popped out for bread, apples, bicarbonate of soda (a Marcus tip for cleaning the fridge), jam doughnuts (Tod's favorite), and bottled water because the stuff from our taps tastes of metal. I've just *happened* to stop by the school. However, I am aware that this kind of behavior alerts the attention of vigilant parents and even the police. In fact I probably have the sinister air of someone planning to offer one of those children a drugged toffee, and my actions are being noted in a lined jotter by the school secretary.

"Suspicious-looking adult spotted lurking outside primary school." It wouldn't look good in the *Lexley Gazette.*

What's worse is that I can't see Tod anywhere. A cluster of boys is tackling a ball, but there's no shoving or shouting. They are playing tidy football. A skinny figure is huddled in a far corner of the playground, trying to wedge his foot between the railings, and for a moment I think it's Tod. It's the kind of thing he might do, trap his foot deliberately. Attention seeking. Requiring careful maneuvering to free the foot, or a screeching power tool to slice through the railing. But when the boy swings round, a wide mouth gyrating all over his face, I see he's not Tod.

Maybe he's hiding somewhere, eating his shameful egg sandwiches in a toilet cubicle with the door bolted shut. What if he's tried to come home and was unable to remember the simple layout of the village? Is he lost, blundering around the common, or even trying to make his way back to London? The *Gazette* reported that a boy of Tod's age had become separated from his mother outside Finesse Bathrooms in Lexley High Street. A guard at Charing Cross spotted the lost boy. The kid had boarded the train at Lexley and wound up in central London without anyone wondering who he belonged to. He and his mother were pictured on the front page of the *Gazette*. She blamed modern life. "It comes to something," she said, "when a little boy is left to fend for himself."

I gaze at the playground where none of the kids look like my son. The carrier-bag handles are digging into my palm. These boots are too big; the woman in the outdoor shop in

Lexley assured me that I needed this gigantic size, as I'd be wearing them with thick socks. Tod laughed and said, "They look like coal miners' boots."

"Waiting for someone?" asks the voice at my ear. It's Lucille, the woman who popped in yesterday and suggested that I join clubs. She is job-interview groomed. Her makeup is the natural kind that doesn't look like much but involves an extensive lineup of beige cosmetics and takes several hours to apply.

"Just shopping," I say. To prove it, I give the carrier bag a little shake.

She smiles prettily. Each tip of her fingernails is white. I wonder why anyone would bother to do that.

"It's natural to worry," she says, kindly.

"I'm not worried at all. He'll be *fine.*"

There's so much of her perfume that I suspect she buys the soap, body lotion, all the toiletries in a matching scent. It's called layering your fragrance. My mother does it, but with Yardley's Blue Grass.

"Of course he will," she says. "It's a lovely, friendly school."

Then I see Tod. He is sitting on the ground, at the school's back entrance, even though it's been raining. Tod never liked playtimes; that's when stuff happened to him. He prefers being at a desk, with Dog stashed in the schoolbag at his feet.

He's waiting to be let back in. He'll have a wet patch on the seat of his trousers and Miss Cruickshank might think he's had an accident.

"Is that Tod," Lucille asks, "over there, in the corner?"

I nod. "It's difficult for him. He's—"

I wonder what to tell her. Before we moved, I made an appointment for Tod with our GP, and forced Marcus to accompany us. After Dr. Cohen confirmed that our son had an ear infection, I asked for a private chat. Marcus took Tod to the waiting room. "I'm worried about Tod," I told Dr. Cohen. "There's something…different about him."

"What sort of different, Mrs. Skews?"

I stared down at my black leather boots. "I'm scared that he might be autistic."

Dr. Cohen smiled and shook his head. "From what I've seen, he's a very bright, articulate boy with an excellent vocabulary and a keen interest in—"

"But he's obsessive. You know what he's into? Mazes. Is that normal for a five-year-old boy?"

"Children are obsessive. They fixate on one thing, then eventually move on to something else."

"And he won't make friends. Apart from his cousins, he's not interested in other children."

"I'd say," Dr. Cohen said gently, "that your son is just very selective."

I look at Lucille now, then over at Tod, who's still hunched at the back entrance. "He's very shy," I murmur.

"Leo, my boy, was a loner, too," Lucille says. "They grow out of it. He's ever so popular now, thank goodness."

I drop the carrier bag and march across the road, toward the blue railing, and yell, "Tod!" I'm waving madly but he doesn't look up. The football boys swing round and gaze at me.

Lucille's heels click toward me. "Come on," she says, patting my arm. "You'll make it worse for yourself."

"I just want to talk to him."

"I'll make you a coffee," she insists. "Can't have you going back to that miserable house."

Carl and Lucille bought the show house with all of its furnishings. "Curtains, dining suite, sofas," she says, showing me into a peach and cream living room. It smells freshly polished. The shaggy off-white circular rug is so smooth, its pile all lying in one direction, that I suspect she grooms it. I pull off my boots and hope that my socks don't create foul marks on the carpet.

"It saved touring endless showrooms," Lucille continues. "That's when the kids were younger, more of a handful." She places two coasters depicting Constable landscapes on the polished coffee table. "Adele's ten now, Leo's nearly fifteen. Do their own thing. Adele, she's in the top majorette troupe in the county. What kind of sports does Tod like?"

I want to say football, but on the one occasion that Marcus took him to a match, Tod kept asking why men were waving flags and didn't watch the game at all. "Tod's not really sporty," I tell her. "He's more indoorsy. Likes being in his bedroom, at least he did, in our old—"

"I'm sure he'll grow into it," she cuts in. "There's a football club in Lexley—and karate, gymnastics, swimming club…plenty for young, active boys."

"I'll see what he thinks, when he's had the chance to settle in."

There's a boy on Lucille's mantelpiece, gilt-framed with extremely large teeth, like he has borrowed a set from an older person. This must be Leo, who is, no doubt, good at football, as well as being immensely popular. Beside him, Adele is tightly packed into a maroon and silver majorette's outfit. There's a picture of a teenage couple perching uncomfortably on a dry stone wall. The girl's pale hair is so tightly permed it looks knitted. The boy's looks like it's been subjected to an ill-advised lemon-juice-blonding experiment.

"Who's that?" I ask.

Lucille sets down mugs bearing mottos—"boss of the house," "world's best mum"—on the coasters. "That's me and Carl. Childhood sweethearts. I'd just started training at his mum's beauty salon."

I am always amazed when a couple has stuck together after witnessing each other's most unappealing phases: overenthusiastic sebaceous glands and a fondness for door slamming. At that age, mid-teens, I was still practicing kissing on my forearm and wearing an extra pair of knickers to hold up my tights. I didn't even have a proper boyfriend, let alone a future husband. Yet, as a way of conducting one's love life, the Lucille/Carl tactic is pretty low maintenance. No harrowing breakups or mistaking one-night stands for the beginnings of proper relationships. Maybe I should have tried it myself, persisted with Kevin O'Driscoll, the sarky individual who wrote dirty things about me on the school corridor wall.

Lucille sinks into the peach leather sofa. "I'm off on Monday and Friday mornings," she says. "You're always welcome to pop round for coffee." Even through her layered perfume, she can sense my settling-in difficulties.

As I leave, Lucille scribbles a list of useful numbers: doctor, dentist, taxis, plus the best restaurants in Lexley. "I'm happy to babysit," she adds.

"That would be wonderful, thank you."

Perhaps a night out might help me to recover from a lack of spousal Christmas present. Marcus said, "I thought we'd agreed, being so frantic with moving. We said we'd just buy something for the house." Did Gorby Cottage deserve its very own present?

Back home, I pin Lucille's list next to Marcus's list on the kitchen wall. I notice that she put the doctor's number first, with double underlines. On top of feeling too new, I must look really ill.

Conversation one, on the way home from school: "How was school, Tod?" Silence. "Were the other children friendly?" Silence. "What's Miss Cruickshank like—did she look after you?" Sniff, scratch of the groin. "Want a doughnut? I've bought you some. Tod, will you answer me, please?"

"What?"

"I'm asking you about—"

"A doughnut," he repeats, jabbing our door buzzer even though nobody's home. "What kind?"

"Jam." I once made the mistake of buying him a ring one that he rejected because there was nothing inside it, just a hole.

"How do they get the jam in?" he asks.

"With an injection thing. A kind of syringe, I suppose."

"Who does it?"

I let us into the house. "I don't know. A jam injector?"

Tod flings down his bag. I unpack his barely touched lunchbox and wonder why I don't just cut out the middleman: prepare sandwiches, and lob them straight into the bin. Tod plonks himself at the table, receives his doughnut.

"It's fine," he says, sinking teeth into the sinister combination of refined sugar and saturated fat.

"What, school?"

"No. Doughnut. Good."

Conversation two: "How was your journey?"

Marcus says fine, drops his briefcase in the hall, and nods at Tod who is watching an educational program about dinosaurs. I have postponed his bath because he wanted to see an entire triceratops skeleton being reconstructed from one genuine rib.

"Not too tiring?" I ask.

"No, why—do I look tired?"

"No, you look fine. You look *great*."

He gives me a quick smile, and a kiss on the cheek, an afterthought kiss. "What are you up to tonight?" he asks.

"More unpacking."

"Me, too." Marcus checks how much longer the dinosaur thing will be on because there's a program about Second World War code breakers at seven-thirty. "School okay, Tod?" he asks over the dinosaur commentary.

"Yuh."

Clearly, country life is enhancing our ability to communicate as a family.

That night, at around two-ish, I hear a voice and think it's Marcus sleep talking, which he does sometimes, although rarely in any identifiable language. Then I realize it's coming from Tod's room where something awful is happening. I land on the bed beside him. He's bolt upright, his eyes two gobstopper balls, gleaming with tears and real fear.

"It's coming," he shouts. "Get over, over the wall. *Help* me."

I hold him tightly to my chest and say, "Nothing's coming, Tod. It's just you, me and Dad, in our new house."

"Cows," he pants.

I lift him out of bed. His pajamas are damp with sweat. He has also had a small accident, so I pull off his pj bottoms and carry him into our bed. His hair is soft against my chin, his arm featherlight around my waist.

"They were coming," he mumbles.

"Just a nightmare, darling."

Not any old nightmare, a *livestock* nightmare. My son is allergic to the country.

chapter 5

The Trouble with Tod's Hair

After being abandoned by Dad, my mother was approached by a man with an oblong moustache and powerful upper arms in an electrical appliance shop. The shop was having a closing-down sale. Mum was hoping to buy a cut-price washing machine as her old one had expired, choked with the contents of pockets—coins, keys—and the underwires from bras. At first she suspected that this man was being friendly through sheer desperation, and was trying to flog the last of his stock. But when he offered to plumb in the new machine himself, at no extra cost, she detected a glimmer of something.

Perry Spencer plumbed in the machine, accepted Mum's offer of a sandwich made with tongue from a tin, and started taking her to dances. Before long, he had brought round his extensive collection of board games, and moved in. My mother had her hair lightened to beige and bought black dresses shot through with metallic thread. They swapped the end-of-terrace she'd shared with Dad since before my birth for a grand, pink-roofed bungalow with an en suite bathroom and kidney-shaped pond in which koi carp meandered dolefully.

Mum and Perry had a small wedding ceremony in a huddled gray church in Barnet and a buffet afterward in a restaurant called Expressions, done out in jarring blues and tangerines. Marcus entertained Mum's friends from her flower-arranging group with tales about the property letting business. "Such a charming man," gushed a lady with a pewter-colored bob, patting his wrist. Women couldn't help touching Marcus. He had a knack for knowing when to wind up an anecdote and let the other person speak.

My mother introduced him to fierce Aunt Isa, saying, "And here is Ro's brand-new husband, Marcus. Isn't he super?"

The way she said it, it sounded like I'd had several, inferior husbands before him.

Marcus laughed in an embarrassed way, which heightened his appeal. Aunt Isa scowled at him over her gin and tonic.

In fact he wasn't brand new—we'd been married nine months, and I was already pregnant—but he still whispered rude things in my ear. I snorted, causing Perry's frail father to lurch up from his chair and clutch the buffet table for support.

My sister Natalie kept glancing at my tidy bump and smiling conspiratorially. She had already produced two children of her own, and made child rearing look as easy as introducing new cushions into the house. Her husband Hugh, a bounding PE teacher, gripped a glass of sparkling water and chatted politely to Perry's workmates from the now-defunct electrical appliance shop. Natalie's children, Daniel and Jessica, piled half-eaten vol-au-vents into an ashtray.

Mum's friends from her flower-arranging group raised glasses and emitted sparkly laughter whenever the newlyweds kissed. Mum and Perry were flying to Cyprus next morning. Not Majorca, obviously. Those mixed fish days, they were over.

Monday. "All settled in, Rowena?" My mother is the only person who uses my full name. She also phones at inappropriate moments: as I'm lacing up Tod's school shoes or at story time when we're seconds away from the climax of the Minotaur bit. Right now I am gripping the phone while trying to locate Dog, which Tod will not go to school without. I have made every effort to locate the wretched creature, thus making us late. Mum is making us doubly late.

"I'll call you later," I say, peering behind the living room radiator for evidence of the missing stuffed beast.

"It sounds like your house needs an awful lot of doing," Mum says, launching into her old houses versus new houses debate. "Why couldn't you have bought a modern bungalow?"

"I need Dog," whines Tod.

"We wanted something with character," I say, wondering why I am even bothering to explain at 8:55 a.m., the precise moment at which a shrill school bell is piercing the air. Mum seems to have forgotten that school even exists. These days, she doesn't behave like a parent at all, or even a grandparent. She sends Tod money instead of real presents and thinks nothing of fondling Perry's backside in front of her impressionable grandson.

"You could have saved yourself all this trouble," she adds.

"It's no trouble," I insist, as if the modernization of a century-old property is equal, in terms of effort required, to fetching a glass of tap water.

"I hope you know what you're doing."

"I'm not doing the work myself, Mum." I march into the kitchen where Tod has returned to the table to mash wet Golden Nuggets in their bowl. I glimpse the tradespeople list on the wall. Marcus stuck it there, to propel me into action. He used to get me going with heart-shaped pralines hidden under my pillow. Now he tantalizes me with stern messages that read: RO! URGENT. CALL OIL.

"Old houses are always going wrong," Mum continues. "Look at the drainage at our old place. That silly bend in the big pipe, always clogging up with solids."

"I know that," I sigh. "It's hard to figure out what comes first. You want to get a wall plastered but realize they'll hack it to bits to squirt damp-proof chemicals in."

"Where's Dog?" Tod shouts. He has yet to comprehend that it is impossible to conduct a face-to-face conversation, and another by telephone, simultaneously.

"Perry says it sounds like there's something wrong with your foundations," Mum adds.

Perry knows everything, although neither he nor Mum has seen Gorby Cottage yet. "The thing is," I tell Mum, "old houses last forever. The walls are at least a foot thick."

"Why do they need to be that thick? It's a family home, not a castle. You're not likely to be besieged."

"Mum, I've got to go. We're already late for school."

"School?" she trills. "Why didn't you say?"

"Of course Tod goes to school. It's the law."

"Call me when you're in a better mood," she huffs. "This old house is obviously affecting your temper. You never used to be like this, Rowena."

I replace the receiver.

"*You* put him somewhere," Tod thunders.

"Put what somewhere?"

"Dog."

On the school walk I add to Tod's displeasure by delivering a lecture about being responsible for his own possessions. Then I catch sight of his drooping face, and feel myself shrinking. Mean mother, barking at a child who has just started a new school. A tear slides down his cheek. I am the size of a pea.

"What's your school topic about?" I ask, to take his mind off Dog.

"Jipshuns."

"What?"

"Egyptians."

Ah, one-word territory. Designed to cause further shrinkage, until mother withers to a barley pearl.

"You like that?" I ask.

"Yuh."

"And you're getting along with Miss Cruickshank?"

"Yuh."

Coming from Tod, this counts as crazed enthusiasm. And the Egyptian thing, that's promising. Could become a hobby. Kids should have a range of interests, not just one. I decide to drive to Lexley, locate the library and bring home books about sphinxes and tombs. Photocopied images of dead people wrapped in filthy bandages might cheer up his bedroom.

After dropping off Tod, I put off the evil business of calling tradespeople by going for a walk. Isn't that what you do in the country? You follow signposts and footpaths. But there aren't any paths, at least not leading from Chetsley Common, where I had expected to find a sign depicting a walking figure and the instruction Walk This Way.

City dwellers assume that country people spend weekends striding through woodland and catching trout with their bare hands. They forget that most of the countryside actually belongs to someone, possibly someone with slavering dogs and a gun. On these walks, we townies expect to stumble upon bushes bearing fat bubbles of fruit, not realizing that raspberries do not burst forth in January. Even if they did, we would have nothing to take them home in. We never have the right kind of receptacle.

I march across the common, following the stream in which some bright spark has placed a traffic cone—not Best-Kept Village behavior—but reach a dead end where there's only beer cans and a barbed wire fence. Marcus calls my mobile, asking if I've been on to the oil man yet.

I must get a job.

At teatime, Lucille taps on the window and invites herself in. She has brought me a present, a scented candle called "Tranquility," which they had loads of at the salon and couldn't sell. "I thought it might make you feel at home," she says.

"That's lovely, thank you."

Tod looks up from his workbook and says, "You know what the ancient Egyptians did? They pulled out dead people's brains through their nostrils, with a spike."

Lucille laughs nervously.

"His school project," I explain. "Want to show Lucille your hieroglyphics, Tod?"

He shuts his workbook and slaps a hand on top of it.

At the front door I whisper, "Take no notice of Tod. He's just iffy with people he doesn't know very well."

"He'll grow out of it," she says, as if it's that simple.

Tuesday. Despite having no paid job, and therefore no real excuse, I still have masses of unpacking to do. Moving house forces you to admit that your precious possessions, which you lovingly wrapped in newspaper and gently placed into tea chests, amount to one gigantic pile of crap. Now I wish that we had decluttered before moving, binning pointless items donated by Marcus's parents: the three-tier cake stand, several yards of navy moon-patterned fabric, a Corby trouser press.

Actually, the trouser press came as part of the package when Marcus moved into my flat. It has, to my knowledge, been used only once, during Tod's fourth birthday party. Unbeknownst to the adults present, Suzie's eldest kid Laura used it to heat up a pizza. The resulting four-cheese mess was a nightmare to scrape off, and Laura received a non-PC slap on the backside.

You cannot bin your belongings when they have been transported, at great expense, by courteous removal men.

I leaf through my folder of drawings: scribblings from my illustration course, most of the same disheveled boy. I'd draw him carefully, then place a second sheet over the first so I could still see my lines, and sketch him as fast as I could so he'd look like a real boy who couldn't stay still. I wanted to make a book of this boy with his dirty face and hair flying, but my lecturer said I'd never make a living out of that.

I stuff the drawings back into their folder, wishing I was more like Natalie. She doesn't live in one gigantic lost-and-found depot. As I unpack boxes of cheap vases and candlesticks I remember Natalie's warning: "Clutter is bad for your heath, Ro. It collects dust and triggers allergies."

"But I don't have any allergies," I told her.

"That doesn't matter. All your stuff—it's blocking your *chi*. It can't flow properly." I knew that already. My *chi* had always been bunged up. Natalie is so efficient that you can feel the *chi* whooshing through her house, whipping your face.

The oil man cometh. I am ridiculously pleased about this, and watch as he struggles with his whopping pipe. He has sore-looking hands and one leg several inches shorter than the other. I fire questions about the workings of his tanker and pipe. When he's gone, I feel bereft. I must get a job/life.

Marcus comes home in a sullen mood despite the fact that I have worked like a slave, unpacking tea chests and packing them again, because I couldn't decide where to put stuff. Instead of talking, he delves into his filing cabinet, which glowers sternly from the breakfast room. His goal is to file every aspect of our lives. Drawers are labeled Finances, House & Cars, Skews Prop Let and so on. I suspect that the entire filing enterprise is a ploy to enable him to duck out of teaching Tod to ride his bike.

The Hobbies drawer is empty apart from Marcus's octopush training schedule and match fixtures. When Marcus first moved into my flat, I found it intriguing that he liked to waggle a big stick in a swimming pool. But when I saw a match, I didn't get it at all. Why would anyone wish to make hockey—a tortuous game that had forced me to fake period cramps and, on one occasion, an impressively authentic faint—even more difficult, and wetter? With snorkels on, and all that frantic flapping of flippers, it was impossible to distinguish Marcus from his teammates. "Fantastic goal," I said after the match.

"I didn't score," Marcus said. "That was Will, our captain."

The exhaustion of filing, plus the fact that I have cranked up our central heating to its hottest setting, sends Marcus into an open-mouthed slumber on the sofa. At midnight he's unwakeable, so I go to bed without him.

Wednesday. I phone Mr. Leech, the damp-proof specialist. His name has a reassuring, sucking-out-badness feel about it. However, I speak only to Mr. Leech's answering machine, then the builder's answering machine and the plumber's answering machine. None of these people is scrambling to transform Gorby Cottage into a model of style and efficiency.

After my fruitless calls I spy Tod's schoolbag on the kitchen table. How could he have walked to school without sensing a lack of bag against his back? I should have noticed. I should have found Dog. I light Lucille's Tranquility candle but it fails to have a calming effect. I need something else, like real people, not machines, to talk to.

I need London.

The restaurant is tucked down a dank side street, close to Leicester Square, and is staffed by grinning waitresses wearing headdresses adorned with dazzling feathers. "I'd love to meet up," Suzie had said, "but not at my place. The guy who took our boiler away found loads of asbestos. They're coming today to remove it." She suggested that we meet at Geronimo's. The restaurant has a Native American theme, hence the headdresses.

"How's Gorgeous?" she asks, plonking Barney on a gummy chair and thrusting him a color-in menu. "Gorgeous" is her name for Marcus. Gorgeous Marcus or, usually, just Gorgeous.

"We're probably adjusting, nothing's *really* wrong…"

"Stop that," she snaps, "or we're leaving." Barney has tired of the color-in menu, peeled the paper off the crayons and is making swirling patterns on the table with salt. "Why are we at Geronimo's?" she asks him.

"To see Auntie Ro."

"Yes, that's true, but we're also here because it's your favorite place. Otherwise we would not be at Geronimo's."

Barney snatches the vinegar bottle and upends it. Some children are capable of eating out in a sophisticated fashion; these kids tuck into olives and salami and can inhabit a chair without flipping over its back. The parents of such infants say, "If you expect your child to misbehave, they will," as if it's your fault. They brag that their offspring has been eating out since birth and never caused a problem; they'd barely cut the umbilical cord and he was chomping braised wood pigeon in a raspberry jus.

These people are liars. In restaurants, small people need the loo every ten minutes—a ploy to enable them to play with the hand dryer—or they're under the table, as Barney is now, rapping adult shins with a spiteful-looking plastic figure called Falcon Man.

Children cannot keep still. Boys especially have an inability to remain stationary for long enough to nibble the wafer from their ice cream. It's their testosterone, bubbling madly. You can hear it, swishing about their insides.

"Anyway," Suzie says, "there's a new bunch of us, lovely women, we meet every—you should come up more, look like you need a…" She's drowned out by the squaw waitresses who are bellowing "happy birthday" to a sprawly assortment of little girls wearing gauzy wings and tiaras.

Before I rush off to catch my train, she says, "I've been meeting up with Colette, the French girl who bought your flat. Baby's due any day. Lovely girl."

"That's great," I say.

On the train I think: I needed London, but not Geronimo's.

Thursday. Marcus has been whacked by the sledgehammer that is the common cold. This strain turns eyes into moist pink slits, and is definitely flu. Despite the fact that he could quite possibly be dead by lunchtime, Marcus staggers into the car to catch the 7:45 to Charing Cross.

The plumber shows up with a broiled face, smelling of last night's lager, and I spend the day loading putrid clothing into the washing machine.

Job. Need one.

Marcus calls. "I'm too ill to face the journey home," he says.

"You'll only be sitting on a train," I protest. "Come home and go straight to bed."

"Just can't face it."

"Can't face what?"

"I'm not having a row when I feel awful."

"It's a cold, Marcus."

My terminally ill husband will sleep on the sofa in the back room of the office. Nettie has whisked him up a concoction of lemon juice, honey and whiskey. Good, kind Nettie.

He says, "At least you could sound sympathetic."

Friday. Tod is having his hair cut. The spooky dome requires urgent attention and so I have assembled a variety of bribes (doughnuts, shopping trip tomorrow to purchase 3-D maze components) if he cooperates. Tod is not a friend of scissors. Before the thing happened at his old school, he would cut up gummed paper to make pictures and didn't even mind having his nails trimmed. Then I was called to the school, and he was wary of scissors after that.

"Hop into the racing car seat," commands Tina the hairdresser. "Are you in Miss Cruickshank's class? Then you'll know my son Harry. Mad about this seat, he is. I have to drag him out of it."

"Want an ordinary chair," Tod announces.

"Don't you like racing cars?" Tina asks. She has apricot-colored cheeks and a small, upturned nose, like a child's.

Tod thrusts his hands into his trouser pockets where he stores pebbles and bits of stick. He has never exhibited a glimmer of interest in vehicles. Suzie often complains that her children's obsessions with diggers and forklift trucks have resulted in her spending vast portions of her life on the fringes of building sites. I'm glad Tod's not like that. At least his mazes don't require me to loiter on churned-up ground, gawping at cement mixers.

As Tod peers at his reflection, I see how truly dreadful his hair has become.

"Goodness," Tina says. "Let's go much shorter, thinned out all over, smarter for school. Would you like that, Tod?"

"All right," he says carefully.

Tina starts trimming with such speed that I worry that her prices—a third of what we were charged at Clippers in Bethnal Green—reflect the fact that she is no more capable of cutting hair than removing a bunion.

"Settling into the village?" Tina asks.

"Oh, yes," I tell her, "we're very happy."

"Planning to do much with your garden?"

"Lots," I say. In fact, I have never been in charge of a garden before. Behind my old flat was a patch of communal ground. Lydia from the basement flat potted up insipid pink geraniums that turned sick, then got knocked over and rolled out of their containers. Marcus made Tod a wooden sandpit and bought plastic molds for stamping fish shapes, but Tod just traced coils in the sand with a finger.

"If you need any help or ideas," says Tina, now raking the back of Tod's neck with a buzzing device, "there's the Chetsley In Bloom committee. We're always looking for new members."

"I'll think about that." Could gardening become enticing to me? Certain aspects—like writing "nasturtiums" in a smart leather-bound notebook—are appealing. But that's not what it's about. Real gardening, as any idiot knows, involves weeding and the extermination of slugs.

"Pity," Tina says over the buzzer, "about Wyn Beadie. Have you heard? Collapsed in her garden on Wednesday. Found by the post girl, the new one with the attitude. Carted off to Lexley General, but of course it was too late by then."

"Wyn Beadie?" I repeat.

"Didn't you meet her? Lovely lady, across the road from you. Lived in that house all her life."

The lawn tidier. "That's terrible," I say.

Tod regards Tina with moon eyes. Death doesn't scare him—in fact he enjoys it. I thought he'd be upset when I ran over a rabbit, but he nagged me to perform a swift U-turn and drive back, so he could examine the corpse.

"All done," Tina says. "Want me to do something with his eyebrow?" Tod jerks his head around to face me. "I could trim it," she suggests, "make it less…dramatic."

"Let's just leave it," I say.

Tod has been clippered into respectability. He has best-kept hair. I take my mini accountant home.

Marcus shows up in sizzling good humor, having fully recovered, thanks to Nettie's whiskey and lemon. He is being Good Dad, up there in Tod's room, admiring the haircut and quizzing him on the Egyptian project.

Much later, in bed, I think about faking, but worry that I'll overact and wake Tod or trigger a livestock nightmare. He had another last night. I found him babbling about being overpowered by flapping poultry, and when I grasped his quivering hand, he sobbed, "Don't like it, Mum, that nasty red skin on their heads."

Marcus rolls off and turns away from me. Only our feet are touching.

"I know," I say suddenly.

"What? You know what?" He springs up and stares at me.

"I know where Dog is. Tod was playing in the shed at the weekend. That's where he left Dog."

"Christ, Ro. Is that what you think about when we have sex?"

part two

A complex pattern of pathways can disorient the unsuspect-
ing visitor.

chapter 6

Happy Birthday

Re: Gorby Cottage, 18 Main Street, Chetsley
Date: February 10
Observations:
— High moisture content readings noted at several locations esp at rear of property indicating severe rising damp.
— Softness in timber floors indicative of sub-floor rot.
— Severe infestation of woodborer *Anobium punctatum* noted in roof timbers above main dwelling house.
Recommendations:
— Remove plaster to height of one meter at rear wall. Inject with chemical damp-proof course.
— Install sub-floor ventilation.
— Chemical eradication of *Anobium punctatum* and replacing of floor timbers where necessary.

DAMPBLASTERS: FOR WOODWORM,
DRY/WET ROT AND RISING DAMP ∗
PERSONAL ATTENTION ALWAYS

I slip Mr. Leech's quote into our House & Cars file, grateful now for Marcus's organizational skills. You want words
like *infestation* and *eradication* well out of sight. Knowing that
woodworm has a proper name, a creature name, makes it
seem more threatening. You imagine it gnawing and punc-
turing, lunching on the very fabric of your home.

Our other post is a postcard from Dad, depicting a Span-
ish dancer with a red and gold stuck-on satin skirt. It reads:
Hope you're settling into your new home, we are all fine, love, Dad.
It must have taken him weeks to come up with such a heart-
felt message.

Of course there was someone else, my mother was sure
of it. Would Dad have swished off to Majorca alone? Someone would be with him at that fish restaurant. She would be
wearing a sarong and bikini top. "One of those skimpy ones,"
Mum raged down the phone, "like two hankies that tie at
the bust."

Actually, I knew the real story, at least the version Dad had
told Natalie in a letter. He had become close—that's the word
he used, *close*—to a woman called Freda who manned the
cheese counter at our local deli. My parents weren't comfortable with delis; those enormous sausages were too
strange, with their streaks of fat and gnarled-looking skins.
But Dad loved those pale, mild cheeses—Wensleydale,
Cheshire—and Freda would often throw in an extra slice and
not charge him. Sometimes he would come home with a
new kind of olive, which no one in our family liked, but
which Dad would nibble at gamely.

He left Mum for her, the kind cheese lady. They moved to Majorca—I haven't seen Dad in nearly six years—and set up several ill-advised businesses, the latest of which is a soft play center called The Funhouse. I cannot imagine why anyone would wish to endure a visit to an indoor playground where five drops of rain fall all summer.

I stick Dad's postcard next to the tradespeople list, and glimpse Lucille's card on the shelf. Those *Anobium punctatum* are making me itch. I need treatment.

Fab-U-Look smells of vanilla. The reception area teeters with glass shelving bearing bottles of honey-colored fluids. Lucille greets me in a crisp white tunic with her hair pulled back, flat against her scalp.

I am waxed by a younger girl with baby skin and cotton-thin eyebrows. She talks constantly about her boyfriend, who is a butcher and can do me an excellent deal on half a lamb, if my freezer could accommodate such a beast. "Has your husband ever had anything done?" the girl asks, ripping gauze and possibly several layers of skin from my shins.

"Do men have their legs waxed?"

"Mostly backs, shoulders, chests—that's pretty painful. Their hair's coarser than ours. It's much worse for a man." Maybe ordinary men, who get nervous when confronted with salad, have hot wax applied and torn off at great speed. But not Marcus. His only problem area is the nasal hair, and he has the trimmer for that.

When the girl has finished, I touch my legs. Though angrily mottled, the epidermis is intact. I feel cleaner, less infested by woodworm. Unaccustomed to having anything done—apart from the odd speedy haircut—I thank her too much and leave an embarrassingly generous tip on the re-

ception desk. "Gosh," Lucille says, "that's way too much." I
am acting like a poncey Londoner, flinging money about.

In Hamiltons toyshop I am aware of smelling oddly, like
plant juice. My shins still feel raw. I buy a metal robot with
a key stuck in its hip, and yellow binoculars on a cord. They
come to less than the waxing girl's tip.

These are extra birthday presents for Tod to open when
he wakes up tomorrow. Marcus has decided to stay over in
London tonight and spend the morning choosing something really special in the West End. For a fan of the countryside, he was distinctly unkeen to shop for our son in
Lexley High Street. "You could have planned it," I said, when
he called me earlier, "so he'd have his big present when he
wakes up tomorrow." So you'll be there, to say happy birthday in person, is what I meant.

"Does it matter?" he asked.

"Of course it matters. I suggested lots of things you could
have picked up during the week. You promised—"

"And I don't *work* in the week. I don't have a business
to run."

"Fuck your business, Marcus. This is Tod's—"

The phone went dead.

I should have bought Tod's main present. I don't work,
Tod's at school; what do I do all day? As his mother, I should
have had this sorted out weeks ago.

Does it matter? Marcus said. Didn't he tell me that his parents made every birthday perfect for him, with a cake shaped
like a tank or a racing car, or a replica of the red-and-white
rocket from Tintin? He can remember which cake he received each year from age five to eleven.

Don't tell me that birthdays don't matter.

I wrap the robot and binoculars in blue tissue, and deco-
rate the parcels with a silver pen. Beneath my feet, the *Ano-*

bium punctatum will be settling down for a post-lunch nap. Across the street, Wyn Beadie's front door is wide open, but there's no one around. I must stop this, prowling at windows, staring out.

I call Suzie to rant about Marcus who won't be there on his son's sixth birthday, at least not until lunchtime. She says, "Ro? Hang on. Barney get down from that stool—you'll crack your skull open. Remember last time?"

There's a yelp, like a young animal having its foot run over. Suzie visits casualty so often, her kids are familiar with every toy in the waiting room. She reckons she deserves a loyalty card. "I'll post Tod's present on Monday," she says, then, "Shit, there's blood on your forehead. Are you trying to give me a breakdown?"

"Suzie?" I say into the crackling air.

I want to phone Marcus, to say sorry for shouting and swearing, or swear some more, or suggest that we should invest in a new fridge that's large enough to house half a lamb.

I don't know why I need to hear his voice. I just do.

Saturday. My son is six. Last year he was up at five-thirty, ripping off paper, but today I find him still asleep at nine a.m. He must have got up in the night and done a drawing. It's been stuck wonkily to the wall, a cross-section of a pyramid—entitled PIRIMID—with a tangle of passageways inside.

I draw the single curtain and when I look back, his eyes are open, peering stickily.

"Can I have my presents?" he asks.

I want to put off the opening ceremony in case he's disappointed by the tin robot and cheap binoculars. We seem to have lost track of what to buy him, how to excite him.

Last birthday, Marcus presented him with a white rat in a cage with a clear Perspex tunnel to make its life more interesting. I'd never been able to stomach rodents—rats, mice, even hamsters and gerbils—since that time I wandered into the bathroom of our old house. I must have been around ten. I know I was allowed to run my own bath, that Mum had decided that I was unlikely to boil myself alive. There, in the toilet, its rear end and tail jutting out from the water, was the creature. A glossy, nutty brown rat. Its tail looked like thick, wet rope. I turned to run, screaming, and slammed my forehead on the door frame, requiring seven stitches at St. Luke's Hospital.

"Don't you think it's quite sweet?" Marcus asked, as he carried Tod's rat through to his room.

"Marcus," I said, "I'm not sharing a flat with a rat."

The animal stayed, filling Tod's old room with the whiff of neglect. After a month, I called the shop to enquire about their pet-minding service for families on holiday, and handed the animal over.

We weren't really going on holiday. I wanted to conduct an experiment to see if Tod would miss it. The rat hadn't even been named. It was just an it. But still, I felt mean, as if I had conned the animal into thinking that this was a trial separation, when the relationship was definitely over. Two weeks later, the pet shop man left a message, asking if we were back from holiday. The animal had outstayed its welcome. "We have limited space in the shop," the man said. "I'm sure you understand our position."

Marcus disapproved of my tactic. He said that I should have coaxed Tod into connecting with the animal and forming a relationship with it. But Tod didn't even notice it had gone. I never went back to collect it. As far as I know, a nameless rat still resides at Healthy Pets, 119 Lyall Road, London E3.

Tod now opens the robot parcel. He seems pleased, more pleased than he was with the bike that accompanied the rat. He winds up the robot and sends it skittering across the worn bedroom carpet.

Mum and Perry have sent a card depicting a goalkeeper leaping for a ball, plus ten pounds. My sister Natalie—Ms. Efficiency—has had each of her children make Tod a card (involving paint, smudged chalk and gummed shapes—she always has the right kind of art materials), and sent a sporty red V-neck top, which Tod pulls on over his pajamas. Suzie's card comes with an "I am six" badge, loose cola bottle sweets that have gummed themselves to the back of the card and a scrawled note that reads, *Present late sorry.*

"Where's Dad?" Tod asks, examining me through the yellow binoculars.

"He's in London, choosing something really special for you."

"More presents?"

"Well, these are just little things."

"I like them," he says, hugging me with unexpected force, overwhelmed with the joy of being six.

To take Tod's mind off the fact Marcus has failed to appear by two p.m., I am taking him on a birthday outing to Summerlea House. I am beyond angry now, and have banned myself from calling Marcus. Verbal communication would require shouting and overuse of the f-word, which you simply don't do on a birthday.

From the leaflet I picked up in the library, Summerlea House appears to offer your usual stately home fare: the heads of dead antlered animals, weapons in glass cases, a tearoom offering thin sandwiches. But in the grounds is a maze. It's planted with yew hedges, which swirl gracefully around a small mound at its center. On the mound is an octagonal summerhouse, from which you can admire the pathways from above. Tod prepares a picnic, battering Cheddar with a blunt knife. He snaps breadsticks in two so they'll fit in his lunchbox. The binoculars bulge from his back pocket.

Summerlea House is around ten miles the other side of Lexley. Tod flumps in the passenger seat, clutching the map. He is aware that his mother has a shoddy sense of direction. I am not proud of this; nothing is more irritating than grown women boasting that they are unable to perform simple tasks, like remove jam jar lids or hold a screwdriver correctly. Tod hums to himself, examining Lexley High Street through his binoculars.

"It's that building again," he reports.

"That's the library," I tell him. We have passed it three times due to a section of the High Street being dug up and traffic being diverted down the narrow lane beside Fab-U-Look.

"Are we lost?" Tod enquires.

"Of course we're not lost. We will be, if you keep asking. I'm trying to keep my mind on the road."

Tod opens his lunchbox and nibbles the plastic-looking cheese. We are out of Lexley now, but not on the road to Summerlea House. The map on Tod's lap is smattered with cheese particles. He traces roads with a finger. "Left," he shouts, and I swing the car into a cul-de-sac of immaculate bungalows with a clump of toddlers straddling toy vehicles on the pavement.

I am expecting too much, that a boy who turned six only this morning should be able to map-read with any accuracy. How dumb to assume that he'd make some whopping developmental leap.

"It's that building again," he retorts, pointing out—quite rightly—that we have arrived back in Lexley. "I feel sick," he adds.

"Do you? Stop looking at the map. Open the window." Tod winds the window down fully and shivers. "Didn't you bring a jumper?" I ask.

He shakes his head and stares at his lap, as if deliberately wanting to upset his insides. He chews cheese mournfully. It's freezing in the car with the window wide open. "I'll be all right," he says weakly, "as long as you drive slow."

"This *is* slow."

"There's that building again," he mutters.

I am angry now, dithering at nine miles per hour with a silver Espace crawling up my rear end, flashing and tooting impatiently. Tod burps into cupped hands. He opens his lunchbox and piles more cheese into his mouth.

"Stop eating," I shout. "It'll make you feel even more sick."

He is sniveling now, batting back tears with inky fingers. I've upset him, on his birthday. I wonder what good I do him—really, if it's the best thing for Tod, being around me so much. Does it matter who meets him at the school gates? It's not like we talk much on the way home. Would his world shatter if a child-minder picked him up while I commuted to London with Marcus? Anna would have me back in a blink. She said that the place is collapsing without me. Unable to add new acquisitions to the PC, she has resorted to the old card index system.

"Are we nearly there yet?" Tod asks.

We have successfully located a road out of Lexley that leads to an expanse of muddy ground where a supermarket is being built. A sign boasts that the supermarket will offer a café, post office and banking facilities. "It's round the next corner," I snap.

Back in Lexley High Street I take the next left, which looks like a proper road but leads to a primary school playground where elderly women are setting out potted cacti on trestle tables. *"The maze,"* reads the inside cover of Tod's favorite book, *"is simply a puzzle to be navigated from start to finish. Will you ever find your way out?"*

"I need the toilet," reports Tod.

We are on the right road. I'm awash with euphoria. Here I am, a lone mother in control, negotiating her way through unfamiliar surroundings to take her birthday son to a maze that will remain forever etched in his memory.

"Toilet," Tod repeats, writhing in his seat.

"Wait until we're properly out of town. You can pee at the roadside."

"It's not a pee. It's a poo."

I drive faster now, with cold air blasting my cheek.

"I'm desperate," Tod says.

"You can't do a poo until we get to the big house. I haven't brought any tissues."

"Or my jumper," Tod adds, banging his teeth together.

We're pushing seventy now, and there's a brown sign, the kind used for places of interest, saying Summerlea House Next Left. I speed up, crunching a breadstick, letting it hang out of my mouth like a cigarette. We zip past a slow-moving car. The driver glances at me, looking alarmed. I wish Marcus was here, to witness me traveling from A to B so efficiently. He enjoys driving and planning how to get places. When he gives me directions, I gawp until his mouth becomes a gyrating sausage and he stares, as if checking that the vital facts—first exit at roundabout, sharp right turn after Shell garage—have attached themselves to my brain.

"Stop the car," demands Tod. His face is contorted, like genuine pain's going on.

"Hang on two minutes. Stop thinking about it."

He shuts his lunchbox firmly. "There's a smell," he says.

"You haven't," I say, glaring at him.

"Not that. A burning smell."

I turn left, confident that Summerlea House will offer adequate toilet facilities including the roaring hand dryers that Tod enjoys so much.

"There's a stink," he says.

"It's manure, Tod. That's what the countryside smells like."

But it's not manure. When I inhale there's a rubbery burning, accompanied by subtle, then more dramatic smoke effects eking from the bonnet.

"Are we nearly there yet?" Tod asks, as I point the car into a graveled lane.

"We'll have to stop. Something's wrong with the engine."

"What is it?" he shouts, ogling me through his binoculars.

The car judders to a halt. Turning the key triggers a metallic screech, like a sheet of aluminum being rammed through a sewing machine.

"What's happened?" Tod asks.

My car has died. My son will celebrate his birthday in a golf course parking lot. "Nothing serious," I say.

chapter 7

Needing a Cigarette

According to Lucille's husband Carl, Lexley Golf Club is the kind of establishment to which Marcus should belong. Its members wear turquoise LGC sweaters bearing a logo of a skinny man with bowed legs, jauntily swinging a club. Carl is a wedding photographer, requiring him to wear a suit and tie, but when he's not working he sports his LGC sweater, and the sort of trousers you'd call slacks. Carl looked rather worried when Marcus explained the rudiments of octopush and said, "If you change your mind, Marcus, I'm happy to recommend you. What's your handicap?"

And now Tod and I are stranded in Lexley Golf Club car park, having not been recommended by anyone. I am in possession of a terminally sick Mondeo with a cheesy interior and a son firing questions: "What's this place? You said we were going to a maze. Where is it? Why can't we go? It's not *fair.*" Tod uses a grubby nail to dislodge cheese from between his teeth, and extends his bottom lip like a table leaf.

A man raps on our windscreen. I open the driver's door to see what he wants and discover which rule I'm breaking.

"Great place to break down," the man says.

"Yes, we're very lucky."

"Use the phone," the man says, "in the clubhouse. You can wait there until the AA arrive." He has a large, pink face, like a ham. The ends of his golf clubs sport knitted bonnets, possibly to keep them warm.

In the clubhouse Tod plunges into a toilet cubicle, banging the door with such force that the paper towel dispenser reverberates uneasily. In the members' bar he pauses to apply oily fingerprints to a glass trophy cabinet, then installs himself in a fat leather armchair as if he, like Carl, is a fully paid-up member of the club.

"At least it's stopped raining," says the girl at the bar. She hands me an orange juice for Tod and tells me to help myself to coffee or tea. By now, with my good fortune on a par with that of a rollover lottery winner, I tap out the AA number on my mobile, feeling chuffed to belong to such an organization. It's the kind of reassuring thing Mum's husband Perry does, like pulling plugs out at night, and owning a rake.

Tod crunches brown sugar cubes and licks crystals from a finger, making himself suitably sticky for further fouling up of the trophy cabinet.

"So you've changed address," says the AA lady. "What was your previous postcode?"

My brain seizes. "E-something," I say, watching Tod as he experiments with the hot water dispenser intended for golfers' beverages. He has placed a saucer beneath the tap, and is filling it with quick spurts. I could have just brought him here for his birthday outing instead of bothering with Summer-

lea House with its entrance fees. Children are thrilled by ordinary things. When I took him to London Zoo, Tod showed
little interest in the animals. He wasn't even thrilled by the
baboons' red bottoms. We spent most of the afternoon clam-
bering up and down a short flight of concrete steps, which
he told Marcus was "fantastic fun."

"Can you be more specific?" the AA woman asks.

"E2." Or was that Suzie's street? "E3," I say. She runs a
search and discovers that only Marcus is eligible for rescue.
"But I'm his wife," I plead. "A woman alone with a child.
Anything could happen to us."

"That's boiling water," the barmaid warns Tod. "You'll
scald yourself."

"We are *vulnerable,*" I bark into the phone.

The AA woman sighs. "Please call to update your address.
Someone's on their way."

I have never been in a clubhouse before. Occasionally, I
have wondered what goes on in such places, but not enough
to participate in a sport requiring the lugging of a massive
bag of metal. Carl mentioned that there's a ladies' division I
could join ("You've got powerful arms, Ro. I'm sure you
could master a swing") but I can cope with that term—
"ladies"—only in a public convenience context.

However, I can see that such a grown-up establishment
holds a certain appeal. Tod is certainly enjoying himself. He's
back at the trophy cabinet, clouding the glass with his breath.
Outside, our Mondeo sags pitifully among sportier models.
Marcus still has his harlotty motor. It's good for business, he
says. When he takes high-caliber clients to view properties,
the car shouts: *I am successful and rich. I will show you a successful, rich person's flat.* My lumbering tank, with elderly sandwiches decaying in its crevices, says only: *mother.*

Tod needs the loo again. He makes grunting noises, insists

on leaving the cubicle door open and regards me through his yellow binoculars.

"Hello?" the barmaid says, poking her head round the door. "Your AA man's here."

The man has tight silver curls and a turned-down mouth. While he examines our car's innards, Tod busies himself by picking out loose mortar from a brick wall. I show him the Summerlea House leaflet, a poor substitute, admittedly, for the real thing with its maze and raised summerhouse.

"We'll still go," I reassure him. "I'm sure it's just some piddly thing." I leave a terse message on Marcus's voice mail, informing him of our situation.

The AA man beckons me over and says, "Cylinder head gasket."

"I thought it might be that. Is it fixable?"

He shakes his head.

"Shit," I mutter.

"When can we go to the maze?" Tod demands.

"Sorry, love, we can't go."

"Can we go somewhere else instead?"

"Tod, we're not going anywhere. The car's broken."

This is all my fault. For five years I have treated the Mondeo shoddily—despising its murky blueness, never topping up oil or water—as if it's a boyfriend I've wanted to be rid of and hoped would desert me due to maltreatment. I realize now that the Mondeo is my only means of escaping from Chetsley, from which three buses leave daily, and only to mysterious places called Rippenden and Newton Meadows.

"Anyone you can call?" the AA man asks.

"Dad's coming to help us," Tod informs him. "Mum just phoned him."

"You're not going to be stuck?"

"We'll be fine," I say. I sign the form on the AA man's clipboard and tap out Marcus's number again, then try home. It rings and rings.

And we wait. Tod gnaws the last lump of cheese from his lunchbox, and we share the remaining breadsticks. A white truck pulls into the car park. A tall, long-limbed man climbs out and investigates a skip loaded with wood. He selects an armful of planks, and flings them into the back of the truck where they land with a *crack*.

This man does not belong here. His jeans hang baggily about his legs and his enormous boots are daubed with paint. They are even bigger than *my* boots. Tod observes him through the binoculars.

"Stop that," I hiss.

The man notices that he is being spied on, and coils fingers around his eyes as if he's wearing binoculars, too.

"Our car's broken," Tod shouts. The man strides toward us and looks sympathetically at the Mondeo. "Mum said 'shit,'" Tod adds.

"That's understandable," the man says, "in the circumstances. Where are you going?"

"We need to get back to Chetsley. I've called my husband, he should be along pretty soon—"

"That's where I'm going," the man says.

Never accept lifts from strangers. How many times have I told Tod that? Not that he would. He is fearful of people he doesn't know—even those he does know, like Mum's husband Perry, who thinks you befriend children by whirling them like windmill sails or flinging them on to the sofa and being a fierce bear. My scaredy-cat son has already opened the truck's passenger door and plonked himself in the middle, next to the driver's seat. I climb in beside him.

This man, Joe, lives at the perfect white cottage across the road from Gorby Cottage. "So I'm your new neighbor," he says.

I don't know if he is, by Carl's standards, the *right* kind of neighbor. He doesn't look like someone who belongs to clubs. Not a joiner-inner.

"You bought the old lady's house?" I ask.

"It was my mother's place."

"Oh, I'm sorry," I say, which feels fake, as I didn't know her. The one time I shouted hello over the fence, she plucked a plastic peg from her washing line and gripped it between her lips, like a small yellow beak.

Both windows of Joe's van are wide open. Fine rain sprays the side of my face, like wet breath. My feet rest among a jumble of crushed coffee cartons, cigarette packets and an open toolbox spewing chisels.

"Mum was seventy-four," Joe continues. "Lived in that house all her life. I've been telling her for years that it was too much, but stubborn wasn't the word."

"How old are *you?*" Tod asks.

I give him a sharp nudge with my knee.

"Ancient," Joe says.

"Like the Egyptians?"

"Way older than the Egyptians."

"I'm six," Tod announces. "It's my birthday. I got these." He puts the binoculars to his eyes and gawps at the driver until I tell him to stop, Joe needs to concentrate on the road. Tod puts the binoculars down, but keeps gazing at Joe. Children love men, boy children especially. They spend so much time among females—their mother, her friends, women teachers—that a mere whiff of maleness has them babbling excitedly and trying to clamber on to their backs. The effect is heightened when they don't see dad much.

Joe pulls into his drive. "Want to come in?" he asks abruptly.

"Yes, please," chirps Tod.

"We'd better not. Dad will be home any minute."

Joe smiles at me, and I'm horribly aware of my burning face. Damn this blushing gene. I read once that it can be suppressed by taking pills to stimulate seratonin levels in the brain. Perhaps blushing is due to my brain being stuffed with largely useless information: remembering to pack Tod's gym kit, Egyptian topic work, sandwiches that won't be laughed at. Since moving to Chetsley, I feel like my brain's congealed, like a flabby rice pudding. There's no room for any seratonin in there.

Joe's still smiling, kind of cheekily.

"Thanks for the lift," I say.

"Shame about your car."

"That's okay. At least it saves me cleaning it out." Now he thinks that, whenever my car's interior starts to stink unbearably, I just throw it away.

"Let me know," Joe says, "if you're ever stuck and need a lift somewhere." He pushes back a tangle of dark hair, and rests a hand on Tod's shoulder.

"I'll do that," I say, hauling Tod across the road, his binoculars bouncing against his damp birthday top and his face blasted by smiles.

"But I didn't *know* you'd broken down," Marcus says. "I had no idea." He is crouching on the kitchen floor, hastily wrapping an enormous glass box in paper emblazoned with dancing fairies. I'm not saying that boys' presents must be wrapped in paper with a repeat BIRTHDAY BOY pattern, but there are limits.

"I called you," I tell him. "Why is your phone always off? Where the hell were you?"

"Ro, I was rushing about like crazy, getting this." The fact that he is wrapping it in full view of Tod—he's loitering in the kitchen doorway, slapping the rolled-up road map against his thigh—rather spoils the surprise.

"You don't care about us," I announce.

"Of course I do. You're just getting more…ridiculous." The tape keeps tangling itself up. He jams a gummy ball on to the floor beside the half-wrapped present. Then he looks up at me and reaches for my hand. "I'm so sorry, Ro. I wish I'd known. Is the garage collecting the car?"

"Yes, I think it's wrecked." A relationship over, like Tod's white rat.

"And you never got to that natural history place."

"Stately home," I correct him.

"We went to a car park," Tod announces, "and this building with trophies and a boiling water machine. It was great. The AA man came and another man drove us home in his truck and Mum said 'shit.'"

"What man?" Marcus asks.

"A stranger," Tod says dramatically. "He took wood from a skip without asking. He *stole* it."

Marcus frowns at me. "Was that wise, Ro?"

"What choice did I have? Anyway, he's not a stranger. He's just moved into that old lady's place across the road."

Marcus shakes his head, and tries to cover the naked section of glass with a leftover strip of fairy paper. He wouldn't have passed the library three times, triggered carsickness or tried to drive into a school playground. And he certainly wouldn't have broken down, because he looks after his car. He *nurtures* it.

"Well," he says, "aren't you going to open your present, Tod?"

Tod steps forward warily, as if he's at school prize-giving with mums and dads all staring. He peels away the paper carefully. It's a fish tank; we knew that already. There are two speckled fish: one silver, one black.

"What are they for?" Tod asks.

"They're *pets,*" says Marcus. "Dalmatian fish. They're for you to look after."

Tod nods solemnly and says, "Thank you, Dad."

"Happy birthday, son," Marcus says, ruffling Tod's hair like a Christmas uncle.

I find Tod still awake at eleven-thirty, wide-eyed in the glow from the fish tank.

Marcus realized too late he shouldn't have filled it and dropped the fish into their new habitat before placing the tank on Tod's chest of drawers. We lifted it together, with the water slapping over the edge, dousing the front of Marcus's work shirt. He was annoyed, too, that the chest of drawers hadn't been cleared of unfinished collages made from clumsily glued lichen that Tod and I picked off the shed. Like I should have known that a fish tank was about to enter our lives.

"I can't sleep," Tod complains. "The tank's noisy."

A humming sound is coming from the water heater, or maybe the gadget that will enable the tank to self-cleanse, requiring no effort whatsoever on my part. "If I turn it off," I tell him, "the water will go cold and the fish might die."

"Can't sleep," Tod repeats.

I climb into the bed with him, pull the spaceman duvet around us and lie there until his breath comes warm and steady against my chest.

Later I find Marcus awake with the bedroom light blazing and work papers littering the duvet.

"I met Carl at the station," he says, without looking at me. "Helped me lift the fish tank in the car. Said he'd seen you earlier, driving terribly fast. He reckons you must have been doing seventy on a B-road."

"Tod needed the loo," I explain. *He was desperate, Officer.* Yes, I should have stopped at the roadside. Isn't that an offence, too? Fouling a public place? I should have taken him to the bathroom before we set off, like an organized mother would.

"Were you smoking in the car?" Marcus asks.

"What?"

"Carl saw you."

"You know I don't smoke. I haven't had a cigarette since—" I realize I'm shouting, propelling Tod into another livestock nightmare. He's had two this week, woken up yelling about horses—not sleek, elegant creatures, but snorting beasts with foul breath and decaying teeth.

"He said," Marcus continues, "you had something hanging out of your mouth. He said you were *puffing away.*" He gathers his papers together and gives me a strange look, as if I'm a child who's just knocked her lunch off the table. He's not angry, just disappointed. I undress, slide under the duvet and Marcus's paperwork, and curl up with my back to him.

It's much later when Tod's voice comes again, wanting me. I find him perched stiffly on the edge of his bed.

"I can't look after them," he mutters.

"Look after what?"

"The fish. It's my job, Dad said."

"Don't worry. Just forget about them."

"I can't because of that noise."

With patience dwindling I leave him, bundled angrily in bed, and make insipid tea, which I drink while sitting on an unopened box containing the crockery Marcus's parents have forced upon us over the years. In this box is a set of earthenware pots that might come in handy if we are ever seized by an urge to make eleven casseroles at once. Scraps of fairy wrapping paper litter the floor.

One male in this house doubts his fish-parenting skills. The other takes work to bed, and accuses me of smoking. I remember now, as I dunk plain biscuits into my tea, what I had in my mouth in the car: a breadstick. The snack favored by modern parents to guard children's teeth against sugar decay and acid attack. My habit of puffing on over-long sticks, devoid of taste or pleasure, will no doubt make it into the *Lexley Gazette.*

For the first time in years, I could murder a Silk Cut.

Before leaving for work, Marcus reminds me to feed the fish daily with colorful flakes that reek of rank seafood. When the water needs changing, I should remove only a third and replace it with fresh water at room temperature so I don't upset the fish. On no account should I slosh in icy water straight from the cold tap. The shock could kill them.

Thoughtfully, Marcus bought a red plastic sieve that I must use when washing the gravel from the bottom of the tank. I must not confuse this with the other sieve, the blue one, which we use for straining vegetables.

"I thought the tank was supposed to self-cleanse," I remind him.

"Let's just try to look after them," Marcus says. "They're live breeders, the pet man told me. We could have lots of little fish, a whole family."

Live breeders. We are heading for a tank stuffed with juvenile fish, a school of Dalmatians, with potential for sibling rivalry and shoddy parenting. I wonder when this breeding might start, and whether Tod will realize what's going on. On the sex front I have attempted to palm him off by explaining that the man's seed meets the woman's egg, like they have a coffee and chat and, somehow, a baby is made. "But how does the seed get to the egg?" Tod asked once in our old East London park. We were sharing the bench with a prim-looking lady who was deconstructing a slice of Battenburg.

"It kind of swims," I explained.

"Where does it swim?"

"Into the woman," I whispered.

The lady had peeled off the Battenburg's marzipan layer, and was now rolling it into a ball between her thumb and forefinger.

"Yes," Tod said, "but how does it get *into* the woman?"

I said that we'd better go home as it looked like rain, although the sky was clear blue and cloudless.

"Does it go in her fer-*gina?*" he shouted.

I jumped up from the bench. The woman broke the cake into four squares—two pink, two yellow—and flung them down on the path.

Unprotected fishy intercourse will now be happening, on a daily basis, in my impressionable son's bedroom, and we haven't even got around to naming the parents.

"Fishy?" I suggest over breakfast. "Fishy and Dishy?"

"That's stupid," snorts Tod. This is the boy who, when presented with a cuddly dog one Christmas, racked his brain for a name until our decorations had been put away for next year, and finally came up with Dog.

"Bill and Ben?"

Tod gapes at me as if to say, why?

"Fuckwit and Arse," I murmur, delving into the fruit bowl to find acceptable lunchbox components and discovering only peaches shrouded in blue fur.

"What?" Tod asks. "What did you say?"

I feign deafness and remind myself that it's hardly fair to take out my ill humor on Tod, when it's Marcus who appears to have forgotten Valentine's Day. Who cares about a corny institution that propels intelligent adults into Hallmark shops to buy teddies bearing the message I Wuv You? Presenting an adult with a soft toy is an offence that should carry an extremely stiff penalty, like being forced to eat the thing, plastic eyeballs and all.

I don't need a card to reassure me that I am adored by my husband. I did notice, however, that Marcus failed to open the fuchsia envelope I placed on his bedside table this morning, and that his parting shot before leaving for work was to remind me to call the drain man because something bubbles up into the shower every time we flush the loo, which suggests that we have a plumbing problem. This, I felt, was hardly in the spirit of Valentine's Day.

We set off for school. Tod is dawdling, trying to peek into other people's front rooms. He stops before the middle cottage in a terrace of three, and jams his binoculars against the front window.

"That's *so* rude," I hiss, tugging his jacket.

Inside the cottage a man slowly raises himself from an armchair and shuffles toward the window. He has two black thumb smudges for eyebrows, which wiggle angrily. Tod grins and waves.

I drag him onward, past the hairdresser where Tina's son Harry is sucking a lolly. It's a whistling lolly, which he blasts as we stride past. Tina has the smug flush of a woman who has just received roses. She is certainly being taken for dinner tonight to a restaurant where desserts come with a heart-shaped dribble of raspberry sauce.

At the school gate, Tod kisses me goodbye and mooches away to assume his usual position, squashed next to the main entrance. Chetsley Primary has a system to help newcomers settle in. An older child—a "buddy"—is supposed to help them make friends. Adele, Lucille's ten-year-old, is Tod's buddy. She stands now among a group of similar-size girls, her calves bulging above white ankle socks, her face flatly unwelcoming. I hope she exhibits more enthusiasm in her majorette displays.

The bell sounds. Miss Cruickshank ushers children in through the door. Her hair is a pinkish gray puff. She waves and beckons me over. The children are indoors now, the playground empty and speckled with the beginnings of rain. "Mrs. Skews," she begins. Being Mrs. Skews makes me feel ancient. Call me Ro, I think, or even Rowena. "Could you pop in sometime," she says, "for a chat?"

"Yes, of course."

"Around two today?"

My eyes are fixed on the marble cake swirls of her blouse. I have never seen her wear the same one twice. Jumble sales are, I suspect, entirely stocked with Miss Cruickshank's discarded blouses. This one is certainly a fire hazard. I want to ask, "What's this about?" but she has hurried in from the drizzle, banging the heavy blue door behind her.

Back home, I intend to call Dampblasters to find out when someone will inject our back wall with foul chemicals, but can't motivate myself. Why does Miss Cruickshank want to see me?

Tod isn't fitting in.

He won't speak.

Bigger boys are picking on him.

He is exhibiting an over-fondness for images of dead people wrapped in bandages.

He is a genius and must be moved immediately to the year above. Miss Cruickshank wants to congratulate me on raising such a gifted, articulate child.

I call Marcus, who says, "You're worrying too much. She just wants a chat."

"Yes, but what about? Teachers don't just chat, not at two o'clock, when they're supposed to be in charge of twenty-six kids."

"I'm pretty busy," Marcus adds. "Call me later, after your meeting."

"You think it'll be a *meeting?* Like, a formal thing?" I picture Miss Cruickshank with a clipboard, on which she has attached her agenda entitled: Worrying Things About Tod.

"It'll be fine, darling," he says.

"It must be something urgent."

"Ro, I'm with a client. Let's talk later."

He thinks I'm a fussy mother. Even Tod bats me away as if I'm a wasp. That's what happens when you have an only child. They hog all your brain space, permeate every cell. I never planned to have just one kid. When Tod turned three, broodiness started to rise in my throat. I couldn't gulp it back down. It was Nappy Rejection Day that made me decide to suggest we have another baby.

My attempts to force Tod into pants had resulted only in perpetual wee smells, and a humiliating incident when a nugget of solid matter rolled out of his trouser leg and on to the mottled gray carpet in the doctor's waiting room. Everyone fell silent and stared as I picked it up with a paper towel from the loo. Then one spring afternoon, at an art installation in Victoria Park, Tod toilet trained himself.

Anna, my old boss, had dragged us along. A friend of hers with an aubergine crop had erected nylon structures, like enormous, billowing knickers, on the scrubby grass. Tunnels led from one silken tent to the next. The idea was, young babies and children would be stimulated by the colors and wafting fabrics. Most babies were whimpering miserably or bellowing to be liberated from the tents. Tod ran through the tunnels, losing himself. I found him glowing beneath red silk, trousers bunched at his ankles as he ripped off the nappy.

"No Pamper," he roared. "Big boy now."

Later I told Marcus that, with Tod having reached this developmental milestone, we should think about having another baby.

He said, "Why?"

"I want one," I said, as if it were as simple as buying a jumper.

He shook his head. "I just think Tod's…enough"

"I don't want him being an only child."

"It's Suzie," Marcus said suddenly. "You want to be like Suzie." She had two children by this point, and her third was pushing her belly outward and causing her to crave boulder-size jacket potatoes. "There's this pressure," he ranted on, "to keep reproducing, like we're animals."

"We *are* animals," I pointed out.

"Let's just focus on Tod. We can give him everything he needs."

Suzie suggested that I stab a hole in my diaphragm. I couldn't, even if I'd wanted to. On Marcus's insistence, we had started using condoms by then. "It's not fair," Suzie insisted, "that he decides how many children you have, when you're desperate for another."

"I'm not desperate," I lied. The truth was, Marcus could spout sensible reasons why having another child was a bad idea.

And my reasons were simple: want, need.

Suitable attire for meeting Miss Cruickshank: a simple, coordinating outfit to lend an air of efficiency. I flap through black trousers with their blackness washed out, and spy the charcoal-gray trouser suit Marcus bought for me. When I first tried it on he said it made me look sexy in a smart, extremely *capable* sort of way, and was so excited about this sexy/capable combination that he pulled me into bed and missed octopush.

My strappy black sandals haven't been out of their box since we left London. They are certainly unsuitable for walking to school. For one thing, we're usually running. Together, though, the suit and heels create a pleasingly grown-up, if rather job interviewish, effect.

I comb my eyebrows, examine my teeth and smile broadly at my reflection. The molar dentist again. *Don't look so tense, fussy mother. It's just a chat, that's all.*

chapter 8

How To Make Friends

Miss Cruickshank has a sturdy bosom like a sandwich loaf. The room she shows me into has too many chairs upholstered in bobbly oatmeal and not enough daylight. I peer at her through the gloom.

"So," she says, smiling. "Tod."

"Yes," I say, aware of my breathing and blinking. The desk that separates us is scattered with pamphlets entitled "All About Me." Each one has a child's drawing of a face on the front, and a name. Joely has drawn herself with shifty eyes, peering sideways, and yellow plaits that curl outward as if stiffened by wire.

"Tod is a very bright boy," Miss Cruickshank begins. "He takes great care over his work. So particular."

I wonder if Joely's mother is ever summonsed to sit on this oatmeal chair and wait for the *but.*

"His artwork is excellent," she rattles on. "I assume you do a lot with him, Mrs. Skews."

"Well, we tried swimming but he wasn't…and his bike, there's a problem with balance. The stabilizers should be off by now, but last time we tried—"

"Art," she says gently. "Painting, drawing. I imagine he's had a lot of encouragement in that area."

"Yes," I say, staring at the pink ribbons that secure Joely's plaits. "Tod draws a lot, mostly mazes. He's very interested in—"

"But he doesn't mix," Miss Cruickshank butts in. "He doesn't play with other children or even talk to them." She finishes this with a little laugh. *Imagine, a child who doesn't like children!*

"He's not used to being around lots of kids. He's an only child."

"But he had friends, at his last school?"

"Heaps," I protest.

Miss Cruickshank is trying to smile but her top lip is too short for her mouth. She looks like she's sucking on an invisible straw. "Social development is an important aspect of school," she adds.

What does she expect me to do? He's just selective, that's all. I was like Tod, as a child. Natalie's bedroom buzzed with babbling girls competing to style the hair of Dolly Delicious, a hideous severed plastic head that came with waxy lipsticks and glittery hair bands. It seemed too busy in that room, and confusing. Whenever I did Dolly Delicious's makeup, she just looked cheap.

"Tod seems happy at home," I say firmly. "And we've only lived in Chetsley for six weeks. He hasn't had time to make friends."

"You're right," she says.

Of course I am—I gave birth to him.

"But it might help if he socialized outside school. Maybe you could invite one of his classmates for tea."

"We'll do that," I say.

Miss Cruickshank knocks the "All About Me" pamphlets into a tidy pile. I interpret this gesture as my cue to leave the room, and embark on my Help Tod Make Friends project.

First come the flowers, a startling combination of orange and purple bursting from a cellophane cone. Behind them, clutching the outlandish bouquet, is Marcus, pink around the cheeks, saying, "Darling, I totally forgot, I'm so sorry."

"Forgot what?"

He drops the blooms on to the kitchen table and blinks at my suit and heels. "Valentine's Day. Have you been for an interview?"

"What? No, just that meeting at school."

"Have you been to my school?" Tod calls from the living room where he's dismantling a deceased clock radio and examining the circuits. He charged out of school with a heart-shaped biscuit studded with Jelly Tots (for me) and lips speckled with sugar. Sweet-overload had made him jumpy, and I'd hoped that picking apart the radio's interior might calm him down.

"What meeting?" Marcus asks.

"I told you, Miss Cruickshank wanted to see me."

"Why?" Tod yells.

"To tell me…how well you're doing." Tod appears in the kitchen with Marcus's Phillips screwdriver, which he has decided to name Phillip.

"Really?" Marcus says. "That's great, Tod."

I peel the cellophane from the flowers and wonder what to put them in. None of our vases is large enough to accommodate this dramatic display. In the utility room I find a bucket, half fill it with water, and dump in the blooms.

Marcus has also brought me a card that reads, You're Cute, Kiss Me, I Like You. The card is supposed to play a tune when you open it, but something's gone wrong with its workings and all that comes out is a strangled *peep*.

Still, it's the thought that counts.

It has taken me three days to select a child for Tod to befriend. I have stalked mothers and their offspring to school, sizing up potentially suitable matches, and quizzed Tod on who he likes in his class. He just said Miss Cruickshank, which wasn't the right answer at all.

"Do you like that boy with the massive forehead?" I asked. He looked at me blankly. "Or that blond girl who wears a fur coat?"

"Tabitha," he mumbled.

I hoped that he wouldn't choose Tabitha. Despite her Dalmatian fur coat, and matching gloves, scarf and hat, the child is always complaining to her mother that she's cold. "Am *coe*-wuld," she whines in the street.

Tod has never expressed any interest in Harry, but if I waited for Tod to choose his own friend, he'd be heading for university and the damage would have been done. I chose Harry because Tina once cut Tod's hair, which means that we know them, and he doesn't appear to possess any worrying traits, apart from a fervent attachment to a whistling lolly.

Before inviting a child to tea, you need to ask permission. I spotted Tina this morning, marching stiffly with Harry as he strained to admire a display of miniature teapots in the grocer's window.

"Could we have Harry for tea?" I barked into her ear.

She looked startled, as if I was a stranger demanding

money. Harry pressed his back against the shop window. His mouth trembled, as if he were nibbling ants. "That's kind of you," Tina blustered. "Would you like that, Harry?"

He didn't reply, but here he is now, clutching Doctor X, Action Man's foul-looking opponent. Doctor X has a Mohican hairdo and veins bulging from his upper arms. Perhaps Harry thinks that Tod will steal it if he lays it down on the table. I call Suzie, hoping for tips on handling other people's kids, but am met by her stultified tone on her answering machine.

Harry can eat, at least. He forks in spaghetti, splattering his school polo shirt with globules of sauce. He has a fuzz of grayish brown hair, like mouse fur, and sullen eyes that flit about the fixtures and fittings of our kitchen.

Tod eats his spaghetti painfully slowly, sucking in one strand at a time. Both boys are silent.

I feel like a matchmaker, trying to ease two social outcasts through painful first-date procedures. I fire questions at Harry: "Aren't you lucky, having a mum who can cut your hair?"

"Yeah," he says, licking his fork.

"I can't do that," I rant on. "I tried once, didn't I, Tod? Chopped the fringe so short it didn't match the rest of his hair. He looked like a TV screen."

"No, I didn't," Tod mutters. Harry shoves away his empty bowl and stares at me, mournfully.

After our jolly tea, I suggest, "Want to show Harry your bedroom, Tod? You could check if the fish have had babies yet."

"Can I draw?" Tod asks.

"Of course you can. Do you like drawing, Harry?"

"Nah," he says, through a stuffed mouth. "I'm going upstairs."

He's up there now, creeping from room to room. There's the occasional *bang,* like a drawer being slammed shut. I should follow him, make sure he doesn't tamper with the wires at the back of the fish tank or spy Marcus's octopush kit spilling from its zip-up bag and tell his mum: *"They have rubber flippers in their bedroom."*

"Go up and see if Harry's all right," I tell Tod.

"I don't want to." He's hunched over the kitchen table, drawing an underwater scene. The fish have row upon row of tiny scales. Filling every fish with scales is going to take him all night.

"Then play Action Man with him. *Do* something."

He looks up from his drawing. "Why?"

Harry reappears in the kitchen, chewing on something. What's he guzzling now? There's nothing to eat upstairs, except fish food and maybe a collection of ancient toast crusts under Tod's bed. Should I make him open his mouth and show me?

"Let's do homework," I suggest, eagerly. Harry yawns at me. It's okay, he still has a mouthful of spaghetti. "Lego?" I suggest. "I'll get the Lego out."

"I'm drawing," Tod murmurs.

Harry wanders over to the kitchen bin, opens his mouth and lets the spaghetti fall out. "Spaghetti's pasta," he announces. "Pasta's wheat. I can't have wheat because I get this thing where my stomach blows up and I can't go to the toilet."

You still ate a bowlful, greedy tyke.

I glance at the clock. Five-fifteen. Forty-five minutes to fill before Tina comes to collect him. Each of these minutes will suck even more life out of me. I can feel my blood curdling.

"What videos have you got?" Harry demands.

"Sorry, the video got busted in the move. Let's see what's on TV." All that's on offer is a program in which enthusiastic children are brushing dirt from old bottles which they've dug up at a dump.

"This is boring," Harry announces.

Doctor X is lying facedown on the carpet with his trousers off. I wonder if the wheat effect is kicking in, whether Harry's stomach has started to inflate. He catches me staring at his belly and folds his arms firmly.

"Shall we make something?" I ask, wondering how much longer I can keep this up, whether Tina will turn up to find two unattended children, and me, dead on the carpet.

"What do you mean?" Harry asks.

"Maybe biscuits, or something from card and glue…like a rocket. Do you like outer space?"

Harry blinks at me, as if I have arrived from some distant planet whose inhabitants look like normal humans but ask too many questions and force wheat on people. "Yeah," he brightens, "or I could go home."

Tod and I drop Harry off at the hairdresser where Tina and her customer are discussing illness. The woman, who has had vivid custardy stripes put through her hair, says, "He's had the all-clear, but his bowels, they're the main worry now."

Harry clambers into the racing car seat.

"Back already?" chirps Tina.

"Yes," I say, "I think he's had enough."

"That's not like Harry. He's usually very sociable." She gives him a concerned look and doses her customer with hairspray. "Say thank you, Harry," Tina adds. "We must have Tod over for tea sometime."

This, I realize, is the play-date equivalent of "I'll call you."

"He's clogged up," the yellow-striped woman continues. "What he needs is that chronic irrigation."

When I glance back into the shop, Tina has lifted the front of Harry's polo shirt and appears to be inspecting his stomach.

★ ★ ★

We're nearly home when Tod stops at Joe's fence and says, "What's he doing?"

Crouching, with his back to us, Joe is laying out planks on the lawn.

"Come on, it's really late."

"No, it's not. It's not even properly dark yet."

"Stop *staring*."

Joe turns around and sees us and, I think, smiles. I pull on Tod's arm, the way Suzie yanks Barney, her youngest, when he clings to the door handle of the bakers in Bethnal Green Road, bellowing for cake.

"You said," Tod protests, "that if ever I want to know something, I just have to ask."

"What do you want to know?" Joe asks at the gate.

"What you're making," Tod says.

"Want to see? You can help, if you like."

His hands, I notice, are brown and very smooth, more like a child's hands than those of a man who hauls wood from skips.

"Tod," I say, "it's past teatime." I give his arm a gentler tug.

"We've had tea," Tod points out. "We had spaghetti that made Harry's stomach blow up."

"That sounds serious," Joe says, laughing.

Tod is springing from foot to foot, saying, "*Please* let me help."

"Some other time, darling."

As we cross the road, I try to wipe the smile off my face but can't.

"Mum," Tod says, as I stab my key in the door, "you look funny."

Later, with Tod huddled over homework—he has to an-swer ten questions about the Egyptians—I stand at the kitchen window, where Betty and Gordon's net curtains still hang. Joe is hammering now. I think he's nailing wood together. He keeps standing back, viewing the thing from a distance.

Marcus wants to keep the net curtain because it stops people staring in. I despise it. I can think of no torture method more awful than being entirely cocooned in floral net. Tod likes to wrap his face in it, like it's mummy bandages. I don't know how he can stand it against his skin.

"How do you spell Tutankhamen?" he asks.

Joe's outside light is on now and I can see him clearly, measuring planks with a tape. *"T, U, T,"* I begin. A fold of net curtain is trapped between my thumb and forefinger.

"Then what?" Tod asks.

"What?"

"Tutankhamen."

"T, U…"

"You *said* that."

"What was the question?" I am tweaking this curtain. Not tweaking, but *twitching*.

"Mum," comes the cry, "why won't you *listen* to me?"

I watch Joe as he straightens up, glances at our house, and carries an armful of planks to his front door. He turns, and although the nets are supposed to stop strangers from peeping in, I'm sure he sees me: Ro Skews, the curtain twitcher of Chetsley.

chapter 9

Daredevil

March brings rain as unrelenting as Marcus's workload.
I assume that Nettie, his business partner, has stopped
doing anything remotely useful, as he complains about
running the place single-handedly, which is impossible, as
not even Marcus can accompany clients to view properties and man the office simultaneously. As a result, he now
catches a later train home, showing up when Tod is asleep.
At least one night a week, he stays over in London for octopush. I am so starved of adult male company that I am
ridiculously excited when the Dampblasters man bangs on
our door.

Mr. Leech has an air of mild disappointment, as if the
eradication of rising damp and *Anobium punctatum* is having
a detrimental effect on his psyche. "What I'll do," he explains,
"is take off the plaster up to here." He indicates a point on

the back wall at around Tod's height. "I'll be injecting," he adds sadly, "and it will be very disruptive."

It appears that I have acquired the job title of Boss of Renovations. I am unqualified for this position, and have been flung into this highly responsible role, involving the spending of thousands of pounds, with no previous experience or training.

Mr. Leech blows softly into the tea I've made him. His head is sparsely covered with sandy hair, with pink scalp showing through. "This place has potential," he says, "but you've got your work cut out."

My mother, Carl and now Mr. Leech are eager to stress the enormity of renovating an antique property. *It's a lot to take on.* Like a difficult child, prone to mood swings and erratic behavior. You don't "take on" a new place like Lucille and Carl's, you just move in and hang your clothes in the wardrobe.

Mr. Leech has brought a power tool called a Kangol hammer. He will use it to hack away plaster up to a yard above floor level. The Gordon-and-Betty layer will crumble away. It's like an exfoliation treatment, but noisier.

Lucille raps on the kitchen window. I must have invited her for coffee, because she saunters in, shrugs off a turquoise jacket and looks for somewhere to put it, as every item of furniture has been covered with sheets and a fine coating of dust.

"We're being damp-proofed," I roar as the Kangol hammer rams into the wall.

"Poor you," Lucille says. Her hair is pulled back into a complicated French plait that looks as if it took several hands to construct. She fishes papers from her bag: a page from a lined jotter, on which she has listed temp agencies in Lexley, and the appointments page from the *Lexley Gazette.* "I'm sure you'll find something here," she says.

"Thanks," I say, scanning Situations Vacant: bar person, part-time gardener for country estate, general dogsbody at Barking Mad boarding kennels.

"I'm looking for someone for the salon," Lucille adds.

"It's not really me. I don't know how to wax someone's hair off."

"Not a therapist—for reception. I'm thinking of cutting down my hours. After school I'm a taxi service, running Adele to majorettes, ballet and tap…you know how it is." She spreads out the pages from the *Gazette* on the sheet-covered table.

I make her coffee and we sit in the dank conservatory which is as far as we can be from the Kangol hammer without going upstairs. Rain splats the windows, seeping in where the conservatory meets the house.

"What did you do before that film archive thing?" she asks.

"I worked for a greeting cards company, designing birthday cards."

"So that's where Tod's artistic streak comes from."

I shrug, swig my coffee. "I didn't exactly design the cards. I thought I'd be drawing and painting all day, but mostly I just added lettering to other illustrators' work." I don't add that this was the best bit; some days, I was sent out to collect dry cleaning for Donald, my obese boss, who lounged on a swivel chair, sprinkling ash onto his stomach. Four years at art college, and I'd wound up fetching the fat man's trousers.

"What do you want to do next?" Lucille asks.

"I'm thinking of working from home, maybe dig out my portfolio, see if local businesses need posters or flyers."

"Wouldn't you be lonely? I couldn't stand it," she says, shuddering, "being trapped in the house."

In fact I do worry about being shut indoors for too long,

and wonder whether I would get any work done, being in such close proximity to the fridge. Home workers notice that the streetlights have come on, and they're still wearing a dressing gown with gravy splattered down the front. They call their office-bound partners to report, "I've bought frozen peas," and take an entire afternoon to seal an envelope.

I might start caring about the condition of other people's property. Marcus has moaned about the garden over the road, with planks strewn all over the grass, and suggested that I say something to that Joe person, since I know him well enough to accept a lift. I snapped that I didn't know him, that his planks were none of our business and our garden wasn't much better with its slimy shed and exhausted plants.

"There's a job at the bookshop," Lucille says. "Part-time, I think. There's a card in the window. You should speak to Julia." She examines her nails, which are filed square at the tips.

As she's leaving, I catch Mr. Leech admiring her graceful brown legs, which are so utterly pampered—waxed, bronzed and moisturized—that they don't even mind the cold. Then he looks sadly at me and rams his Kangol hammer back into the wall.

Julia's hair flows down her back like a streak of fox. She has a satin-smooth face and wears a Biro pen on a cord around her neck. I don't like to come straight out with it, demanding a job, so I browse the shelves and work myself up to say something.

Coffee & Books is lit with dim spotlights sunk into the ceiling. I flip through gardening books: *Easy Herbaceous Borders, The Ultimate Lawn Guide.*

"Looking for something?" Julia asks.

"Just browsing, thanks." My tongue feels like it's coated with chalk. I stare at a display stand of cardboard cubes

called *Boxed Brainwaves,* which squeaks as I turn it. Each
box contains fifty cards telling you what to do with your
life. In the Beach Box, a card suggests having a treasure
hunt of shells: who can find the most species? The gardening box includes hints on constructing a teepee from
twigs, twine and a sheet, which it promises will take "one
fun afternoon," but you know will stretch over weeks and
result in a tremulous structure and emergency couples
counseling.

The Seduction Box contains the following advice: *"Play
hide and cheek! Ask your partner to count to twenty. Go hide—
wearing delectable undies—and wait for your lover to find you.
Warmer, warmer, hotter, hotter…WOW!"* I wonder how long I'd
spend crouching behind Marcus's filing cabinet, in my raspberry bra and knicker set, before he'd realize I was missing.

"Brainwave 37: Saucy striptease! Don your favorite lingerie—
raspberry knickers again—*and your day clothes on top. To the
sound of sensuous music, slowly peel off your outer layer to reveal
the luscious delights beneath."*

I am uncomfortable with the idea of peeling off layers
while being stared at. I worry that, like a rubbish joke-teller,
I'll lose confidence and freeze, trapped in my knickers and
massive boots. Marcus would snort at me, or assume that I
needed medication.

I have flipped through so many cards that I feel obliged to
buy the Seduction Box, and hope that Julia doesn't put it
about that the new people in Gorby Cottage are experiencing sexual difficulties.

"Anything else?" she asks.

"A job?" I say hopefully.

Me, Tod and a bike called Daredevil, minus stabilizers. We
bought it last year, for Tod's fifth birthday. To enhance its ap-

peal, I had added an old-fashioned bell, squeezy horn and camouflage-printed panniers. Together, Marcus and I wrapped Daredevil in silver paper, crept into Tod's bedroom and rested it against the wall. Of course he'd know what it was. You can't wrap a bike and not make it bike-shaped.

"Are you sure he'll like it?" I asked.

"Of course he will," Marcus said. "He'll be riding it by teatime."

Tod regarded Daredevil with the same level of enthusiasm he demonstrated with the rat. My last attempt to teach him to ride it, in the park opposite our old flat, resulted in Tod careering off the path and into the main road. He slammed into a decrepit car that was parked outside the mini-cab office. The car's owner, a vexed little man who looked like he'd been squashed into a brick shape by a car-crushing machine, raced out of the office and examined the car, as if he cared about its condition.

"I want to go home," Tod says now. We are on Chetsley Common, facing each other over the bike, which lies on its side. Tod is wearing his school uniform, plus a cycling helmet with a bright yellow peak, which creates a top-heavy duck effect. There is a glimmer of sun, but Tod is shivering, forcing hands up opposite sleeves of his sweatshirt. "It's too cold," he adds, "for riding."

"Let's just try. Come on, Tod, you should be able to—" I nearly said it: *at your age.*

I hold him upright, cling onto the saddle and trot behind. Tod pedals with his knees thrust outward. He has already outgrown Daredevil. His helmet, which is still too big for him, shakes dangerously. Nothing fits properly. I break into a canter, and Tod lurches to the left, landing with a yelp on the gravel path.

"You okay?" I ask, gathering him up.

He shrugs me off and stomps away from the bike. "Tod, come back," I yell after him. "Try again. It's like horses—you have to get straight back on if you fall off."

"It's *not* like horses," he rages, pulling off the helmet and tossing it to the ground.

This isn't right. He's six and he lives in the country. *Babies* can ride bikes around here. I've seen Harry streaking across the common on his sporty blue model, no stabilizers or panting mother, running behind. Tod is sulking on a bench, his face smeared with mud and tears. I am angry now, not with Tod, but with Marcus: aren't bike lessons part of Dad's job description? There's a rip in the left shoulder of Tod's sweatshirt, from his fall. Daredevil lies on the ground with its chain off.

I hold him and say, "Think how proud you'll feel when Dad comes home and you tell him you rode your bike."

He probes the gravel with the toe of his trainer. "I'm asleep when Dad comes home."

"Not tonight, you won't be. You can stay up late. Watch a video. I'll make vanilla popcorn in the microwave."

He manages a weak smile. "And doughnuts?" he asks.

"We'll get some."

Tod pulls up his sweatshirt to wipe his face. I fix the chain, and he straddles the bike. He exhales noisily, complains that his nose is cold, and we set off: *Sit up straight, you're leaning to the left again, that's better—no, don't look sideways, look ahead,* LOOK WHERE YOU'RE GOING…

This can't possibly work. He'll clang into the swings and crack his head open. This child still clonks his forehead on the wing mirrors of parked cars. We're heading for A&E at Lexley General. Where *is* Lexley General? We'll get lost again, wind up in that playground, with the cacti on trestle tables. *Get me to a hospital. My son has a bleeding head.*

There's no accident, no head injury. He is riding Daredevil.

Then I see Joe striding along the top path—he has an armful of wood, he's been collecting again—and run toward him, yelling, "Joe, he's done it—look!"

"That's so brilliant," Joe says, dumping the wood at his feet.

"Letting go, that's the scariest bit."

"Go, Tod!" Joe yells, clapping as if Tod's achievement is something to him.

Tod jiggles to a halt, slams down the bike and runs toward us. "Phone Dad," he pants. "Tell him I did it."

Joe takes Tod's hand, leads him back to the bike and helps him to climb on. I call Marcus's mobile, which is switched off, then his office.

"He's showing a flat in Fulham," Nettie says. "I'd expected him back by now. Is there a problem, Ro? You sound quite worked up."

"Tod rode his bike without stabilizers. I can't believe it, Nettie. One minute he was hopeless, falling off every—"

"Lovely," Nettie says.

"It's his very first time."

"I'll pass on the message."

Tod pedals furiously back to me. "What did Dad say?" he asks.

"He's very proud."

"Did you tell him I'm staying up late with popcorn?"

"Yes, he says he can't wait to see you." As Tod sets off again, I text Marcus: *TOD RODE BIKE PLS COME HOME ASAP.*

Then Tod, Joe and I walk home together.

He lived in Perth, and at first I think he means Perth, Scotland, but he's talking about Australia. That's where his girlfriend lived as a child. They came back for his mother's funeral and he's decided to stay.

"It feels right," Joe says, "living in the house I grew up in. Same garden, same tree—though it doesn't look as big and powerful as when I was a kid."

"What was it like then?" Tod asks, trotting beside him.

"Still big enough to fall out of. You like climbing trees, Tod?"

Tod shrugs uncertainly.

"I fell out of it once—must have been about your age. Crawling along a branch that couldn't take my weight. Four stitches in the forehead at Lexley General."

I wheel Daredevil into the shed.

"Show me," Tod says, pulling off the cycling helmet. Joe pushes an abundant fringe away from his forehead. There's a small scar, pearly against darker skin.

"Did you cry?" Tod asks.

"Oh, buckets, until the doctor gave me a barley sugar. I was okay after that."

I point to my forehead scar. "I got mine," I tell him, "from running away from a rat."

"Let me see," Joe says. He touches the scar very lightly.

I step back quickly.

"What's your girlfriend's name?" Tod asks. He's in an inquisitive mood. Once, when I told him to stop asking the librarian how her bleeper machine worked, he announced: "I am a question gun."

"Vicky," Joe says. He hasn't put his fringe back in its proper position. It sticks up in peaks, like badly cut grass.

"Never seen her," Tod says.

"She's in Dorset now—decided to move near her parents."

"So why—" Tod begins.

"We split up," Joe says.

I had planned to offer him coffee but the Kangol hammer is still screeching and Tod is revving up for a full interrogation. When he asked the librarian "But *how* does it read the bar code?" she slammed her gadget on the desk and snapped, "It just does."

I wish Joe would leave now, before Tod starts on the really personal stuff.

"Like your mum and dad," Tod continues, turning to me. "They fell out, so they left each other."

"That's right," I say, smiling tightly.

"Will that ever happen to you and Dad?"

Joe turns to leave. "See you again, Tod," he says, "for more bike practice." Tod grins and bounds toward the house.

"Of course not," I say after him. "That'll never happen to me and Dad."

I have cleared up Mr. Leech's debris and acquired a fine coating of pale gray dust. I can feel it clinging to my teeth. Now I am pairing up Tod's socks, ensuring that they are inside out, as he cannot bear the sensation of seam against toes.

"I'm not *that* late," Marcus says.

"Tod waited up for you. He stayed up till half-past nine."

"Why, is something wrong?" Marcus pulls off his tie and drops it on the bed.

"He watched a video and had popcorn and we waited and waited. Where were you? Didn't you get my messages?"

"I just missed the train."

"You missed lots of trains."

He lands heavily on the edge of the bed.

"Tod rode his bike," I add, "if you're interested."

"Of course I'm interested. That's fantastic."

Now I feel stupid for blowing up Tod's achievement into a major event. It's a mother's trait; we lose perspective. We wake up at four a.m., panicking that we don't have a non-embarrassing T-shirt for our child to use as an art overall at school. Before Tod, I was normal. I worked normal hours, barely thought about Anna's Archives at weekends, and never babbled to strangers in parks.

"My mobile battery's flat," Marcus says quietly. He stands up, wipes dust from the seat of his work trousers and strides out of the bedroom, leaving me with my seething bad mood and the stupid *Boxed Brainwaves* scattered all over the bed.

"Brainwave number 49: sensual bathtime. Surprise your lover by stepping into his bath. Have your own foam party!"

He's running a bath now, and when I look into the bathroom he is lying flat out, gazing at the shelf where Betty kept her toilet-roll doll. "Marcus," I say from the doorway, "Tod wanted to show off to you. These things are really important."

"You're saying I'm a terrible dad."

"Of course not. I didn't mean that."

"I do everything I can for him, Ro. Those fish—do you know how much trekking about I had to do to get them?"

He can't help it that Tod hasn't connected with the fish. He can't help being late. He's been working, that's all. He reaches for me with a wet hand and grips my fingers. I squeeze his hand back. I remember being in my old bathroom with him, that first evening, feeling trapped but not wanting him to leave. When he'd gone, I stared at his card for a long time. I picked up the phone several times and started to dial, but slammed it down before anyone answered. Then I forced myself to speak. My lips had dried out and my mouth had taken on a startling new shape, so when I spoke, it sounded like I didn't have any teeth. He said, "I'm so glad I came to the wrong flat."

I pull off my clothes now and step into the bath. Marcus gives me a surprised look, then pulls up his knees to make space for me. I stretch my legs around his hips, and lower my shoulders into the water. Now that I'm here, I'm not sure what to do. It doesn't feel like the right moment for a foam party.

From Tod's room comes a sharp, dry cough, an old person's cough. Marcus has started hacking at his toenails with the silver clippers.

"I've got a job," I tell him.

"Have you? Where?" He stops clipping.

"At the bookshop in the High Street."

"How did that happen?"

"I just walked in and asked. I start in May, when their temporary girl finishes." It had been too easy. Julia checked that I didn't keel over at the sight of a computer, and listened politely as I blathered on about managing Anna's Archives and creating my own range of greetings cards. Then she offered me Monday to Thursday, school hours. "It's just a shop job," I add.

"It might be good for you. You've been—"

"What?"

He grinds a fingernail into my apple soap. I feel jammed in, like Tod in that racing car seat at the hairdresser's. We used to fit into a bath, Marcus and me. On our wedding night, when we'd drunk the minibar dry, he filled the tub so full that the suds clung to our shoulders. Our kisses tasted of gin. Space wasn't a problem then.

Now my knees are too close to my face. My legs are sprouting hairs again. Lucille keeps offering me a discount, and told me about a new seaweed body-wrap treatment, which she can do for half price, as her therapist needs the practice.

"The cold tap's dripping on my back," Marcus says.

"We could swap places."

He leans forward, and I think he's going to kiss me, but he climbs out and grabs a towel from the rail. "You seem tense,

Ro," he says, roughly drying his back. "Maybe you'll feel better when you're working and have something to do."

"Smother each other with kisses and sweet-smelling bubbles."
Another time, maybe.

chapter 10

More Treasure

Marcus owns the king of car stereos. It takes six CDs that you insert into a box in the boot. The box is covered in carpet, like the rest of the boot, so you wouldn't even know it was there. He usually listens to light jazz, the kind that's played in wine bars or shops selling expensive plain vases, but right now it's not on, because Tod is playing a story tape in the back, on a yellow plastic tape recorder with pointy buttons like the tips of wax crayons.

I love Marcus's car. When I'm being driven by him, I can easily slip into a fantasy that we are en route to a country wedding or garden party where Pimm's will be served. I'm not a mother—or, if I am, my child has been spirited away to my fantasy parents' house where they are still married, and Tod is not being whirled by a man with an oblong moustache, and there's no story tape playing.

Apart from the stereo, Marcus's car boasts many pleasing features: it's never too cold, nor too hot. Nothing is sticky. In my old Mondeo, Ribena pools quivered on the dashboard and the car stunk so bad—a rank blend of molding Mini Cheddars and festering apple cores—that Tod, chief litter-lout, would retch on entering the vehicle. This car smells only of vacuumed upholstery. We are in Marcus's car because mine never recovered from Golf Club Day, and was towed away for scrap. Marcus hinted that I might be charged for the safe disposal of its battery and Mini Cheddars.

He has allowed acres of time to catch the three-twenty ferry from Southampton to the Isle of Wight. The story tape is *Danny the Champion of the World,* borrowed from Lexley library. Tod insists on a tape for journeys of more than forty minutes. Danny's dad, who has raised the boy by himself, is a wonderful man. He smiles a lot, not with his mouth but his eyes. Danny is glad that his dad is an eye-smiler. You can't fake that sort of smile.

"Looking forward to your holiday, Tod?" Marcus asks.

Tod is lost in the story, lolling on a bunched-up sweater against the window.

"Playing on the beach, learning to swim?" Marcus continues.

The narrator says that Danny, a child of nine, can drive a car all by himself.

"Well, *I* am," says Marcus. "Will you speak to me, Tod?"

"Dad, I'm trying to listen." He nudges up the volume.

When I booked the chalet, I tried to picture the three of us laughing and running on beaches, like a proper family who do things together. The chalet is set in an arc of similar properties and was the only vacant place I could find. I am hoping for basic amenities, but not somewhere intimidatingly posh. Can't have Tod expecting a similar standard of fixtures and fittings—like a Jacuzzi bath or a shower that blasts you from all angles—at home.

It's a terrible responsibility, propelling your family into an unseen house. You wonder what they're not mentioning on their slick Internet site. Enclosed garden with mature fruit trees? *Adjacent to bubbling septic tank.* I was tempted to book a cute cottage adjoining a working lighthouse, but spied a warning: "Foghorn activates automatically, so guests may wish to bring earplugs to minimize discomfort."

There is a crunching sound in the back. "Are you eating?" Marcus enquires. Cracker crumbs fly out of Tod's mouth. "Is that biscuits?" he asks. "Please, Tod, we'll stop when you're hungry. You can't be hungry yet. We've only just set off."

"I can't hear the tape," Tod complains.

"So no one can talk until your story tape's finished?"

"Shush," mutters Tod.

I study Marcus's profile. His jaw juts proudly, and his hair shows no sign of graying or falling out. His nostrils have become hairier with age, but with regular attention from the nasal hair trimmer, no one would ever know. If he were alone in this car—if Tod and I were catapulted out by convenient ejector seats—women might glance over and flirt at red traffic lights. He's still looked at, still noticed. The girl in the grocer's, who wears a Margaret badge and slams my purchases into a carrier bag, assumes a more sparkly demeanor whenever Marcus is with me.

"You sure Lucille will remember to feed the fish?" he asks.

"Yes, don't worry, I've given her a key."

"Did you leave the food out?"

"Right by the tank."

He exhales loudly, as if he's been fretting wildly about those fish.

The tape player's batteries are failing. The narrator's hon-eyed voice has slumped to a sinister growl.

"Turn it off," I tell Tod. "We'll get new batteries at a garage."

Tod employs his selective-deafness technique. "Give the tape player to Mum," Marcus says.

"It's still working," Tod protests.

"That was the end of the story."

"No, Dad, it wasn't."

"Give it to Mum."

Tod clicks off the tape player and hands it to me. He sits rigidly, his pale face set hard like the jouster model he made from plaster of paris in a rubber mold. "Are we nearly there yet?" he asks.

We have been driving for twenty minutes. We could hardly be less nearly-there-yet. "There's hours to go," I tell him. "Weeks, years. You'll be an old man by the time we get there."

Tod is making a noise, an unappealing blend of whine and groan, designed to infiltrate parental brains, cause the cells to vibrate and ultimately self-destruct. Before I had Tod, my mind worked efficiently: I could remember the name of all of my primary school teachers and the first postcode we ever had, when postcodes were first invented. Now I am wonder-ing if I've brought all our swimming things and Tod's spout cup and directions to the chalet.

Marcus is smiling now. It's an eye smile. He's somewhere else, somewhere he likes better than being trapped in a car, which is slowly being polluted by a whining six-year-old with a mouthful of crackers.

Much later, when Tod wakes from a doze, I check that the batteries have made a partial recovery and pass the tape player back to him. He presses Play.

"My father was in a sort of poacher's trance. For him, this was it. This was the moment of danger, the biggest thrill of all."

Easter Sunday, six-thirty a.m. I am up at this unearthly hour to put my plan into action before Marcus and Tod wake up. Yesterday, when we arrived on the island, I asked Marcus to stop at a garage, supposedly for bread, milk, coffee and batteries, but really to buy treasure. I spotted net bags of chocolate coins—I thought they were only sold at Christmas—and bought six, stuffing them deep in my coat pockets. I hoped Tod wouldn't sniff them out. Children can detect a mere rustle of foil wrapper, smell confectionery on adult breath.

My plan is to hide the coins on the beach and have Marcus and Tod do a treasure hunt. Until Tod was born, and our lives were engulfed by feeding and changing and trips to the doctor's, Marcus would hide surprise gifts all over the flat. He would watch, with an eye-smile, as I searched every room. One birthday he gave me a note bearing the clue: "I think you're grate." Finally, I located my perfume inside the cheese grater, at the back of the pan cupboard.

I'm hoping that a treasure hunt will remind Marcus of how we used to be. He and Tod can do it together, father and son.

I follow the steep path that leads from the chalets' shared garden to the beach. The chalets are in darkness; no one gets up this early on holiday. Some are starting to peel, shedding their skins, and one has hardboard and polythene instead of glass at its window. Ours is one of the neatest. It's tiny—just a shower room, two bedrooms filled by their beds, and a living room–kitchen in one—but feels plenty for three, which makes you wonder why adults are so keen to acquire utility rooms, sheds and conservatories.

I hide chocolate coins under damp knobbled rocks, making sure they stick out and are easy to find. I hope they're not stolen by gulls. There's a sign in front of our chalet that warns: Please Don't Feed Gulls, They Can Be Aggressive. By the time I'm back indoors, Tod has come through from his bedroom to ours and is dozing in Marcus's arms.

Down there on the beach, along with my treasure, are fossils. This is dinosaur land. Bones are found, pieced together with fake bits to fill the gaps, and displayed at the Dino Experience museum, which we plan to visit. The oldest bones are 132 million years old. This makes me feel quite youthful and sprightly.

We might even find a fossil. Our guidebook warns: "Sadly, as they belong to the Crown, you're not allowed to take fossils or dinosaur remains home. Please hand them in to a museum instead." This seems grossly unfair, as the Crown has enough treasures already. Who would gain more pleasure from owning a trapped, coiled creature than a six-year-old child?

Tod could take it to school. That would get him into Miss Cruickshank's good books. She sent a note home that read: "Fridays are show-and-tell days! Could parents help children to find something of natural interest to bring into class! No live bugs, please!" We discovered an abandoned wasps' nest, glued to the eaves of our shed, and carefully wrapped it in loo roll. Tod took it to school in a shoebox. When he opened the box at show-and-tell time, the nest had crumbled to dust, and Miss Cruickshank told him to tip it into the bin. A genuine fossil would win him Good Work stickers and house points, and his house would win the end-of-year trophy, thanks to Tod's ammonite.

"Treasure hunt?" he yelps, catapulting himself out of bed. "Let's go."

"It's not even morning," Marcus protests, pulling on jeans

and a sweater and following me and Tod—who's still wearing his rocket pajamas—out of the chalet.

While Tod hunts, Marcus perches on a rock and fiddles
with his mobile. "Found one," Tod announces. Soon he has
amassed handfuls and starts to rip off their foil. "Want one,
Dad?" he asks.

Marcus accepts a coin and peels off its wrapper. "They're all
spotty," he says. "Tod, don't eat them. They're disgusting." Tod
stretches his mouth, exhibiting its molten chocolate interior.

We head back to the chalet and Marcus drives off in search
of proper breakfast, something more substantial than toast,
to minimize any damage caused by decaying chocolate.

While he's gone, I promise to read to Tod if he'll get dressed
and clean his teeth properly, not just suck the toothbrush. It's
all deals. You do this, I'll do that. And I start reading: "'City
mazes provide a welcome diversion from life's hustle and bus-
tle. At Warren Street tube station, a two-dimensional maze on
the wall gives…' Are you listening, Tod?"

It has finally happened. He has gone off this book. I will
not have to resort to hiding it, like I did with *Guess How Much
I Love You*, dripping with guilt as he tore his bedroom apart
in search of the story, which I had slipped down the back of
the storage heater.

But Tod's not sick of the book, he just *feels* sick. I make
him sip water, which he spits back into the cup. Frothy dribble slides down his chin. Marcus arrives with too much food
to pack into the tiny fridge.

"We don't want anything else going off," he murmurs, carefully arranging cartons and packets to make best use of space.

"Sorry about the treasure hunt," I say to his back. "I
thought you'd have fun."

He turns, and his eyebrows scoot upward. "I am having
fun," he says, bravely.

★ ★ ★

Instead of swimming, Tod does this sand-batting thing. He lies flat on his belly, flapping his limbs as each wave hits him. He is being Salmon Man. "Salmon Maaan!" he shouts. *Flap-flap-flap.* This is why he likes the sea and not swimming pools. Pool water is too deep for him to be Salmon Man.

Marcus lies back on the sand and shuts his eyes. His fatigue must be due to the exertion of watching me lug beach towels, a blanket and the carrier bag containing our picnic to the beach. Marcus has pulled off his sweater to form a thin pillow, and falls asleep instantly.

It's so impressive, the way he can click into slumber. There's no squirming to find a comfy position, no semi-awake state. I suspect that he sleeps on the train to and from work, not using his laptop at all, allowing him two hours' extra kip per day.

Salmon Man becomes Tod again, and is instantly hungry and freezing. "What is there to eat?" he asks through banging teeth. Rarely does Tod want to eat at mealtimes. He expects a constant supply of appetizing snacks, as if life comes packaged with round-the-clock room service.

"Ham rolls," I say.

He peers into the carrier bag where wet, pink scraps have escaped their bread casings. "What else?"

"The barbecued boar will be ready in a minute, darling."

"Huh," Tod mutters. Really, I should take tips on picnic preparation from my sister. Her outdoor offerings include cloudy lemonade she makes herself and some fancy dessert involving loganberries. Natalie never has to babble an apologetic "It'll taste just fine. It's just a bit squashed, that's all."

Tod takes a filling-less roll and sucks it, then drops it into the burrow which he's made in the sand. "Dad, is there water down there?" he asks.

"Your dad's asleep," I point out.

Tod has yet to master the art of recognizing whether a person is asleep or not. He often blunders into our bedroom at night, announcing, "The sheep won't be *quiet,* Mum," when I can't hear a living thing, and had been enjoying a particularly pleasing dream about being massaged by a man with incredibly sensitive fingers and no filing cabinet.

Tod is burying the roll and muttering about our lack of bucket and spade. His hair needs cutting again—the back of his head looks like a matted cushion—but I can't face jamming him into Tina's racing car seat. Marcus shows no sign of regaining consciousness. If he were a different dad—the dad who's in the sea now, towing a squealing girl on a fluorescent pink raft—we might bury him in sand. We'd pile it on his legs and chest and leave only his head poking out. He would pretend to be trapped, and struggle to free himself.

I don't think it's good that I imagine Tod having a different dad.

chapter 11

Sleep Talking

Dinosaurs had clever protective accessories like armored backs, pointed thumbs and spiky frills around their necks. Their remains reside at Dino Experience museum. These creatures are dead, obviously, and therefore don't do very much, but at least they require no feeding or cleaning out. As far as Tod is concerned, one of the smaller dinosaur species— a *Hypsilophodon,* perhaps—would make an excellent pet.

Dino Experience is packed with family groups who are escaping the fine rain. A small group has clustered around a life-size replica of a *Neovenator* which, says the taped commentary, "was a ferocious predator, ripping its victims with its razor-sharp—" We miss the next bit because a man in a wet navy anorak is barking, "Are you writing that down, Tristan? Come on, you've got your worksheets to fill out."

Tristan uses his knees as a desk. His flat, damp hair looks

like it's been licked. "Lean on something," the dad goes on. "Look, you're rumpling the paper."

I wonder whether Marcus would have made Tod fill in a worksheet if he hadn't decided to stay at the chalet, resting.

We're so used to it just being the two of us that Tod rarely asks why Dad hasn't come. It's as if he's forgotten that dads can go out to places other than work.

"It's the dinosaur journey," Tod says, yanking my sleeve.

We step into a dimly lit passage that leads to a moving pavement. Creatures with abundant teeth and gnarled complexions peer through the undergrowth.

"How do you know that's a meat eater?" asks the worksheet dad behind us.

"His sharp claws?" suggests Tristan. He is a perky, well-spoken kid who, I imagine, uses cutlery in a tidy manner.

"Wrong. Come *on*. You know this."

"His big mouth?"

The moving pavement stops. We are trapped in the Triassic period, being eyeballed by life-size *Tyrannosaurus rex*.

"What happened?" Tristan asks.

The dad sighs and looks around for a staff member. A man with a jaunty orange Dino Experience T-shirt stretched tight across his bulbous chest strides along the pavement. "Did someone press the red button?" he asks. "It's only for emergencies."

"I did it," whispers Tod. His finger is still on the red button. He jerks it away, and tries to hide it behind his back.

"Can't you control your child?" scolds Tristan's dad. "He's spoiled the whole experience."

"For God's sake," I snap. "What's a child supposed to do with a whopping red button like that?"

The dad ushers Tristan away from us, as if button-pushing tendencies are contagious.

Later, we see the Dino Experience man mopping up a puddle in the Early Life section. "Sorry about the button," I say. "I bet children do that all the time."

"No," he says, "they don't."

The small restaurant sits alone and stranded on the hilltop. It's nine-thirty and too cold to eat outside; we're all wearing our coats. Tod has a scarf around his head, tied under his chin, like a bandage.

"You sure you're okay out here?" asks the waitress.

I mean to say that we're fine and it's lovely out here, but blurt, "We're all lovely, thanks."

"Beautiful night," she says, smiling. She rubs her delicate hands together.

Tod has the wide-eyed delight of a child allowed to stay up way past bedtime. Marcus and Tod are trying to identify star constellations, but can't find any discernable patterns. Now they're debating whether the brightest one is the Pole Star or Venus or a UFO heading for the garden in front of the chalets.

"If aliens try and take me," Tod says, "you're coming with me, Dad."

"Of course I am. I wouldn't let them take you by yourself."

I rest my hand on Marcus's thigh under the table. The UFO has gone, must have landed.

"Me and Dad are going to their planet," Tod announces.

"What would I do without the two of you?"

Marcus shifts his leg and calls the waitress over; she has forgotten his mustard.

"So sorry," she says. He flashes a Marcus smile to make her feel better. The waitress keeps fluttering around Marcus, checking that his steak has been cooked the way he likes it. "It's perfect," he says.

At Dino Experience, Tod had found a lift-the-flap section. When you raised one of the wooden doors, the smell of rotting corpse wafted out. He kept lifting and shutting the thing, forcing me to inhale until the stench had embedded itself in my throat.

Tonight I ordered lamb but can't taste it—only the horrible thing behind the flap.

Our last night. We have functioned well as a family. Marcus and Tod have constructed a giant sand castle with a maze of moats that filled each time a wave hit the entrance, then melted beneath the tide. Marcus bought Tod a football, saying, "He just needs practice, he'll soon get the gist of it." Tod was more excited about the plastic snow dome, also purchased by Marcus, with its miniature lighthouse inside.

We leave first thing tomorrow. Tod is in bed and Marcus is curled up sideways on the sofa, reading a book about Stalingrad. At least I think he's reading, but he doesn't seem to be turning the pages. Each time I speak to him, he says, "Hmm."

If you want to know something, just ask. That's what I tell Tod. If he asks again, I'll tell him how babies are really made. How the sperm meets the egg.

"Marcus?" I say.

"Hmm?"

"Is everything all right?"

He sets the book on the sofa arm and turns down the page corner. "Is what all right, darling?"

Ask. Come out with it. "It's just a feeling I get."

He comes over and perches on the arm of my chair, which makes him look enormous. He kisses my head, like you might that of a child who has damaged itself, when it really is possible to kiss things better.

"What kind of feeling?" he asks.

"I don't think things are right with us."

"Since when?"

"Since ages ago, Marcus."

He sighs, and glances at the book that he wants to carry on reading. "Why do you say that? Everything's fine. It's *always* been fine. What's different?"

I can't tell him, because whatever I say will come out sounding needy. I don't want to be that kind of person. All I manage to say is, "We're not like we used to be."

He strokes my hair and says, "We just need more time together, all by ourselves." Then he pats my head, stands up and carefully smoothes out the folded page corner of the Stalingrad book.

I don't point out that that's what we're having right now.

When Tod went to bed, I read from the dinosaur book we bought at the Dino Experience gift shop, but he kept sniffing and fidgeting and setting his spout cup on its side so it dribbled on the rose-patterned pillowcase. He wouldn't pay attention. It was probably my flat voice. I was reading but thinking about my first holiday with Marcus, on the Basque coast of Spain, in a rank hotel owned by an Englishman who swigged wine from a plastic carton, the kind that usually contains car oil.

There was a small, rectangular swimming pool in the hotel grounds, with an oily film on its surface. The owner dangled a small white gadget into the water, checked a reading and ran away, muttering to himself. Nothing could have spoiled that holiday, not even a poisonous pool.

I remembered calling Anna, saying I was sick, and lying in bed all day with Marcus and not feeling one speckle of guilt.

And him actually offering to sit at the tap end.

And Anna saying I looked thin, and was I on some stupid juice-only diet, when in fact I was so Marcus-demented that I could hardly eat.

When we had Tod, Marcus didn't seem to want me so much. He said it was sleep deprivation, that everything would work out fine, and I believed him.

I remember really minding when he was asleep, because I couldn't talk to him.

And telling Nettie that Tod was roaring the flat down—holding the phone to his face so she could hear for herself—so could Marcus please not work late and just hurry home?

She never seemed to know where he was.

He said that having a baby had made me suspicious, not so much fun anymore.

He said: "You never used to be like this," and I wanted to rewind to Easter egg day, but still have Tod.

I wanted to have my cake and eat it.

"Mum. *Mum*." Tod has crept into the living room. His cup is empty but he keeps sucking the spout, filling his belly with air.

"You should be asleep, sweetheart."

He flings himself next to me on the sofa. "Can I ask you a question?"

"Sure."

"It's late, Tod," Marcus says, glancing up from his book. "Just five minutes, okay?"

Tod straddles the sofa arm as if it's a horse. "Mum, if you could be a dinosaur, what would you be?"

"Dinosaurs are too old. What's a bit newer than dinosaurs?"

"Mammoths."

"I'd be a mammoth. I'd spurt you with my trunk. How about you?"

"*Hypsilophodon.* They were little, so they went around in gangs to keep safe. They had friends."

"What about Dad?" I ask him.

"A *Neovenator,*" Tod announces.

Big, powerful, top of its food chain. The *Neovenator* can do whatever the hell it likes.

Two twenty-seven a.m. I have been woken by something, but by the time I'm properly conscious, whatever it was has stopped.

On the windowsill is the snow dome Marcus bought for Tod. Inside the plastic dome is a lighthouse. I collected domes like this as a child. I must have been older than Tod is now, because I can remember each one.

Mum and Dad let me choose one every holiday. My favorite dome had York Minster inside. It wasn't the building itself that I loved—as far as I was concerned, one church looked much like another—but the snow. In the York Minster snow dome, it looked soft, like real snow, instead of the obviously synthetic flakes in my inferior domes.

Dad bought me a microscope the Christmas after our York holiday. I had examined my hair, a fragment of scab I had picked from my elbow and the wet beads from a pomegranate that Mum, thrilled to introduce such an exotic fruit to our home, had let me dissect.

I still wasn't satisfied. I wanted to examine the snow from the York Minster dome. I tried to unscrew it, but of course the dome couldn't be separated from its black plastic base. So I smashed it against the washbasin, mopped up the water with a towel—it was just ordinary water, I dunked my finger into the puddle and tasted it—and picked up as many flakes as I could. I set three on a glass slide, placed a square of clear plastic film on top and jammed my eye against the microscope.

They were real. Each flake had its own, perfectly symmetrical shape.

Dad came into the bathroom and found me crouching on the wet lino with my microscope and bits of smashed plastic. The base, with York Minster attached, had landed in one of Mum's pink zip-up slippers. All Dad said was, "I think you'd better dry that floor."

I shake Tod's lighthouse dome, and wonder how I could have thought that the York Minster snow was real when it showed no sign of melting.

Marcus is sleep talking, that's what must have woken me. It's a family trait. Tod has mumbled at night since the thing at his old school, when the head teacher called me at work, saying that there had been an incident. He started talking about scissors after that, and has since moved on to beasts with flaring nostrils and hooves.

It's hard to hear what Marcus is saying because he's lying facedown, muffled by pillow. Then one word escapes, as clear as if he were speaking right to my face.

He says, "Sarah."

part three

When you're lost, or feel trapped, the worst thing you can do is panic.

chapter 12

Mayday

Dear parents,
Don't forget the fancy dress contest at the Spring Fair
on Chetsley Common, 10 a.m. on Sunday May 3rd!
Entry fee £2—all proceeds to the Chetsley Primary
PTA! So get creative! Contributions to the PTA cakes
and candies stall also appreciated!

I am more alarmed by the date on the letter than Miss
Cruickshank's overuse of exclamation marks. This note has
lain in Tod's schoolbag since before the Easter holidays. The
fair is in two days' time. While other parents have been bea-
vering away, sparks flying from their sewing machines, I have
been supervising the rewiring of our home and trying to
look unconcerned as the electrician announced—rather
gleefully, I thought—that we could have burned in our beds.

"Why didn't you show me this letter?" I ask, waving it in Tod's face. He is poring over a library book about animals' underground homes.

"I did tell you," he says. "I reminded you *three times.*"

I didn't listen. I can't sew. I don't even own a sewing machine. Bad, bad mother. "Well, do you mind going in your ordinary clothes?"

"Yes," he says, giving me a sharp look. "Harry's going as a knight. I *do* mind."

"So what do you want to go as?" I hope he says a ghost—a sheet with eye holes cut out—or even a mummy. He's still engrossed in Miss Cruickshank's Egyptian project. I could simply bandage him in kitchen roll and it would look fantastically authentic, unless this rain keeps up. It could also prove rather problematic if he needed the toilet.

"Harry's mum made him a real chain-mail outfit," Tod adds helpfully.

"Did she now."

"And a real horse on wheels for him to pull along."

"Horses don't have wheels," Marcus says. He has just come in from the garden where he appeared to spend more time chatting over the wall to Carl than cutting back our beleaguered plants so everything will look tidy and Best-Kept-Villagey come summer. "They have hooves," he adds. He pours himself a pint glass of orange juice and gulps it noisily, as if to emphasize how hard he's been working.

"I'm going to be Minotaur," Tod announces.

"Half man, half horse," says Marcus. He lands heavily on a kitchen chair and flips open the *Lexley Gazette.* There's an article about a local children's entertainer who drove his car through the chip shop window in Lexley, stopping inches in front of the fryer. The entire facade of the shop will have to be replaced. This isn't the kind of behavior you'd expect from a magician called Professor Tickles.

"Half man, half *bull*," Tod retorts.

I am uncomfortable with the concept of composite animals. Where does one part finish and the other bit start?

"He's got an ordinary body, hairy legs and a big bull's head with horns," Tod explains.

"How am I supposed to make that, Tod? I haven't a clue how to—"

"I'll help," he says.

The matter apparently settled, he traces a finger along an illustration of a cutaway burrow, in which small mammals live happily in darkness, unencumbered by needlework projects or mythical half this, half that creatures.

The most worrying aspect of fancy dress contests is the real possibility of appearing foolish in public. You feel exposed enough in a village like Chetsley. Tina, creator of chain-mail masterpieces, occasionally says things like "I saw you in your garden—planning to do anything with that straggly red currant bush?" or "I hear Tod brought in worms for show-and-tell and Miss Cruickshank didn't like them." I could have told him that would happen, had I known that he had dug them out of the garden, and stashed them in an ice-cream carton in his bag. Now my son will be observed by the entire population of Chetsley in a botched animal outfit. *Not his fault, of course, poor boy—and isn't it weird how one of his eyebrows flares up like that? You'd think his mother would do something about it.*

I phone Suzie, who says, "Just buy an outfit. What's this country thing about making stuff?" I can't explain why that's all wrong.

I call Lucille. As creator of outlandish majorette outfits, she will surely know where I might purchase suitably bull-colored fabric.

"Meet me tomorrow," she says. "My break's at two. Don't worry, I'm sure we'll find some…what are Minotaurs made of again?"

I tell her that some kind of fur will be involved.

Jackson & Peel is a haberdashery shop. Being a non-sewer, I have never been in such an establishment before. As well as fabric rolls, the tiny shop also boasts a small selection of ornamental coal scuttles. The elderly lady who works here regards my unkempt hair with interest, as if the growing-out crop might benefit from harsh scissoring.

Lucille hums to herself, and examines fabrics. She is wearing her white Fab-U-Look tunic, which makes her appear infinitely hygienic and capable. "Do you have any fur, Mrs. Jackson?" Lucille asks. That sounds terribly personal. Any superfluous hair, Mrs. Jackson? Scars? Piercings? Tattoos?

"What color, Lucille?" the woman asks. She is drinking tea from a fluted-edged china cup, which she sets down on its saucer.

Lucille shrugs. "Brown? Gray? What color are bulls, Ro?"

She should know this, being a country person. "Gray, I think. The Minotaur's a kind of dirty gray in Tod's book."

Mrs. Jackson disappears into a mysterious room where, I suspect, more sinister goods are stored: illegal knives or DVDs where everyone wears shiny black rubber and there's no plot or dialogue. Surely Jackson & Peel cannot exist solely on sales of fabric, zip fasteners and coal scuttles.

Mrs. Jackson returns with a hefty roll of gray fur, which she lobs onto the cutting table. "Two meters, Ro?" Lucille suggests.

"That should be enough," I bluff. The fur is vaguely bull colored and textured, but not bull shaped. Not even Lucille can help me with that bit.

We stop off in the café at the back of the baker's where they appear to make coffee with three granules of Nescafé.

"Is Marcus around this evening?" Lucille asks.

"Yes, why?"

"Carl was hoping to catch up with him. He's got a bee in his bonnet about that garden opposite you."

I'm developing an allergic reaction to Carl. I suspect that he's the kind of man who says, "Shall I be mum?" before pouring tea. Worryingly, he appears to have taken a shine to Marcus, and has started to ask him for the occasional beer at the Poacher's Retreat. Marcus is noncommittal about Carl, but said, "We're new here. We should make an effort, be friendly. Try to be open-minded."

Lucille dips a plain biscuit into her coffee and sucks its melting edge.

"What's wrong with Joe's garden?" I ask.

"I'd leave it. It's none of our business. But Carl likes to get involved, can't help himself—"

"What does Carl plan to do?" My coffee is having a soporific effect. I thought that it was supposed to contain caffeine and jolt your system—isn't that the whole point?

"He wants to have a word, wonders if Marcus might back him up."

"Why Marcus?"

"Well, you live opposite. You're the ones most affected by—"

"Honestly, I don't think he'll want to get involved."

"Have you noticed that thing he's building?" she continues. "Bits of old wood, flung all over the lawn?"

"I think it's a shed." Skin crinkles the surface of my coffee. I scoop it off with a spoon and dump it in my saucer.

"What does he want that for? It's not like he does any gardening."

"His garden's not that bad. It's only May—it hasn't had time to get bad." In fact, the first thing that struck me after our Isle of Wight trip was how quickly the grass and weeds had sprung up, as if doused with some kind of growth hormone. You could virtually see it growing, hear the sprouting of grasses and leaves.

Lucille posts the last fragment of biscuit into her mouth, and pulls a compact mirror and mascara from her bag. She brushes on the mascara, stretching her mouth wide, like Mum and Perry's koi carp. "Carl's planning to pop over and offer to help. Nothing nasty." She snaps the compact mirror shut.

"Can I borrow that?" I ask. Lucille hands me her mirror. I look sickly, the color of anemic coffee, possibly due to the prospect of Marcus being cajoled into harassing Joe, but more likely, the horror of my impending needlework challenge.

I lay out gray fake fur on the living room floor and wonder what to do first. What use is school, really? Did I learn anything useful? Tod often declares, "I don't understand why I have to know sums." I explain that he's clever and that learning even more will help him to have a wonderful life. He always says that he doesn't want a wonderful life; he'll live with Marcus and me forever. Sometimes I add that school is useful for stuff other than learning—making friends, for instance—but he never looks convinced.

And he's right to question the school system. What can I remember now? My big sister winning gymnastics trophies and pretending not to notice the adoring boys who watched her displays.

This library book, *Easy Sew Fancy Dress Outfits,* includes instructions to construct a clown mask from a paper plate with pan scourers for hair. There are tigers and spacemen and rabbits with bendable ears, but no bulls.

Marcus has gone to meet Carl at the Poacher's. I'm glad that he's out. He would suggest that I abandon the Minotaur and persuade Tod to squeeze into his age-three-to-four skeleton outfit, which is still in its original packet.

Tod creeps into the living room, stares at the fur and says, "New rug."

"It's not a rug, Tod, it's your Minotaur. Lie down on that newspaper. I'm going to draw round your legs to make a pattern." He gives me a worried look, as if I am on the brink of attempting a task way beyond my capabilities, involving gas and naked flames.

"How?" he asks.

"You know how to lie down. You're really good at it. Do you want this costume or not?" Obediently, he lies on his back. I draw around his lower half, allowing extra space for…seamage, I think you call it. "Off to bed now. I can't have you hanging around me, putting me off."

"I'm not *doing* anything," Tod protests.

"Yes, you are. You're breathing."

I have cut out enormous, furry trousers. How will they stay up? He'll be standing in front of important judges and the *Lexley Gazette* photographer and they'll flump to the floor, showing his milk-lolly thighs. He'll have to wear one of Marcus's belts, also too big. I'll stab in an extra hole. Marcus won't notice.

"Is it finished yet?" Tod shouts from the bathroom.

At what point does a child acquire patience? They want everything *now*. They want it before they've even thought about wanting it.

"Get dry and put your pajamas on," I yell back. "I can't read to you tonight. I'll come up and tuck you in a minute."

Hand-stitching the fur takes ages and I wonder if my sewing will hold, whether Tod will have to move in slow motion to avoid putting seams under pressure. Now for the head. I have figured out how to do this: two ovals for sides, and a thick strip for the middle. I'm picturing a kind of furry bonnet.

Ears. How to make ears? I'll come back to that bit. The nose ring is easy. I bought curtain rings at Jackson & Peel. There's a pot of gold enamel paint in the kit for Anne Boleyn, which Tod needed in order to carry on living but never got around to making.

I creep into his bedroom to fetch it.

"Can I see it yet?" he demands, throwing off his duvet in a dramatic swoop.

"Not until it's ready."

"Are you going to make Anne Boleyn? Can I help?"

"Go to sleep."

Mazes and Labyrinths lies open on the floor. "Keep one hand on the wall. You might hit dead ends but you will, eventually, solve the puzzle."

"You didn't tuck me in," he shouts after me.

I make ears from two leaf shapes of fur. One is bigger than the other. Now they're too small, and might have belonged to a guinea pig. I spike my finger, and daub the crimson bead on to my jeans.

Sarah, he said, as if he was waking up next to her: *Sarah*.

Sarah doesn't spend her evenings fretting about the dimensions of ears. She's never stabbed herself with a needle.

Sometimes I cheer myself up by imagining her as a bull, with thick neck folds and gigantic damp nostrils. Mostly, though, I picture her with an airbrushed bottom, like those impossibly perfect models in adverts for thongs.

Upstairs, Tod is chundering on about being unable to sleep because he has been denied his milk, a kiss, and I haven't read to him. I think about Sarah's buoyant breasts and hack out horns from a cardboard box. As I paint them white, I imagine she and Marcus on one of their regular nights out, in a restaurant with candles and waitresses in black dresses and heels, not headdresses. No one sings "Happy Birthday" in that sort of restaurant.

The Minotaur has no teeth. What kind of teeth should it have? Forget teeth. It's past midnight. Tail! How could I have forgotten a tail? I need a furry draught excluder. Would Lucille have one? Or Joe? He doesn't look like a draught-excluder owner. Mum and Perry have one, but it's a brown sausage dog. Wrong color.

The door opens as I'm stitching on pan scourers for the bull's curly fringe. "Hello, love," Marcus says.

I can detect mild drunkenness without looking at him. "Have fun?" I ask.

"Carl was all for going to see that guy who's moved in, you know the one—but he'd had a few and I said it might turn ugly."

"Really," I say, remembering that bulls do have curly bits, but not fringes.

"What's all this fur?" Marcus asks.

I hold up the bull head and make him examine my sore thumb.

"Great horse," he says.

Spring Fair day. Merry-go-rounds and sideshows have already been set up on the common, awaiting the main event.

It's the rain that wakes me, splatting our bedroom window as if being hosed on to the glass. Since I was fifteen, wet fairgrounds have made me sense that something awful is about to happen.

I ran away then. I mean ran away properly. Not to the end of the garden, knowing that I'd hurry back as soon as I got hungry or it started raining, but to Blackpool on the back of a 90cc scooter with a raccoon tail tied to the back, belonging to a boy called Phil.

Phil wasn't even my boyfriend. He was just a boy I had met at a disco, who thrilled me with his spooky gray eyes and obsession with running away. He wanted to go to Brighton, but I insisted on Blackpool because Dad had spent all his childhood holidays there. He had told me about the Pleasure Beach and illuminations and a nightclub called Diamond Lil's. If there was a place where everything was built for fun, it had to be Blackpool.

I had twenty-five pounds, my prize for passing my mock exams, and a skewed belief that running away with Phil was one of my cleverer ideas. Blackpool was shrouded in fog, and smelled of onions and wetness. Rain slapped the phone box as I told my mother where I was. "Get back here this minute," she said. She added something else, in a strangled voice, and I banged the phone down.

Phil stood outside the phone box, holding a wicker basket containing seaside rock shaped like a fried breakfast: egg, bacon and something that was supposed to look like a tomato, but was pink. The raccoon tail was sodden, and hung limply.

Why had I done this? Back home, the air had grown heavy with tension and my mother's overuse of pine-scented furniture polish. Dad had taken to preparing his own doleful meals—usually crackers and pale, milky cheese—which he ate in the garage. I assumed that this was a permanent arrangement as I had spotted a collection of cling-film-wrapped cheeses on a shelf in the garage, next to the varnish and Nitromorse stripper. I worried about him, eating his meals surrounded by inedibles. I was scared that he'd start varnishing his food.

Phil crunched the rock egg. Fairground music rattled along in its tinny way. We tried to sleep on the beach, covered by damp coats, and stared up at the pier's underside.

The next day, I lost Phil at the Pleasure Beach. It rained and rained and he had all my money. Feeling sorry for me, the ghost train boy said, "Cheer up, have a free ride if you like." As I stepped out of the train, I realized I'd been sitting in someone else's wee.

I never felt the same about fairgrounds after that.

"Can I havamumumum?" Tod asks.

"What?"

"Amumalull."

"Can't hear you," I say. "Take your head off." He removes the bull headgear to reveal an overcooked face. "God, you're really sweating. I should have made nose holes. Sure you're not going to suffocate?"

He shakes his head and marches toward the bouncy castle. It has already acquired a thin layer of gray water. Tod's not my favorite person right now, not since he failed to greet the Minotaur costume with appropriate enthusiasm, considering the toil that went into its production. He just said, "Is that it?" and complained that Marcus's belt pinched his stomach.

He was more impressed with the chocolate nests we made for the PTA cakes and candies stall—bashed Shredded Wheat bound with melted Dairy Milk—which I now carry on an uncovered plate, despite the rain, so the entire village can see what a fine, dedicated mother I am. We filled the nests with speckled sugar eggs left over from Easter.

The bouncy castle is manned by a vexed-looking man whose hair sticks flatly to his forehead. Marcus stands a few feet away from us, presumably to disassociate himself from a small, damp bull. For the man bit of Tod's costume, I gave him an old orange fleece of mine that's been washed so many times it's turned peach. Peach makes me look like a dead person.

Adele, Lucille's daughter, is catapulting herself across the bouncy castle. She's supposed to be Tod's school buddy but regards him like she would a woodlouse she's found under a flowerpot. She is wearing a silver and turquoise majorette's outfit, which flips up as she bounces, showing baggy white knickers.

I spot Tina with Harry, whose chain-mail ensemble appears to be unmarred by the rain. Clever Tina, she must have used shower-proof wool. Children are dressed as fairies, queens, dragons, mermaids; intricate costumes bearing up well against unfavorable climatic conditions. Tod's bull head is now sodden. I wish that I had picked a less absorbent fabric.

"These look lovely," says Carl, chair of the PTA and powerhouse behind the cakes and candies stall. He examines our Shredded Wheat nests, each now containing a puddle as well as the eggs, and sips lager from a plastic tumbler.

"I'm cold and wet," Tod informs me.

"We'll just stay for the fancy dress judging, then go home."

We buy one of our Shredded Wheat nests, and huddle under the awning at the Any Odd Number Wins a Prize stall. I'd like to know precisely how many odd numbers are in that box.

"You might win," says the stall woman. She has prominent

nose veins and is sucking a colossal sweet, which forms a ball in her cheek. Tod rummages in the box. "Look at all these lovely soft toys," the woman says. "Dig deep down, right to the bottom."

Where there still aren't any odd numbers, you little twerp.

We have seven goes. Tod outgrew Winnie-the-Pooh years ago but desperately wants a counterfeit Piglet that isn't even wearing the right color jacket. We shell out double the cost of a shop-bought Piglet and still don't win.

"Better luck next time," growls the woman, rolling the ball to her opposite cheek.

Nearly everyone has hurried to the marquee now, although Adele is still on the bouncy castle, slithering in a small lake. At the marquee's entrance, on a rickety looking platform, Mr. Tickles is fashioning swans from sausage balloons. He hands them to children who mistake them for presents, then demands five pounds. I suspect that he is trying to raise funds to pay for the chip shop window.

A girl dressed as a witch with a raffia wig is grumbling about not being allowed an eleventh go on the odd-numbers stall.

"Let's find Dad," I suggest, dragging Tod around the muddy common. The merry-go-round man looks far from merry. He is wearing a carrier bag as a rain hat and waggles a finger when Tod leans against the rumbling generator.

Still hunting for Marcus, we dive into a smaller tent with a soggy paper sign announcing: Tea Tray Contest. The most spectacular trays are marked Winner, Second, Third and Highly Commended. Each component—cake, sandwich, additional item—is marked out of ten. I'm not sure that I approve of Tod seeing these trays. He might expect similar endeavors with his lunchbox.

Sandwiches have been formed by Swiss-rolling the bread

and carving off dainty slivers. When Natalie made sandwiches like these for Mum's Boxing Day buffet, I seriously
wondered whether I could carry on being her sister. I am
staring at a pyramid of tiny pink cakes, which have somehow been piled up without any of their icing being dented,
when I hear Tod behind me, at the tent's entrance, shouting,
"Joe, Joe, come here, look at *me.*"

Joe strides into the tent and takes a step back from Tod,
appraising his costume. "You look fantastic," he says.

"Guess what I am."

"You're a Minotaur. The monster in the maze."

"How did you know?" I ask, astounded.

"Isn't it obvious?" Joe says, laughing. "Furry legs, soggy
sweatshirt, terrifying-looking ears—think you've lost one,
Tod, not that it—"

"Will I win?" Tod asks. "Am I the best out of everyone?"

"I bet you're the most original. I haven't seen any other
Minotaurs around here." Joe is wearing an enormous, baggy
sweater, which looks as sodden as Tod's bull head. Even his
eyelashes are wet.

"You're building something in your garden," Tod
announces.

"That's right. It's a tree house."

"But it's on the ground."

"Some of it is. You build the main supports around the
trunk and then you add the house. It's much easier to make
the house on the ground. That way, you cause less damage
to the tree."

"I know," Tod says. "I've been looking from my bedroom.
I watch you all the time—"

"He's just curious," I cut in quickly.

"What's it for?" Tod asks.

"Well, what would *you* do in a tree house?"

"I'd climb up," Tod says, poking a finger through the mesh fence in an attempt to access a Highly Commended fruit scone bursting cream and blackcurrant jam. "I'd sit all by myself and look out."

"That's what I'm planning to do," Joe says.

An announcement: *"Could children please make their way to the main marquee for fancy dress judging."* Where's Marcus? He only gets lost when he wants to, like at IKEA or a Spring Fair.

"I'm going to find Dad," Tod yelps, charging out of the tent and across the muddied common toward the main marquee. His tail—I made it too long, from a strip of leftover fur—wraps itself between his legs, and he steps on it, flipping backward and landing on his rump in mud and discarded May Fair programs. It splatters his peach sweatshirt body, the back of his bull head, and somehow works its way up his nose.

I expect him to cry but he ploughs onward into the marquee where sodden grown-ups step back, as if scared of mud contamination, past fairies and mermaids who stare with gobstopper eyes at the state of him. He climbs on the stage and joins the end of the line. The other children tilt their faces toward him. I wonder if Marcus simply grew tired of the rain and Mr. Tickles's balloon tricks, and sneaked off home. I start to tap out our home number on my mobile, then ram it back into my pocket.

Behind me, someone says, "What's that furry thing supposed to be?"

"A dog?" comes the reply.

An elderly lady with an embroidered shawl pulled around her shoulders talks to each child in turn. She clasps the microphone at the center of the stage. "This is extremely difficult," she begins.

She should have seen me at midnight last night, hacking

out those blasted ears. We didn't have time to look for the lost one. It's probably lying by the even-numbers stall.

"You all look wonderful," the woman continues, "but I'd like to award third prize to Veronica Hines, a beautiful mermaid." Veronica flutters to center stage to collect a small silver parcel.

"Second prize, Juliette Shandler, the human pyramid." Juliette is in Tod's class. Her tiny, delighted face pokes out of the top of the pyramid, which bobs at her shoulders as she thunders across the stage.

"And first prize, Harry Fisher, our fantastic knight."

My heart is no longer in its proper place. It has plummeted to my stomach at least. Tod pulls off his bull head and drops it at his feet. Now he just looks like a boy in silly fur trousers and his mother's wet, washed-out sweatshirt. I scan the crowd, in case I've missed Marcus, and spot only Lucille, who offers a sympathetic shrug.

"Finally," the woman says, "a special prize for the most original outfit. In all my years of judging the Spring Fair contest, I have never seen anything like it. Please, everyone, a round of applause for a very muddy boy here—Tom Skews."

"You can't even tell what he is," someone growls behind me.

"So, Tom," says the woman on stage. "Let's see—there's a cow's head, a sort of lady's top, and furry legs…you've had us all guessing. What are you?"

"My name is *Tod* and I'm a—" he begins. No one hears because the majorettes have kicked into action, lead by Adele in sparkly silver and turquoise, but even their *bang-bang* racket cannot blot out the walloping grin on my son's face.

I find Marcus, Carl and Joe emitting ill-humor at the cakes and candies stall. "Where have you been?" I ask him.

"Looking for you. Where have *you*—?"

"I won a prize," Tod announces. "I was most original, just like Joe said."

"That's great," Marcus says flatly.

"What we're worried about," Carl says, jutting his jaw toward Joe, "is that it might become a health hazard. Don't you have a mower?"

"I'm not planning to cut it," Joe says.

"It wouldn't be so offensive," Carl continues, "tucked down a side road where no one could see it. But you're smack-bang in the High Street."

"Yes, that's where I live."

"We're only trying to help," Marcus chips in.

I try to tug Tod away, but he won't budge. None of our nests has been sold, I notice, apart from the one we bought, although I spy some of our sugar eggs embedded in mud.

"We all have to live here," Carl adds firmly.

"Do we?" Tod asks. "Why?"

"Let's go home," Marcus says. He reaches for Tod's hand, but Tod needs both to rip silver paper from his prize. It's a kite, which he wants to fly now, but it needs to be built before you can use it.

We stride home with Tod waving the tail above his head. I glance back to see Carl tipping the leftover cakes and candies into a plastic sack. Joe is perched on a bench by the river, smoking. Carl drops the sack on to the muddy ground, and rips the checked plastic cover from the trestle table.

A drooping banner is attached to the footbridge. It reads: Happy May Day. "What does May Day mean?" Tod asks.

"It means 'Help,'" I tell him.

chapter 13

Put Your Shoes On

At Coffee & Books, most customers take care to put books back in their proper places. Rarely would anyone be so badly behaved as to stuff a gardening manual back into the local history section, or slide an author beginning with *B* on to the *S–Z* shelf. Their cups leave no rings on the three circular tables. If a book has taken longer than expected to arrive, the customer doesn't complain or cancel the order. They actually say thank-you, even though they leave empty-handed.

Julia's daughter Sian, and occasionally Julia herself, serves coffees, teas and brittle biscuits for dunking into hot drinks. I man the till, a task which, as our customers are thoughtful enough not to stampede in all at once, is low on stress, and high on caffeinated beverages.

Sian is a dreamy girl of around eighteen who smells of cloves and hums unidentifiable melodies. As she wafts her smells around, I align the spines of paperbacks or draw on the backs of old posters that have been displayed in the shop window. There are notices for church coffee mornings and aqua-natal classes at Lexley Leisure Center. On their plain sides I draw that boy, the one who crept into my head years ago, before Tod, or even Marcus, and sometimes I look up to see a customer, holding a cookbook or a guide to cycling in Southern England, waiting patiently to be served.

Marcus says that since I've started working again, I'm more like my old self. I'm not sure what this means. I don't feel like I've ever been any different. For years now, I've waited for something to happen, to feel suddenly sorted and be seized by an urge to start using the National Trust place mats donated by Marcus's parents. But that hasn't happened. The place mats are still stashed in the box with the casserole dishes.

Some nights I lie with Marcus curled around me, thinking he'll soon complain that his shoulder hurts, or his arm's gone numb, and assume his usual edge-of-bed position. But he doesn't move, and I wake up still wrapped in his arms.

I buy him books from the shop—books about war, with grainy black-and-white covers—and not just because I get a thirty percent discount. I have stopped grumbling if he misses the six–thirty-five, or the seven-twenty, and no longer call him at work because he's either too harassed to talk properly or out with a client.

If you want to know something, just ask. I don't want to know. I have my job now, and Tod after school, and a new kitchen to choose, which I pick from a catalogue without even going to see it in the shop.

"That looks fine," Marcus says when I force him to admire pictures of plain white units.

"Well, I like it. It's very…"

"…white," Marcus says, wandering away from me and the flapping catalogue so I'm left talking to the back of his head. His hair is freshly cut, shorn close to his ears and neck. I wonder how he manages to fit in regular haircuts when he's so busy that he keeps missing trains.

"Or I could paint the old one," I suggest. "That would work out much cheaper."

"Yes, good idea."

"Purple, maybe, with tangerine spots and glittery handles."

"Whatever you think's best," he says.

Natalie and her family burst into our house on a breezy, late-May morning. Daniel and Jessica have matching dappled eyes and smell of fabric conditioner. My sister gleams with efficiency. Her life's compartments—children, husband Hugh, job as a speech therapist, voluntary shifts at a youth center—are held together by a complicated list system involving star stickers, clear plastic wallets and a highly functioning brain.

I was up at six-thirty this morning, bashing Gorby Cottage into shape for the arrival of Health and Efficiency. Natalie once said, "It's great that you don't care what your house looks like," which I interpreted as: "Oh, dear." And so I have baby-wiped every visible surface—even Tod's wellies—and shaken the toaster upside down to liberate its collection of antique crumbs. I was behaving as if a reality TV crew were due any minute, and planning to maximize humiliation by showing close-ups of old bits of sausage poking out from under the cooker.

Why do I do this? I flew the parental nest eighteen years ago. I don't need to prove that I'm a grown-up, I just *am* one. I have a child, a house, an adult-size body and, I think, life insurance. I still dealt with the furred-up fish tank, which requires zero maintenance, yet needed two-thirds of its water replaced, slime wiped from its sides and stale food scraped from the plastic ledge, where most of the stinky flakes land on the rare occasions that Tod takes charge of the fish's nutrition. I have also prepared a picnic to show Natalie and her high-achieving children how fantastically sorted we are here in Chetsley.

Natalie can do many things, simultaneously. Here she is, praising my appearance—"I have to say, Ro, I prefer your hair now it's grown out and looks less severe"—while helping Tod to glue a fiddly curve on the 3-D maze *and* construct the kite he won at the Spring Fair. It's as if she has seventeen hands. Next to her, I feel like an ancient baked spud, left to shrivel at the back of the oven.

"Why don't you show Daniel and Jessica your room, Tod?" Marcus suggests. My nephew and niece bound upstairs.

I must quiz Natalie on how to raise children who do as they are asked and never smear nostrils on cuffs.

Marcus shows Hugh around our garden. Hugh has fine silver hair with a combed-down fringe and wears a shimmery gray tracksuit. Upstairs, the children are playing hide-and-seek. Tod is counting loudly. He likes his older cousins; they never laugh at his eyebrow or do anything scary.

"I've got something to show you," Natalie says. From her bag she pulls out a letter.

Dear Natalie,
I have important news to tell you. Freda and I are expecting a baby and are very happy. Please tell Ro this.
Love and kises,
Dad

At first I think it's a joke or that I've added a bit that's not really there. But Natalie is saying, "Isn't it great that he's made a new life and is finally happy?"

"But he's *old*," I splutter. That woman from the cheese shop—whom I have never met but imagine smells of Gorgonzola, a pong she can never get out of her hair—is having a baby. My dad's baby.

Tod appears at my side. "Are we having a baby?" he asks.

"No, Granddad is." He thinks I mean Marcus's father. He has forgotten he has another granddad.

"I'd like a sister," Tod adds.

"No, you wouldn't. She'd throw all your toys in the fish tank."

He looks pretty excited about this. I am still clutching Dad's letter; the name "Freda" is concealed by my thumb. "When is it due?" I ask.

Natalie shrugs. "No idea. Why don't you write to him?"

"And say what?" *Thanks for the sole visit you made to see Tod, just after his birth, when you kept asking what Tod was short for and I told you it was just Tod. You said it sounded like a nickname, not a real name at all. And thanks for your occasional postcards. I see that you still can't spell "kisses."*

"I'm sure he'd love to hear from you," Natalie says. She hands the finished kite to Tod. It is rainbow striped, with each color bleeding into the next.

"It seems so…reckless."

"It's a baby, Ro. That's what couples do. They make babies."

Last time I suggested that we stop using condoms—just to see what happened—Marcus said, "Please, Ro, I'm too old now to start at square one, with all those sleepless nights."

He was thirty-seven, and looked a decade younger in dim lighting. My dad is sixty-one.

★ ★ ★

"He's a worry," Marcus tells Hugh. We've all flopped out on blankets on the common. Pale smudges of cloud smatter the milky-blue sky. "Up all hours," he continues, "bashing and banging, building some kind of hut in a tree."

"He just sounds eccentric," Hugh says. He has been playing football with the kids, leaping dramatically and missing the ball on purpose. Tod has scored sixteen goals, which gives a distorted impression of his ball skills.

"This friend of ours, Carl, is worked up about it," Marcus adds. "He's spoken to Joe—that's the weirdo—and offered to help, but of course he won't cooperate. Now Carl's thinking of contacting the council."

"What for?" Hugh asks.

"To see what the legal position is. Chetsley's a Best-Kept Village. He can't let it grow rampant like that." I worry that Marcus is going for too many pints at the Poacher's with Carl. He is no longer a neighbor, but a friend, *our* friend.

"I wouldn't get involved," Natalie chips in. "You don't want to get into a dispute. It could turn nasty."

"It's not a dispute. Carl just wants to measure the grass so we can give the council hard facts and figures."

"We?" I say. "Why are you getting involved, Marcus?"

"It doesn't pay to make enemies," Hugh adds.

"Tod says there are noises in your attic," Jessica announces, rolling over and settling in her mother's lap. "He says it keeps him awake."

"We think there's something living up there," I explain. "Probably mice—nothing serious."

"Ugh." Natalie shudders.

"I've been up to check," Marcus says. "Couldn't see anything. He's probably been dreaming. You dream about animals, don't you, Tod? Animals chasing you, going bump in the night."

"I've heard it, too," I tell Natalie.

"I've told you, Ro, there's nothing there." Marcus gives a little laugh, as if I'm as silly as Tod, imagining things.

"Hey, who wants to fly this kite?" Hugh suggests.

"How?" Tod asks.

"Just hold it up, let the wind catch it. That's it, Tod, nice and high. Now let it go. Here, take the spools, go on now—*run*…"

The kite spears the ground. "Let me try," Marcus says, and soon sends it soaring, forgetting that it's Tod's prize, and possibly that there's anyone else on the common.

"I want a go," Tod mutters.

The kite swerves too close to a tree, but Marcus tugs it away, avoiding disaster. "Well done, Uncle Marcus," Jessica chirps, clapping.

"It's *my* kite," Tod thunders. "I won it at fancy dress." My son might whine and be incapable of flushing the loo, but he doesn't have tantrums, not anymore; yet here it comes—mouth crumpling, body arching and a horrible wail, coinciding with the instant that he hits the ground and starts thumping the life out of Chetsley Common.

"Now, Tod," Natalie says.

"He's just excited because you're here," I explain unconvincingly.

Marcus has reined in the kite and carefully winds the string round its spool. He slips it into his rucksack, which he zips up firmly.

The curious sound—part sob, part small mammal with run-over tail—comes from deep in Tod's gut. He's curled up on his side, with his head resting on a small heap of rabbit droppings. Natalie reaches for his hand, but he kicks her away.

"Stop this," I hiss. "It's only a kite."

"Leave me *alone*," he rages.

I offer him a halved boiled egg from my mouthwatering picnic—the yolk has a gray layer around it—but this makes him cry even harder.

"I'm so sorry," I tell Natalie as we walk back to the house.

"Don't worry. They all have their moments."

Tod is still whimpering—and, for some reason, affecting a limp—although he has at least allowed Jessica to hold his hand and offer comfort in the form of a chewy bar made from compressed raspberries.

The men and children have reached the house and are fixing up the Swingball game Natalie brought for Tod as an extra birthday present. Tod is hunched on the wall with his back to the garden. Natalie and I sit on the front step and pick at picnic remains. No one felt like eating much on the common. The children seemed to prefer Natalie's raspberry bars to my boiled eggs and sandwiches.

"Everything okay with you two?" she murmurs, glancing at Marcus.

I busy myself by trying to unflatten a sandwich. It looks like it's been stamped on. "It's probably just the move," I tell her.

"He just seems a bit…tense. The way he shouted at Tod…"

"We all lose it sometimes," I say quickly. "Don't you ever shout at the kids?"

"Of course I do but…"

I want to tell her what's happening, but the words won't come.

"It's so different here," I tell Natalie. "We're still adjusting. We'll be fine, when we've all settled in."

Natalie squeezes my hand. "Yes, of course you will."

Put your shoes on. Putyourshoeson. PUTYOURSHOESON. Monday morning. Late, late, late. There's no excuse: Mar-

cus was up by six, gone by seven-thirty, after giving me a sur-
prisingly tender kiss on the back of the neck as I sloshed
water on my face.

He cooked for me last night. Tiger prawns stir-fried with
garlic, lemon and parsley. When we'd waved off Health and
Efficiency, he said he needed to nip into Lexley. He brought
home ingredients and instructed me to soak in the bath
while he cooked. I heard foul language—I think he was having trouble de-heading and tailing the prawns—then good
smells drifted up and the swearing stopped. Natalie phoned,
and I heard Marcus saying, "Lovely to see you, too. Tod's always wanted Swingball—he's delighted."

We ate in the kitchen, by the light of the Tranquility candle. I wolfed all my prawns, so he gave me some of his, saying, "I'm really not hungry." I think he felt bad about hogging
the kite, and triggering Tod's tantrum in front of my sister.

The last thing he said this morning was "Don't go breathing in those chemicals." Mr. Leech, our Dampblaster, is due
any minute to carry out stage two of the de-rotting process.
Instead of the Kangol hammer, he will bring a joiner to remove and replace rotting timbers, plus poisonous sprays to
kill the *Anobium punctatum* that reside in our floorboards and
loft. I have started to consider these woodborers as part of
the family. They are certainly less bother than the fish.

On the bottom stair, Tod peels open the Velcro fastening
of his left shoe and peers inside, as if checking for bug infestation. He waggles his toes, limbering up for the arduous
task of feeding said foot into shoe. "Tod, we have six minutes before school starts," I inform him. On mornings like
this, Tod behaves as if he ran barefoot, having been raised in
a forest by wolves until ill-tempered adults dragged him away
from his woodland buddies, forced his feet into unwieldy
leather constructions and sent him off every weekday to be

confronted by Miss Cruickshank's blouses. "That's the wrong foot," I snap. "What's wrong with you? I'm not putting your shoes on for you. You're six."

Since his birthday, I have taken to reminding him of his age several times a day. *Of course you can tell a B from a D, Tod. You're six. Put your cycling helmet on by yourself. You're six. Can't you do a wee without spraying the floor? How old are you? Six!* I hear my haranguing voice and have to remind myself that six is young enough to get things wrong occasionally.

A white van pulls up outside our house. The Dampblasters logo is depicted in orange on the van's side: a modern house, like Lucille and Carl's, enclosed in a circle with sunbeams around it. The van is filthy, but someone has cleaned the bit with the house and sunbeams.

Mr. Leech explains that he and the joiner, Bob, will rip up much of our kitchen, hall and living room floors and treat the remaining joists with a vile substance called KillAll. "The fumes are dangerous," he warns. "I assume you'll be vacating the house for at least twenty-four hours."

"I had no idea—"

"Will we die?" Tod asks cheerfully.

"Most people make plans," Mr. Leech says. "Especially people with children."

I hope that if Tod and I run straight upstairs after school and open all windows—even hang out by our ankles—nothing terrible will happen to our respiratory systems. Rich people experience none of this. At the first sight of an unfamiliar male wielding a spirit level, they are off to some spa in Mustique for detoxing treatments, returning home only when everything is lovely again and the van's pulling away from their house. Like one of those rich people, Marcus has decided to stay at the office tonight.

Tod's left foot has now been successfully inserted into its

leather casing. At this rate, I estimate that it will take twenty-five minutes to put on the right one.

"Mum," he says, "how does Velcro work?" Although un-cooperative on the shoe front, he has thoughtfully unpacked his schoolbag. I ram everything—gym kit, crisps, rumpled homework, Dog—back in.

"We're late," I snarl. He turns away and I jiggle two fingers behind his head. Mr. Leech and Bob narrow their eyes at me, as if I have no business raising a child.

Tod straightens up slowly and examines his shoes. "Is it little hooks?" he asks.

"Is what little hooks?"

"Velcro."

I open the front door in the hope that Tod, like a trapped starling, will glimpse the pale rectangle of daylight and flutter out. "Yes, one side is hooks. The other is loops. Let's go."

Natalie's children left a note pinned to Tod's bedroom wall that reads: *Thank you for a lovely time we love your spooky new house.* As we pelt to school I wonder when he'll become polite, a writer of thank-you letters, with each word in a different shade of felt tip.

"Late?" enquires Tina, heading back from school with Harry no doubt installed in the classroom, having successfully completed sixty-five sums.

"Had to let the damp men in," I explain.

"Damp? You've got your work cut out with that house."

In the playground the janitor is chasing a rogue candy wrapper. As I fling Tod through the chipped blue gates, I realize that his lunchbox still rests at home beside an enormous can of KillAll.

I am the proud owner of a new car, purchased from the ticket office man at Lexley station. Although aging, and the fact it must never *ever* be run on less than a quarter of a tank of petrol, the vehicle has been lovingly nurtured and at first boasted a small arrangement of flowers, in palest pink silk, lashed to the rearview mirror. Tod demanded these, and tacked them next to his poster of the mummified head with linen pads in its eye sockets. Occasionally, I manage to convince myself that Sarah bears an uncanny resemblance to this mummy, complete with worn-away teeth, from eating three-thousand-year-old gritty bread. Tod told me that the ancient Egyptians didn't mind the odd bit of gravel in their sandwiches.

I pick him up from school in my new, sweet-smelling car. We are not heading for a country wedding for glasses of Pimm's, but the chip shop in Lexley. It's easy to find. Apart from a hastily painted sign reading Fat Billy's Fast Food, a giant cone spilling fiberglass fries hogs the pavement in front of the shop's dazzling new facade.

Tod and I are eating out in grand style as our kitchen is out of bounds. When I popped in after work, Mr. Leech and Bob were gazing sadly into a hole in the floor by the sink. Bob scratched his belly and pulled his top lip in on itself, exposing his upper teeth.

Tod is playing with a basket of sachets, sorting the horse-radish from the ketchup and brown sauces, so everything is in its proper order. Still feeling bad about the shoe episode and doing the fingers behind his head, I say, "You can choose whatever you like." He orders Dinobites. These are supposed to be dinosaur shaped, but resemble no recognizable species. They have rust-colored crusts, and pale gray interiors.

When they're finished he asks, "Can I have a cake from the counter?"

"Okay, go and choose." He picks a hideous confection

slapped with neon-blue icing and chocolate strands. If he asked for a bag of sugar right now, I'd probably say yes.

After tea we prowl around the greengrocer's. Miss Cruickshank has requested ingredients for an Egyptian feast. They snacked on grapes, figs and pomegranates, apparently, as a change from gravelly bread. As the greengrocer's is devoid of exotic varieties—they don't even have grapes—I assure Tod that the Egyptians would have gone crazy for flaccid bananas, if they'd had them in those days.

In the stationery section of the newsagent's, he caresses a plain black clipboard. "Can I have it?" he asks.

"You really want that? Wouldn't you rather have a comic?"

"I *really* want it. Please–please–please."

Tod clutches the clipboard to his chest the whole drive home. He looks like a health and safety inspector. I wonder if he'll turn out like Marcus, with a filing cabinet of a brain, rather than a cluttered handbag for a head, stuffed with dented Fruit Shoot bottles and the sugary wrappers from doughnuts.

"Great tea," he announces, snapping the clipboard's clip bit open and shut. Parents fritter away at least eighteen years of their lives, worrying about what's good for their children. We're so hung up on figuring out how to please them that we forget it's ridiculously easy to make a kid happy.

Marcus comes home the following evening to a lingering odor of KillAll and a fabulous surprise. His birthday is in two weeks' time. We won't be eating out at Ruby's, the restaurant recommended by Lucille where the owner made a big show of checking the vast, empty pages of his reservations book to make sure we'd really booked a table. And we certainly won't be going to Fat Billy's Fast Food. I've booked us a night at Millington Park, a country hotel frequented by pop stars and curvy-car owners.

One afternoon, when I was just about to leave work, Marcus showed up at Anna's with my suitcase and passport and everything booked. He took me to Paris. He'd forgotten to pack my makeup, so next day we went to Les Halles and I chose a new face. It was only a few months after our wedding. I was still thrilled at being married to him.

Millington Park will be just like Paris. I'm so excited, I could bite my own hand.

Since Marcus returned he's been making sure that Mr. Leech put every board back in its proper place, and hasn't caused any new squeaks. I hand him the page I ripped out of a magazine, a roundup of luxurious hotels: "Each room at Millington Park is individually decorated in sensual reds, golds and purples. Lounge over a late, late breakfast, take a romantic stroll through the hotel's untamed yet beautiful grounds, or relax in the superb spa. Millington Park is the perfect haven for lovers." I'd written "HAPPY BIRTHDAY" next to the bedroom picture.

"What's this?" he asks.

"We're going. I've booked it."

"What, for the whole night?"

"That's the idea, Marcus. It's a hotel."

"What about Tod?"

"Your parents will stay over. They're fine about it. I've checked."

He opens his mouth as if to protest some more, then flings his arms around me and says, "You're my darling."

Later, in bed, it's almost like Sarah never happened.

chapter 14

Mrs. Monoblock

It's Freda who answers the phone. Freda, the mother of my dad's unborn child. "Is Dad—is *Ernest*—there please?" I ask.

I assume she knows who I am, that he's filled her in on his other family.

"Ernest!" she shouts.

I'm phoning to check that this baby is real because I cannot possibly have a half sister or half brother who is not even born yet, is less than zero years old, when I'm ancient enough to remember Funny Feet ice lollies and On the Buses.

"Ro, love," Dad says, sounding as Yorkshire as ever. "So Natalie told you our news."

Runny yolk drips from Tod's spoon on to the front of his school sweatshirt. "It's very exciting," I manage to say.

"We're delighted," Dad says, "and Freda's coping so well, even in this blasted heat."

"Is this her first child?" My voice comes out prim, disapproving.

"Yes," he says, "but she's a natural with children—you should see her."

Freda will cope, but how will Dad manage? Mum reported his parental input consisted of installing us—first Natalie, then me—into a padded seat attached to a metal frame he would crank up with an enormous handle, to cause a swinging action and keep us blissfully silent while he watched golf. I have memories of Dad and me tackling the occasional project together, like making a lie detector from electronic components with sensors to attach to your hands. It was supposed to *bleep* when you told a fib—a liar's hands sweat, apparently—but nothing happened. We tried to grow crystals, but our lumps of rock just sat in neon-orange liquid and never turned into sparkling beauties like the ones on the box.

"Dad, how are you going to manage?" I blurt out.

"Manage? What do you mean?"

I mean how is he planning to support this child, my half-sibling? According to Natalie, Dad has run into trouble with the standard of his soft play equipment at the Happy House. "I'm just worried about you."

"We'll manage just fine."

It occurs to me that Dad has always managed. Even when he wouldn't come into the house, he made a comfortable nest, with a ready supply of crackers and mild cheeses, in the back of the Morris Traveller.

By lunchtime, only three customers have come into the bookshop. As they popped in to collect orders, I couldn't do any advising or hard selling. The trouble with days like these is that Sarah creeps into the shop, with her shirt unbuttoned just enough to reveal a glimpse of her Agent Provocateur bra.

Sarah's car isn't fouled up with festering foodstuffs and the perpetual cry of "Are we nearly there yet?" She has expense account lunches and a secretary who ensures that there are always fresh flowers on her desk (lilies? Yes, white lilies). She has never had to deal with woodworm, or endure nocturnal scratchings above her head, or complaints that a boiled egg is slightly too runny or too hard, or too cold, because the intended consumer of substandard egg has not been eating his breakfast, but rolling Blu-Tack to make maggots.

It worries me that I am less disturbed by what Marcus and Sarah might get up to together, than by the fact that I know for certain that she has really great shoes.

Joe strolls into the shop, and at first I think he's here to buy a gardening book because that's the shelf he looks at. "Can I help you, Joe?" I ask.

"Just looking," he says, still facing the gardening shelf.

He's behaving as if we've never met before. It must be my weird, formal voice. Or maybe I'm out of context, like Miss Cruickshank at the chemist's in Lexley—familiar, but who was she?—asking for that clear liquid, she couldn't remember its name, to burn warts off her hands. Tod shouted, "Hello, Miss Cruickshank!" and she rammed her purchase into her mock-croc handbag.

Joe runs a finger along the books' spines. We sell a lot from this section because even customers with tiny gardens, or hanging baskets, want to do their bit to retain Chetsley's Best-Kept Village title. I put down my drawing book. Even my drawings are starting to look like Sarah, with her perfect teeth, not crumbling, ancient Egyptian teeth.

"We can order anything you like," I tell him.

"Thanks," he murmurs.

His hair curls down his neck. It's kind of mud colored, the color that splats Tod's face when he falls off his bike. I figure that he won't go for any of the gardening manuals about which colors you should and shouldn't put together, or even the pocket-size books on single species, like lavender and peonies. For one stupid moment, I think he's come in to see me.

He turns to face me, looking confused. Maybe he's forgotten what he wants. Customers do that all the time. The dim lighting, or maybe Sian's clove smell, numbs their brains and has them murmuring "There's this book, what's it called again? I think it's by...John somebody."

Joe holds out a large manila envelope. "Here," he says, "this is for you."

"What is it?" I smile at him, can't drag my eyes away from that serious nose. Any woman would have spent her adolescence despising that nose, to the point that she would have refused to go to the cinema with a boy, as that would have meant being seen side on. On Joe, the nose looks elegant and proud.

"Why don't you open it?" he asks.

I rip it open and pull out a brochure from a company called Distinguished Driveways. "Traditional-style paving and contemporary monoblocking to enhance your home, year after year. Available in charcoal, pale gray and sandstone effect for effortless elegance. Let Distinguished Driveways set your home apart from those of your neighbors."

"What is this?" I ask.

"I assume your husband put this through my letterbox after our conversation on the common." His voice is distant, like Tod's when we're in one-word territory.

"This is nothing to do with Marcus," I say. "It must have been Carl, he's a friend of—not a *friend,* we hardly know—"

Joe turns away, brushing past the revolving display stand

of *Boxed Brainwaves,* which wobbles nervously, and marches out of the shop. A handwritten note falls out of the brochure. I pick it up, and read:

> Dear neighbor
> The residents of Chetsley are concerned about the condition of your lawn, in particular as judging for the Best-Kept Village contest takes place at the end of July. Enclosed is a brochure for a reputable local company which specializes in hard landscaping. We hope this will satisfy your needs.

The note is unsigned. Julia saunters in, clutching milk and a catering tin of coffee. "Was that Wyn Beadie's son?" she asks.

"No idea."

"Isn't he living in his mum's old place, across the road from you?"

"Yes, I think I've seen him around."

Julia blinks at me. I pretend to tidy the pens in the beehive-shaped pot.

"You okay?" she asks. "You look awfully hot. I'll put the fan on for you."

"I'm fine, really," I tell her, dropping Distinguished Driveways into the bin at my feet.

Marcus's mother is a retired primary school teacher, Tod's caregiver while her son and I indulge in an utterly *filthy* weekend and unofficial President of the Ro Skews fan club.

"Wonderful house," Maureen gushes, tactfully ignoring the fact that our flooring consists of filthy bare boards and the occasional new replacement, yellow and cheap-looking, where the rot had taken hold. She clasps my hand and says, "After all the upheaval, you deserve this little break."

According to Maureen, there are many great things about me. My prime achievement has been to raise a gifted, articulate son, whom she smothers with lipsticked kisses and knitted waistcoats for the Action Man he never plays with. Action Man owns an entire knitted wardrobe—pants, cardigans, wetsuit and, curiously, a cape with ribbons to tie around his plastic neck. These garments lie in a box beneath Tod's bed, starved of human contact.

The other wonderful thing about me is the fact that I get on with things and never moan. *There isn't a selfish bone in your body,* Maureen once told me. She is unaware that my entire skeleton is constructed from compressed bad feelings. She hasn't seen me doing the fingers behind Tod's head or swearing into the air, making the dust particles dance as I play a phone message from Marcus ("Staying in town tonight, darling, absolutely shattered. Call me if you need anything").

"Tod, sweetheart," Maureen says, gathering him on her knee, "what would you like to do while Mum and Dad are away?" Her elegant skirt is made from squares of purple and pewter-colored velvet. Her nails are filed to sharp points, and painted to match the purple bits.

"Don't know, Gran," Tod says.

"Shall we take you to Leeds Castle?" David suggests. David is my father-in-law. His unruly gray hair falls in springy waves, like Beethoven's. He wears a spotted tie, the point of which is tucked into the waistband of his casual brick-colored trousers. Tod is so excited about Leeds Castle that he leaps off Maureen's knee and twirls around the living room with his eyes shut.

As usual, Maureen and David have brought us an assortment of household items that are surplus to their requirements. The battered cardboard box contains a wicker-edged tray depicting a map of America—each state is a different color—a stainless steel trough that Maureen tells me is a fish steamer, and a miniature Big Ben with a working clock. When relatives offload their possessions, they never give you the good stuff. I hang on to the hope that Maureen and David will pull up in a rented van into which they have loaded their oval mahogany dining table with the secret leaf in the middle.

Tod fetches *Mazes and Labyrinths* from his bedroom and jabs the photo of Leeds Castle's grounds. "The apparently simple design of this maze," he pants, " is enhanced by a tunnel which leads to an underground grotto studded with shells."

"Gosh," says Maureen, "your reading's excellent, Tod."

"He knows it by heart," Marcus says.

He's been packing his black zip-up overnight bag. I can't understand why he's bringing three paperbacks, plus the newspaper folded open at the crossword page.

"Do you, Tod?" Maureen says. "You're my special, clever boy."

I can't understand why children's literary habits are so different from those of an adult. We crave variety; kids want the same old *blah-blah-hedge-maze-at-Hampton-Court, blah-blah*. I don't tell Maureen that I'm tempted to hide the blasted book, like I did with *Guess How Much I Love You*.

"How's work these days?" David asks.

"Good," Marcus says, assuming that he means *his* work. "We're opening another office south of the river."

"Are you?" I ask. "You never mentioned that."

Maureen flashes a quick smile and follows Tod upstairs to his room. I wish she wouldn't, I haven't checked that it's in a respectable state. "You know Tod still has milk at bedtime," I say, stalking them.

"No problem," Maureen says.

"And he likes the landing light on, and you'll find his socks in the top left drawer and his pants in the right."

"We'll be fine. Please don't worry."

"He'll only wear inside-out socks because he hates feeling the seams. And if you hear noises in the attic, it's only—"

"Shouldn't you be on your way?"

I had anticipated a tearful parting—that my son would crumple at the sight of me with my coat on—but he doesn't seem to have registered that I am in the room, let alone about to swish off to a five-star hotel sixty miles from home.

On the windowsill, above the permanently locked cupboard, is Tod's clipboard. The sheet of A4, gripped by the silver clip, is headed "What Joe Does." Tod has written, *Joe is bilding a treehows. He sors wood I am going to asc if I can go in it.*

"Tod," I say.

"What, Mum?"

"Be good."

There's no *Danny the Champion of the World* in the car and Marcus doesn't feel like listening to music. He drives with his mouth tightly set and a glazed look in his tired-looking eyes.

According to the page I ripped out of the magazine, the pool at Millington Park is tiled with tiny mirrors. I wonder how my plain black swimsuit, and lackluster body, will bear up in such grand surroundings, and whether I'll be faced with millions of reflections of myself. Packing was tricky. I have lost the knack of preparing for an overnight stay that does not require the yellow binoculars, *Mazes and Labyrinths* and Dog. I bought a slinky, sapphire-colored dress from a small, dusty shop in Lexley, and only because the shop lady said, "You must have it. Any man would fall in love with you in this dress, my dear."

It felt like we'd only just come down from the excitement

of our wedding when Marcus took me to Paris. We slept in an ornately carved bed and spent all morning kissing and listening to street noises. Eventually Marcus went out, to clear his hungover head, and was gone for ages. Finally he returned with complicated underwear that had to be put on in a certain order. You couldn't, for instance, pull on the knickers before the suspender belt.

The corset thing laced up, like a gigantic baseball boot, and was made from black velvet. It took me forty-five minutes to squash myself into it. After all that sweating and effort, I realized I'd put it on upside down. We brought home an abstract painting—creamy ovals, like eggs, hovering in a blue-gray sky—and the beginnings of our son.

I wonder now what we'll get up to in our room at Millington Park. Maybe I should have brought a book. Clearly, Marcus intends to do lots of reading. I have stopped trying to initiate sex because I hate the way he lifts my hand from his body, like he's putting it away, tidying up.

"Marcus," I say, "what do you think about visiting my dad?"

He clicks on the car radio. "In Majorca, you mean?"

"We could go in the summer holidays, see Dad's baby, meet Freda."

He frowns and says, "For how long?"

"A week, couple of weeks maybe. We wouldn't have to stay with them. We could rent an apartment."

"We can't afford it." He glances at the map on my lap. He has worked out the route but still requires me to check that all's going according to plan. "Where do we turn off again?" he asks.

"Steepden. Why can't we afford it? I thought the company was doing well, with that second office you're opening. You said we could buy a new kitchen."

"I thought you were going to paint the one we have." He starts humming to himself, something like a children's song.

"Well, I want to go," I say suddenly.

"We had that week on the Isle of Wight, Ro."

"Three days," I remind him.

"I can't take any more time off."

"You can't afford the time or the money—" I clamp my mouth shut.

Marcus takes the corner too fast as he turns sharply left, into the undulating wooded grounds of Millington Park, the perfect haven for lovers.

I wonder how he will cope faced with me, close up, in a red and gold bedroom. Whether he'll start reading straight away, in order to plough through three novels in twenty-four hours. Being positive about this, a *Boxed Brainwave* insists that a stay in a hotel—"pack your sauciest undies, plus scented massage oil"—is just the ticket to remind a couple why they liked each other in the first place.

Our room has a deer head on the wall, and a massive TV. When Tod was younger, and we wound up at some National Trust property with antlered creatures' heads gazing mournfully from the walls, he would demand, "I want to look round the back," despite being assured that there wasn't a back, to view the rest of the animal. The magazine was right about opulent decor, but it hadn't mentioned deer heads. I cannot imagine guests even getting around to taking the lid off their massage oil, being eyeballed by a sorrowful-looking animal with frayed ears.

Marcus switches on the TV. I play with the bathroom fittings and discover three buttons that offer a choice of scents for your shower. Lavender, sage or ocean. I must try it out, discover whether the fragrance comes out as a scented steam, or dribbles directly on to your head.

In the mirror, I spy more new wrinkles. When I asked Marcus if he thought I was aging at a terrifying rate, he said, "We're all looking older, Ro," which hardly had me brimming with joie de vivre.

Marcus has a shower, then I do—lavender-scented—and pull on my new dress.

"Like it?" I ask.

"It's fine."

"Does that mean you don't like it?"

He sighs. "I said it's *fine.* It's a lovely color. Now let's go down to dinner."

That dress shop lady told me a lie.

The restaurant tables are laden with too many glasses, ranging from normal-size to vast globes that could accommodate fish. There are two other couples in the restaurant. Being so exposed makes you terribly aware of your eating face.

"I called someone about the attic noises," I blurt out.

"What noises?"

"The scratchings. The man said it's probably mice or birds. He says nests are a problem. They can be swarming with bugs, up to four thousand larvae in one nest, he said."

An underworked waitress refills our glasses. I wish she wouldn't do that. Marcus's was barely touched, mine drained. Having your glass refilled emphasizes what a glugger you are.

"He's coming on Monday," I continue, "to find out what's going on."

Marcus has stopped listening. I can tell when his hearing mechanism has been switched off, because his eyes film over and his jaw slackens. My pâté is an unappealing pinky gray. I know, that's what pâté is supposed to look like. Now it's ruining any beneficial effects from my lavender shower, and I can't figure out why I ordered it.

As we struggle through our main courses I notice how

smart Marcus looks in his light blue shirt, with his hair freshly cropped. He's too clean for a dirty weekend, and not drinking enough.

After dinner, in the bar, I force more wine on him. I can't face our room, with that big telly and deer head. Two girls in beaded tops are chain smoking and bragging that they never eat carbohydrates after eleven a.m. One of the girls adds that it's the only way to remain a size eight. "If I'd discovered this earlier," she says, "I'd never have eaten bread in my life."

The barmaid is dismantling a PC and stabbing its insides with a tiny screwdriver. The thin girls have stopped talking. They keep glancing at Marcus. He smiles, and they beam back at him, two teasing, glossy red mouths.

Marcus lies back on the red satin bedspread and flicks on the TV with the remote. A boy of around Tod's age is playing the clarinet with grim concentration. At this point, according to *Boxed Brainwaves,* I should be rubbing oil all over myself, like I'm a jammed-up engine part, and slipping into my finery. As I've already tried the shower, I run a bath, adding milk-and-honey lotion from a complimentary bottle with a gold top.

If you want to know something, just ask. Sarah, a word, said in his sleep. Well, I say things in my sleep. One morning Marcus told me I'd lurched upright during the night and shouted "Raisin." It didn't mean anything.

I keep topping up the bath with hot water. The clarinet has been replaced by a cello, probably being energetically sawed by a three-year-old protégé. I wonder what Marcus is doing. Rereading the Stalingrad book? Or watching those young musicians and wishing his own son displayed such virtuosity? He didn't watch TV in Paris. We were newer then.

We didn't have an attic, a utility room or Sarah with her wretched professionally plucked eyebrows.

When I climb out of this bath, I will light the candles I brought, turn off the cellist and ask Marcus why this isn't like Paris.

"Ro?" he calls. "What are you doing in there?"

"Still in the bath—won't be long."

"You've been over an hour. Are you okay?"

Sarah, just a name. She could be anybody. In Coffee & Books is a health section where we keep parenting manuals and a small selection of baby name books. I looked up Tod; it means "fox." I liked that—none of your fiery-warrior nonsense. Ro, or rather my full name, Rowena, means "white mane." I chose to interpret this as a streamlined and utterly elegant creature, rather than one destined to go gray prematurely.

I step out of the bath, pull on a Millington Park bathrobe and find Marcus asleep, fully clothed on red satin, a breakfast order form resting in a loosely coiled hand.

I looked up Sarah in that baby name book. It means princess. Sometimes I feel that life is snorting right in my face.

chapter 15

We're All Right

Mum and Dad went away Gran and Grandad lookd after me. I playd in Joe's garden he is bilding a wild garden he is going to paint picturs of it at difrint times of day even at nite. I went in the tree-hows. Grandad cudent get up the ladda.

"Tod? Tod! I want to speak to you." I am yelling out of his bedroom window, to the front garden where he is feebly batting the Swingball.

"What?" he shouts back.

"I didn't say you could go in Joe's garden by yourself."

"I wasn't by myself, I was with—"

"We hardly know him, Tod."

Across the road, Joe emerges from the tree house and jumps down to the grass.

"Don't you like Joe?" Tod yells up.

"It's not that. It's just—"

Joe sees me and waves.

"Can't *hear* you," Tod mutters.

"I said, hadn't you better come in now? It's going to start raining any second."

He stares up at a searing blue sky. Joe starts laughing. I bang Tod's bedroom window shut.

Pest Controller wears a dark green shirt and a lighter green tie. He has manicured nails and glossy black shoes that squeak as he walks. There is nothing about his appearance to suggest that he has anything to do with the extermination of vermin.

Tod is at Harry's for tea today. I was amazed when Tina invited him. "Harry thinks Tod's very funny," she said, and I wasn't sure if that was a good thing.

I reminded Tod several times that Tina would be picking him up from school, and also that he shouldn't have played in Joe's garden with Gran and Grandad. Yes, it was kind of Joe to help Maureen up the rope ladder—she'd been determined, apparently—but he must never do that again, and he'd better not mention it to Dad.

Although I'm concerned that Tina might try to trim Tod's eyebrow with her hairdressing scissors, I am relieved that he's not here. Pest Controller's talk of rodent behavior would undoubtedly trigger bad dreams. "Noticed any evidence of *rats*?" he asks, pacing the edge of our front garden and shouting the last word so all of Chetsley learns of our rodent problem.

"Of course not," I retort. "How would they get into the attic?"

"Rats can climb gutters. You're close to the common—isn't there a stream down there? Look, here are signs of a run." He indicates a flattened strip in the unkempt section of lawn that Marcus missed with Carl's mower.

"And this pigeon," he continues, indicating the torn remains of a bird I have failed to remove from our property. "A rat could have done this. Have you noticed anything nibbled or chewed in the house?"

"No, nothing." I'm starting to wonder if we really like Gorby Cottage or should move to a smart, modern place like Lucille and Carl's, with an automatic garage door and no infestations. There are too many creatures living here: Dalmatian fish, rats, maybe some *Anobium punctatum* that Mr. Leech failed to blast with his spray. I wish now that I hadn't asked Pest Controller to come. Until he started on about rats, I had viewed our attic inhabitants as noisy but ultimately untroublesome guests. It's not as if they require clean linen or create extra washing up.

At least he arrived in an ordinary Fiat Punto and not a van marked Vermin Extermination.

He is heading upstairs now, to the loft, which he accesses via our stepladder. His tie dangles through the hatch as he pokes his head down, reporting, "There are droppings, but they look pretty ancient. Your loft's too awkward a shape for me to check all the crannies."

He clambers down, brushes thick dust from his trousers and checks the bedrooms. In Tod's room he rattles the door of the cupboard under the window. "Can you open this?" he asks.

"Sorry, no. We can't find the key."

"I'll take another look at your garden," he says.

At the back of the house, he steps daintily past the open-topped vat of horse manure Carl asked the chef at the Poacher's to drop round for us. We must dig the manure into our compost to accelerate decomposition; that is, when we have compost to dig it into. Carl is such a believer in the nourishing power of manure that he has been known to wander the streets of Chetsley, shoveling deposits into a carrier bag.

Pest Controller and I trudge round the garden. Across the road, Joe is in the tree house, or I assume he's there because there's hammering going on, then some sawing.

"Does that thing look safe to you?" the man asks.

"What thing?"

"That eyesore in the tree. I wouldn't want that if I lived here. You could take steps, if it was bothering you."

"It's not bothering me at all."

"I wouldn't like it. You could say it's causing a visual disturbance. And that lawn must be at least a foot high. Your mice could be coming from there."

"I thought you said it was rats."

Just then, a bird flies to the eaves and disappears into our roof space. We have a bird, not rats; a timid, brownish thing, whose most dastardly act is to poop on your windscreen.

"Birds are trouble," the man warns, tweaking the end of his tie. "They bring bird mites, carpet beetles, biting insects." He stares at Tod's Swingball on the lawn. "They bite children," he adds. "Their droppings eat into your masonry."

He offers to return with a colleague, block up holes in the eaves and do his utmost to remove the nest. Joe's hammering stops and he steps onto the platform that juts out from the tree house.

"You'll be talking a grand," Pest Controller adds.

Instantly, I go off the idea of disturbing these birds' natural habitat. There's something pleasing about providing temporary accommodation for small creatures who huddle together in nests. Plus there's the educational aspect. In this modern age, crammed with stuff I vowed I would never allow in our home—Quavers, Nesquik, Dairylea Lunchables—Tod can at least while away hours by standing in the garden, noting when the parent birds go in and out. It might even distract him from *Mazes and Labyrinths.*

Pest Controller hands me his card, flicks a cobweb from his thigh and steps into his ordinary car. "There is good news," he adds. "At least it's not rats."

June sixteenth. School sports day. Sunshine pounds onto the playing field, triggering grown men to wear minuscule shorts in shimmery fabrics and expose limbs in shades varying from blue-white to putty. Marcus, who has taken a day off work to encourage Tod to excel at athletics, looks quite dazzling in his white T-shirt, jeans and sunglasses, which Tod has been banned from touching since he was found experimentally bending their arms.

Marcus's presence has been noted by several mothers who stand in a tight circle, their children bounding around them like hares. One boy's T-shirt already bears three winners' rosettes. Most of Tod's classmates—even Harry, with his wheat intolerance—are big for their age, or is it Tod who's underdeveloped? He still wears an age-four-to-five gym kit. His knees look like knots in the threads of his limbs. Rather than limbering up and assessing the track marked out with little triangular flags, he is jamming his left foot into a rabbit hole at the far edge of the field.

"Start by picking up your egg and spoon," Miss Cruickshank booms to a cluster of children. "Run to the hoop, step through, and sack-race the final stretch. Tod? Tod Skews! The race is starting."

Tod squints up at the sun, extracts his foot from the burrow and creeps stealthily across the field toward her.

She blasts the whistle, and there's a roar from the parents, and I'm amazed at how fast small people can run, even with eggs and spoons. A redheaded boy ploughs ahead of the pack. He has powerful thighs and trainers that light up as each foot smacks the ground. He's still panting excitedly as Mr. Quigley, the head teacher, pins on his rosette.

Tod disentangles himself from his sack and folds it neatly, aligning its edges to form a hessian rectangle.

"Good effort," Carl says, patting the top of Tod's head.

Carl's sunglasses are teardrop shaped, the lenses graduating from clear to pink. He came round to our house last night. He and Marcus had stuff to discuss. I slapped emulsion on to our newly plastered kitchen walls and tried to blot out their voices with fierce sweeps of my roller.

Just after ten, they went out. I ran upstairs and watched them cross the road and stride into Joe's garden. His truck was gone, and there were no lights on in the house. I watched them through Tod's yellow binoculars. There was some pointing and crouching in the long grass. I was still clutching the roller, which dripped on Tod's bedroom floor.

Carl marched back in with a puffed-out chest as if he'd got away with doing something really naughty, like stealing a penny sweet. "Thirteen inches tall at its highest point," he announced.

"What is?" I asked.

"The weirdo's grass. That might not sound too bad, Ro, but the thistles are taller and there's bindweed running rampant."

A bubble of laughter rose up my throat and exploded out of my nostrils.

"It's not funny, Ro," Carl said. "The weed seeds will infect other people's gardens."

Weed seeds, I liked that.

"It'll be the weather," Marcus said, pouring a whiskey for Carl. "Highest rainfall for over a decade, the *Gazette* said."

My serious boots were speckled white from the paint. As he was leaving, Carl asked, "Is that bare plaster you're painting?"

"Yes, Carl."

"Then you should have diluted the first coat. Better coverage."

Now, between races, children cluster around a rickety table bearing juice cartons with straws stabbed through their lids.

"Won anything yet, Tod?" Lucille asks.

Tod is guzzling a scary green drink. "Don't like races," he huffs.

The girl from the grocer's is chatting animatedly to Marcus. Her writhing toddler is parked on her shoulders, and keeps slapping his hands over her eyes. When the child's dummy falls out, Marcus picks it up for her. The girl sucks it, and hands it back to the kid.

Sports day ends with a relay race. Each of the three school houses forms a precarious line. I lurk by the drinks stall, away from the other parents, so I don't put Tod off. The race starts. Tod appears to be batting off a flying insect. He's front of the line now. It's his turn. His teammate lurches past, flings him the baton. Tod looks down at it. "Baton!" someone yells, too close to my earhole.

Miss Cruickshank skitters over and presses the baton into Tod's limp hand. He studies it, as if it's a mysterious object you'd find in a museum, possibly used for grinding corn to make ancient Egyptian bread. Sweat patches darken the armpit regions of Miss Cruickshank's silvery blouse. Tod looks up from the baton and scans the cluster of mums and dads. Then he spots me and starts waving. He's so pleased to see me that he's forgotten about sports day and the baton. He hasn't the faintest idea why he's standing at the front of the Medway House line with thirty children, all yelling, behind him.

The mums and dads are laughing now, and no one is watching the other teams, who are passing batons efficiently; they're all looking at Tod. He's frowning at me, like he can't figure out why I'm not waving back. Marcus is pretending to brush grass from his shoe.

When it's over, he takes Tod by the hand and says, "Come on, Wonderboy, let's get you home."

Tod is grinning wildly and springing from foot to foot. He thinks Marcus means it in a good way, like he's a wonderful boy. He thinks he's done the right thing.

Carl is useful for certain difficult tasks. Having learned of our bird problem, he shows up at teatime with his son Leo and a shiny new aluminum ladder with which he will access our eaves. Leo lets his end of the ladder drop on our path with a *crack*.

I have never had a proper conversation with Leo. I am unsure how to relate to a person who speaks like a man, yet requires his mother to airlift the batter from his cod when they eat out at Fat Billy's Fast Food. Lucille is worried about him. He used to be out all the time with his basketball friends, but now spends most of his time in his bedroom, poring over astronomy books.

"Hold it steady," Carl instructs, climbing up to investigate the birds' entry point.

Leo doesn't hold it at all, just picks at the wall of our house where the stone is crumbling, probably due to bird poo corrosion. He is behaving as if he wants his dad to fall off—and who could blame him?

"Seen the state of this guttering?" Carl yells from up high. His enormous shorts billow outward, like pale lemon pillowcases. He is wearing socks the color of Elastoplasts, plus tan sandals. I hope none of the Best-Kept Village judges witness this spectacle.

"I think there's a hole above Tod's bedroom window," Marcus shouts up.

"There are *many* holes," Carl declares.

He has also brought chicken wire with which he will block the gaps. He and Marcus have already scoured the attic as best they could, although I told them that Pest Controller had been up there already. They found only a broken ironing board and a hefty leather-bound bible, but nothing resembling nesting material.

Lucille shows up with Adele when the holes have been fixed. Marcus has asked them all round for supper. I had this great idea of letting everyone design their own pizzas and have laid out dishes of ham, pepperoni, peppers and cheese. I'm feeling quite chuffed at being so organized and child friendly.

"Don't like pizza," Adele announces. Her hair is scraped back into a tight ponytail, a style that makes her head look like an enormous egg. Reluctantly, she drops two slivers of ham onto a tomato-smeared base. She and Leo have passed the age at which it's exciting, getting to design your own dinner. Leo has a milky complexion and the beginnings of sideburns. He appears incapable of using a knife properly, yet can cultivate decorative facial hair.

"I spoke to the council," Carl says through a full mouth. "Passed from department to department—planning, environmental health. They doubt it's a health hazard. It's not like he's letting his household rubbish pile up. People can do what they like with their own gardens—can you believe that?"

"What about the tree house?" Lucille asks.

"They're concerned about that, with this being a conservation area. The planning guy's sending someone round."

Tod has hacked away the center of his pizza, leaving a ring of crust, like a primitive necklace. "I'd like a tree house," he announces. Marcus chooses to ignore this. "Joe says I can play in his tree house whenever I like," Tod adds with a smirk.

Carl laughs, and glances at Marcus. "Is that a good idea, Tod? I'm sure your mum and dad don't like you playing with strangers. He could be *anyone*."

It's parents' night at Chetsley Primary. Miss Cruickshank occupies a table in the farthest corner of the gym hall. Parents are chatting with teachers as if this is some kind of informal get together, with much joking and hilarity. Harry's parents are having such a rollicking time with the head teacher, a doughy-faced man with several trembling chins, that I suspect they're planning a two-family holiday. I hear Tina calling him George, not Mr. Quigley.

The summer term appears to have taken its toll on Miss Cruickshank. Her hair, which once puffed softly and cloud-like, now looks as if it's been sat on. Her rumpled blouse is patterned with peacock feathers. "Tod is *starting* to settle in," she says with a small smile. She waggles her clear plastic wallet of notes. I know what's coming: reading and maths, fair to middling. Handwriting, poor. Concentration, clearly a problem. *Do you do a lot with him, Mrs. Skews? Can you help him to focus at home? Practice his key words?*

Her lips are moving and it's the same old script. Marcus is nodding, but saying nothing. I am mesmerized by one peacock eye, which gawps from the center of Miss Cruickshank's bosom. It's brighter than the others, searing blue with a green ring around it and a hairy brown edge.

"Sometimes," she says, "I feel that he's not paying attention. It's as if he's not all there."

"What do you mean?" It's the first thing I've said. I sound like a damaged cat.

Tina stops bantering with Mr. Quigley—*George*—and gives me a concerned look.

"He seems to live in a dream world," Miss Cruickshank

prattles on. "Tod World, I call it. The trouble is, Mrs. Skews, he often fails to complete his work in the allotted time."

"Shouldn't we have been told about this?" Marcus asks.

"Your wife and I did have a chat," Miss Cruickshank says quickly. Her ring has an emerald in the middle and diamonds around it, like the spikes of a star. I wonder if it leaves a purple groove when she takes it off, or if it's stuck on.

"Well, thank you," I say, shoving back my chair with a clatter.

"Don't look so down, Mrs. Skews. His Egyptian topic work has been wonderful. We've moved on to botany now. Tod told me about a friend whose garden is bursting with wildflowers."

Marcus flings me a look.

"That's great," I manage to say.

Outside school, I call home. "Lucille? Mind if we stay out a bit longer? Just fancy a drink."

"Everything okay at school?" she asks.

"Yes, great."

"See? I told you he'd soon settle in."

The Poacher's is populated by boys who look no older than Leo, boys who can't cut pizza, and an elderly man in a stained navy suit. He is eating humbugs from a brown paper bag, piling up the wrappers in an ashtray on the bar. A dog lies at his feet, an Airedale I think, mottled gray with a box-shaped head. Tod calls this breed a shoebox-head dog.

Marcus sets our drinks on the table. "She might as well say I've done a crap job as a mother," I blurt out.

"You're not doing a crap job. We both know what Tod's like."

"What does she mean, he's not all there? Is there something wrong with him?"

Marcus sips his beer—mine is half-finished already—and

nods at the man with the humbugs. "She's just saying he's easily distracted, which is quite true."

"But he's not. Look at the time he spends on his drawings. The roof could blow off and he wouldn't notice, he's so wrapped up in—"

"You're shouting," Marcus points out.

"I'm not shouting." I need another beer but don't want to blast Lucille with booze breath.

"Tod's fine," Marcus says quietly, "when he's doing what he wants."

"Should he see a psychologist? He might have some kind of syndrome."

"For God's sake," Marcus says.

My son is not all there. Is it any wonder, when his dad's hardly there, either? "You need to do more with Tod," I announce. "Stuff that other dads do with their sons."

"I do my best, Ro."

"I feel like you're not interested."

"What about you?" He bangs his glass on the table, which causes the shoebox-head dog to twitch fretfully. "You're not remotely curious about my work, or octopush. We won last night, beat Fulham Flippers six–two. You never ask about that."

"Stuff octopush," I snap.

"Mind if I join you?" The humbug man lowers himself on to the vacant chair at our table.

"Please do," Marcus mutters.

The man has a Scooby-Doo plaster on the palm of his hand. The dog yawns, and settles between the man's feet. "You're from London?" he asks.

"That's right," Marcus says.

"Come from Kentish Town myself. Glad to leave the dump. Isn't it good to get away from all that, and be normal?"

★ ★ ★

Marcus and I never argue. We might have *disagreements*—
that's what it was, the thing in the pub—but we don't shout,
or throw things. We would never behave badly in front of
our son.

When my dad flung his breakfast across the kitchen, it
didn't make much of a crash. It had landed on the rush mat-
ting and snapped cleanly into three pieces. The Weetabix
didn't break. Disks of banana, still glossy with milk, scattered
close to my mother's feet. She was wearing pink slippers with
sheepskin cuffs. The bananas looked like checkers, as if someone had kicked over the board because they weren't winning.

Mum poured more coffee from a tall brown pot and said,
"Natalie, Rowena, you'll be late for school." We wanted to
stay and see what would happen next, but Mum ushered us
out and banged the front door behind us, as if that would
ensure that we wouldn't try to come back in.

I drove Natalie mad on the school walk because I daw-
dled. Being late made her anxious and sometimes she'd need
a puff of her inhaler. She never needed the inhaler when she
started secondary school, and we no longer walked together.

That banana day, she was staying late after school for gymnastics so I set off for home by myself. The houses were all
red brick, with dressing table mirrors looming at their upstairs windows. Usually, if Natalie was at netball or gymnastics, I would find somebody to walk with. This time there
was no one.

I was thinking about the bananas, whether anyone would
have cleared up the mess or if they'd turned into a kind of
sweet crisp, when a car pulled up ahead of me. The driver
wound down the passenger window.

"Hello, love," he said.

I assumed he was lost. I knew all the street names—I'd lived
in Wood Green all my life—and felt confident that I would

be able to help him. "I'm a friend of your mum and dad's," the man said. "They've had to go out and said you're to come with me."

I stared into the car, at the man's face. He was old. Older than Mum and Dad, but not quite as old as Auntie Isa, who lived on a broken-down farm and was always losing her teeth. The car had raggedy holes where its rust had got really bad. Its top half was gray, with maroon at the bottom. Maroon was my favorite color back then. I thought maroon was exotic.

"Come on, love," the man said.

I could hear a dog yapping, one of those small dogs with sore-looking eyes. The man opened the passenger door.

"Your dad says you're to come."

I looked around for a friend or somebody's mum but there was no one, so I ran until I reached our gate, and our path with weeds jutting up through the cracks, and Mum, who was stitching a bobble on to the bonnet she'd knitted for Dolly Delicious.

The policeman said I did well to remember so much about the man and his car. I could even describe the cigarette packet on the dashboard. I was sandwiched between Mum and Dad on the sofa, and they agreed that I had been very brave. As the policeman left, his heel crunched on a Weetabix.

It's never like that, when Marcus and I fall out. We don't throw our breakfast or start sleeping in the car. What we do is tell Lucille that Miss Cruickshank is delighted with Tod's progress, and that we had a lovely time in the pub.

Which must mean that we're all right.

chapter 16

Will You Miss Me?

According to Lucille, holiday preparation should consist of a three-pronged approach. One: cleanse from the inside, which means drinking two quarts of water per day and adopting a strict juice-based regime. Two: boost the metabolism with aerobic exercise, at least three times per week, for not less than twenty minutes. Three: ensure that one's skin is well-nourished in preparation for a blast of Majorcan sun.

I have bought a juicer just like my sister's. Natalie makes delicious fresh juice every morning, which may account for the pleasing, cooperative natures of her children. She has sent me her book of juice recipes; the phrase "pure energy" appears in virtually every paragraph. Just leafing through its pages makes me feel purer inside. Tod is so enthralled by our new appliance and mountain of fresh produce that he insists on making his own nectarine-and-strawberry cocktail, and shuns my broccoli-and-ginger variety.

By the time Marcus comes home, our worktops are slopped with juice puddles. "For you," I announce, handing him a blend of carrot and celery that has come out a pale terra-cotta shade. These concoctions, while not as pleasing as wine or beer, are quite drinkable.

"Had a coffee on the train, thanks," Marcus says.

The juicing session has become a stressy affair now that Tod is nagging for our old liquidizer with the cracked jug so he can set up a rival juice bar at the other side of the kitchen. He loads it with more fruit, switches it on, and clatters to the front door with the appliance still whizzing.

"Joe," he shouts into the street. "Joe, can I have your wild-flowers for show-and-tell?"

"What, all of them?" Joe calls back.

I follow Tod out and explain. "Whoever brings the most varieties wins a prize. I hope you don't mind."

"The most *species*," Tod corrects me.

"Sure," Joe says, "come over anytime. Help yourself."

I watch him marching down the High Street, smoking in public. He looks back, and gives Tod and me such a gigantic smile that I step back, amazed. It would appear that I have been forgiven for any connection, however remote, to the Distinguished Driveways brochure.

Three days later, when my insides have made a partial recovery from the juice onslaught, Lucille shows up to take me running. I would rather run by myself, so that I could walk if I felt like it, and had hoped that she'd forget about our arrangement.

Lucille is wearing dazzling trainers, an immaculate pale blue tracksuit, and is bouncing lightly on our front step. The plan is to run over the common and round the new estate, which she has figured is about a mile. This seems rather punishing for a beginner. I had hoped that we'd jog to the Poacher's, maybe pop in for a drink and packet of crisps to revive ourselves.

She streaks ahead, able to talk normally, while I worry that I am putting my blood vessels under unnecessary pressure, and will need surgery. Running—I mean proper running—has its place, like when we're late for school, but I can't really see the point when you don't actually need to go anywhere.

"It gets easier," Lucille yells back to me—but does it really? People only say this when you're embarking on something unpleasant, which you'll have to keep up for months—years, even—before visible effects are achieved.

The inside of my mouth has withered, as if vacuumed by a dentist's suction device. My tongue feels like a dried mushroom. There's a drinking fountain on the common, but Lucille says, "We're not stopping, you need to keep up the momentum." I have swallowed a bug—something meaty, like a bluebottle. It's jammed in my throat, I need water, but we're past the fountain now—nearly home, in fact, where Joe will glance down from the tree-house platform and spy a gasping shire horse, staggering to a halt at our gate.

There's no sign of Joe. I am ridiculously pleased about this. My tracksuit bottoms are splattered with mud, as well as the emulsion from my painting session. I lurch into the house. Marcus looks up from his book.

"God, Ro," he says. "You'd better lie down. You look like you're having a seizure."

I spot Anna immediately. Everyone else in the Covent Garden café is wearing black, white or gray, to match the stark decor, but my former boss dazzles in a flowery tea dress with gathered sleeves, and is the only person smoking. In the ashtray are the remains of three cigarettes, smoked down to their filters.

"Hello, country girl," she says, briskly kissing my cheek. "You look well—been exercising?"

I have been forced to accompany Lucille on two more runs, but suspect that my healthy flush is due to the anti-cellulite tights I am wearing in preparation for Majorca. Lucille sells them at Fab-U-Look, and brought some home for me to try. They are impregnated with sea minerals and plant extracts and are supposed to "melt away" dimply flesh.

"I've been running," I tell Anna.

"I suppose you've got to find something to do in the country," she says, sniggering.

Anna has compiled a shopping itinerary to help me select my capsule holiday wardrobe with minimal walking. She's had to learn to be organized since I deserted her; Stanley the assistant is incapable of registering when a phone is ringing, and she seems unwilling to replace me. I suspect that Anna still thinks we'll move back to London.

In the shoe shop, the dainty pink sandals she thinks I should buy have been designed for dolls' feet. Sarah might wear them while padding around her garden flat, where Marcus keeps a toothbrush and dressing gown.

"If you won't buy them, I'm going to buy them for you," Anna threatens.

In the quirky boutique, Anna selects a shift dress in yellow silk. She has never encountered children on holiday with their chocolate ice creams and sunscreened bodies. Silk is impractical, yellow makes me look terminally ill and I don't need anything so grown-up. This isn't a dressing-up holiday.

We wander up Regent Street and into four floors of fashion, all of which appears to be constructed from flimsy fabrics, the kind you could spit through, and which I fear would require a sturdier garment underneath, like a jumper. I pick a plain navy dress, drag Anna into the changing room and strip off.

"Why," she asks, "are you wearing tights under your jeans?"

I glare down at my legs. The tights are pale tea–colored and making my thighs feel quite unwell. That must be the plant extracts, seeping in. "They're for cellulite," I mumble.

"Has something happened to your brain? Take them off. They're disgusting."

I pull off the tights, liberating a powerful foot smell. It's too hot for tights, and for shopping. The navy dress makes me look like a fierce nurse. I dump it, plus the tights, on the changing room bench.

We stop for lunch in the café on the top floor of the shop. Mother-daughter duos are admiring their purchases and tasting each other's desserts. Anna wanted to come here, said the service was quick, allowing us time to hare over to the chemist's where she had spotted a two-for-one offer on sunscreen.

"Marcus okay about you going away?" she asks, picking at her help-yourself salad.

"I suppose so. Actually, he was quite keen."

"Why?"

"He thinks I need a break. He can't take time off. We've spent so much on the house, with the rot and electrics and woodworm, that we can't afford for him to come."

"That's a lot of reasons," Anna says carefully.

"And it would be good for him, too—ideal, really—because I think he's seeing someone else." The words have fallen out before I could stop them. Now they're out there, and it's all real, horribly real.

Anna drops her fork on to a small mound of barely touched leaves. A mother nudges her daughter: *Stop staring, it's rude, turn around and finish your ice cream.* "Oh, my darling," Anna says.

"Anna, I don't feel like shopping anymore. I just want to go home."

My mother says, "You're having separate holidays?"

I have the phone tucked under my jaw while I inspect Tod's nails, which look quite sinister with their long, blackened tips. "Not *separate* holidays. Marcus isn't having one. And I want to see—I want Tod to see Spain." It's not a lie exactly. I just don't want her to start remembering those Majorca days, the mixed fish specials on the seafront. There will never be a right time to tell her that Dad will soon be acquainting himself with nappies.

"You will be back for Perry's sixtieth?" Mum asks.

"Of course. We're only going for a week." I glance at the miniature Big Ben that sits on the hall shelf. Eight forty-nine, six minutes until school bell, and I still have to trim Tod's talons or at least gouge out the black stuff with a chewed match.

"I can't see why you're traveling all that way with a child," Mum continues, "when there are lovely places in this country. There's no foreign food, no language problem. You could go on a Diamond Break to Durham, like we did."

"Maybe next year," I tell her.

"And finally, the project prize is awarded to a boy who has only been with us since Christmas, and has produced—" Mr. Quigley consults his white card—"excellent work on our

Egyptian topic and also collected the most flower species in the whole of Chetsley Primary School."

I am squashed next to a woman with a gigantic backside who is slapping mentholated gum around her mouth. Tod pops up from a sea of burgundy sweatshirts and struts toward the stage. Mr. Quigley shakes Tod's hand vigorously, and everyone's clapping, apart from the mentholated woman who pulls a string of gum from her mouth and winds it tightly around her index finger.

Tod bobs back down to the floor. His collection has been illustrated with cutout drawings of flowers stuck to a roll of paper, roughly painted to look like grass: long grass, which the council should do something about.

"Happy holidays, everyone," booms Mr. Quigley.

There's a cheer, and the children scatter, the older ones crying because they're going to big school, and the younger kids scanning rows of parents for the right face. Tod waves his white envelope, thunders toward me and lands on my lap like a comet.

"Will you miss us?" I ask.

"Of course I'll miss you," Marcus says.

"How much?" Tod shouts from the back seat. In that children's book—the one I hid behind the storage heater—the little brown hare asks, "How much do you love me?" The dad hare stretches his arms as wide as he can and says, "This much." Of course Marcus can't do that, because he's driving.

At Gatwick, Marcus buys a Meccano crane for Tod to make on the plane, but is disappointed to discover that this Meccano is plastic, not metal. He browses in The Tie Rack, visits the toilet twice, and buys three toasted cheese sandwiches which come in waxy packets and cost almost as much as my pink sandals.

"I don't want this," Tod says from a precarious stool. "I want plain food."

"It is plain," Marcus says. "You can't get much plainer than a toasted cheese sandwich."

"I want *plane* food," Tod insists. "It comes in a tray from the hostess lady."

"They're called flight attendants," Marcus tells him, "or cabin crew."

"Yeah," Tod says, nudging away the toasted slab. "I want flight attendant food."

At the next table a woman with fragile hands is unwrapping her lunch. You're not supposed to eat your own food in the café. She removes three layers of wrapping—kitchen roll, foil and a clear plastic bag—from her sandwich. She is telling someone, possibly us, that her legs are going and her daughter has already gone, accused her of trying to rule her life. The woman pokes a hand up her sleeve. "I can't find my hankie," she announces. "I've looked in my bag and it's not there, either. I must have left it on the bus."

I don't have tissues, but offer to fetch her some loo roll from the ladies. "I shop at Iceland," she tells me. "The girls there are kind. I can't read the coins so they help me. The doctor said I'd better forget about reading, so I took all my books to charity."

"You could get books with big writing," Tod suggests.

The woman studies him for a moment, and delves into her handbag. I assume that she's looking for her hankie again but she pulls out a pound coin and hands it to Tod.

"No, please, don't do that," I protest.

"That's for your holiday," she tells Tod. "Have a lovely time with your mum and dad."

At the departure gate Marcus puts his arms around Tod, who is clutching the Meccano crane and pound coin and standing rigidly, as if waiting for the hug to be over. Marcus drops his arms and says, "Tod, your shoes are on the wrong feet."

Tod is staring at me and frowning. "What's the matter?" he asks.

"Nothing."

"Oh, darling," Marcus says, "it's only a week. Don't be upset."

I dump our case at my feet. "Wish you were coming," I tell him.

He grasps my hand and says, "You want to make things right with your dad. It's important for you. You don't need me around."

I do need you around.

His kiss lands on the bridge of my nose. "Have the best time," he says.

"You, too."

"I'll just be working."

"Yes, of course you will."

As he walks away I want to yell that word he said in his sleep: the word that has grown in my brain, swelling like pizza dough, and acquired a face, an extensive collection of delectable shoes and a waxed bikini line. I wanted to ask him that night, not long ago, before morning had begun to sneak into our room. His mouth was on mine, his arms wrapped tightly around my back. When it was over he fell away from me, like he hadn't really woken up.

Marcus is striding along the concourse, away from us. Tod is still waving.

"Marcus!" I shout after him.

He turns and mouths, *What?*

"Don't forget to feed the fish."

chapter 17

My Baby Sister

He looks like my old dad, but dipped in nutty brown paint and dressed in a startling ensemble of lobster-colored shorts and faded lime-green T-shirt with a fifties car on the front. Dad does not drive a car like the Chevrolet on his T-shirt but a decrepit tin vehicle, held together by thick silver tape and kind words. There is a hole in its underside, allowing the person occupying the passenger seat to view the road surface. Dad calls the car "girl." "Come on, girl, good girl," he says, as the engine strains to manage a slight incline.

Tod sits in the back with his tape player on his lap, his Meccano model and pound coin in one hand and Dog in the other. Around his neck are the binoculars and a hairy scarf he insisted on bringing in case Majorca was cold. He wouldn't believe me when I tried to explain how hot it would be. "Even hotter than sports day," I told him. He still brought the scarf, just in case.

Tod has never been in another country and is thrilled that my dad can drive on the wrong side of the road without crashing or being arrested. He's so excited, he forgets about playing a story tape. "Is this Majorca?" he keeps asking. "Is this Majorca, as well?"

"It's all Majorca," Dad says, laughing. Other cars, and even loose dogs without collars or owners, zip past us like rockets.

"So how's fatherhood?" I ask him.

"Fantastic. You know, Lily smiled at just three days old."

"Really? That's amazing."

"It's all new to Freda but she knows just what Lily wants. She understands her. It's like they're…telepathic."

I assume that they haven't purchased a seat that rocks all by itself, like the one I had.

In town, shuttered buildings with scuffed edges huddle beneath scarlet flowers. The car fills with the smells of warm dust and cooking. Dad and Freda live on the town's scrubbier edge in a basement flat, which is accessed by a spiral staircase. In the small, square yard, a wiry cat springs out of the baby's pram.

Freda has pale lemon lines in her toffee-colored hair, and no discernable age. Lily, a bald, pink bean of a child, is attached to her breast. "Hello, Ro, Tod," Freda says, trying to haul herself up from the worn corduroy sofa to greet us properly. Lily roars her disapproval at having supper interrupted, and Freda flops back into her feeding position. I'd forgotten how small new babies are, how their elbow skin hangs baggily. Freda smiles unsteadily. It hadn't occurred to me that she might be nervous about meeting us.

"She's a beautiful baby," I say.

"We think so—don't we, Ernest?"

Dad nods and rests a hand on her shoulder.

Tod steps carefully toward Freda and the baby. "It was in her tummy," he announces. "It was made with a seed and her egg. Seeds can swim. They get in where she goes to the toilet and—"

"She's not an it," I cut in. "She's Lily." What is she to him? A half aunt? It doesn't seem possible that an aunt can own a Three Little Pigs play mat.

There are so many items of baby equipment in the living room that it's hard to believe that adults actually live here. A wicker crib on a stand is festooned with pink and white frills. The play mat, which fills most of the floor, is littered with knitted animals, velour bricks and pastel-colored rattles.

Tod waggles his Meccano crane too close to Lily's drowsy eyes. "She can have this," he announces.

"That's very kind of you," Freda says, "but she can't hold anything yet."

"She can have it when she's older."

"Thank you," Freda says. "Ernest, do you think Lily needs changing again?"

"What time did we put that nappy on?" asks Dad.

"About three, just before you set off for the airport."

"Let's do it—don't want that rash springing up again." Together, Dad and Freda place Lily on a plastic mat patterned with butterflies. Freda unbuttons the Babygro and removes the nappy, which looks perfectly clean and dry to me. Dad wipes Lily's bottom, then pats it dry, then polishes it with a towel. I realize that I'm holding my breath. Freda lifts the child's lower half, which Dad secures, tongue poked out in rapt concentration, with the new nappy. Twenty fingers are required to fix the adhesive strips. "There," Dad says.

I feel as if I should clap, or at least should have videoed the procedure.

When Lily has fallen asleep, and they've checked several times that she's not too cold or too hot, Dad cooks for us. It's stew from a tin that retains its cylindrical shape as it plops into the pan. It smells like pet food. Dad serves it with rice, which he's boiled to mush. Our plates are flooded with water from the rice pan.

"This is great," Tod enthuses.

"Ernest's been such a support," Freda says, "taking over the shopping and cooking."

Mum called him Ern. She called him lots of other things, too, like idiot, nitwit and good-for-nothing-get-back-in-the-garage, but never Ernest.

The stew coats the roof of my mouth, like engine oil. Tod has walloped his portion down and wants more.

"Mum never makes nice food like this," he announces.

After dinner, Dad takes us for an evening walk and everywhere I look there are families with fathers. Some children have ice-lolly-stained lips and dads who let them jump down to the beach from the yellow stone promenade and race each other. One of the dads joins in and falls over on purpose, making himself lose the race. Another dad is roaring, "If you do that again, your bike's going back to the shop the minute we get home and you're not going out again, ever." He tries to smack the child's rear but the boy zooms forward and the dad is left slapping air.

We sit on the warm, yellow stone of the promenade, dangling our legs over the edge. Tod is telling my dad about his 3-D maze.

"I found this wood in the shed and cut pieces of green stuff to make hedges. It's really brilliant," he says.

"Remember getting lost in that maze just outside York when you were little?" Dad asks me.

"No, I don't think so."

"It was in some botanical gardens. You spotted it in our guidebook and nagged so much that we agreed to take you."

"What was it like?" Tod asks, eagerly.

"Natalie was the first to run in. She was tall enough to see over the hedges and started guiding other families who were sick of the heat and finding themselves back at the same dead end."

"Typical Natalie," I say.

"You followed her in, but you couldn't keep up and no one could see you over the hedges. I kept shouting for you, telling you to just squeeze through the hedges and make your way to my voice. By the time you finally stumbled out, your mum was sunburned and her eyes had started to puff up. We had to take her to the doctor."

"Why didn't you do what he said, Mum?" Tod asks.

Dad laughs. "She said she didn't want to cheat."

By the time we reach Dad's apartment, Lily has woken up and shows no sign of settling. Freda is standing at the top of the spiral staircase, rocking the child in her arms. I remember this part—a child's inability to distinguish day from night. Marcus said, "If I'm sleep deprived I can't work, simple as that, and the business could go under." That's why he started to spend the occasional night at Will's.

Dad's apartment still smells of tinned stew, with a hint of regurgitated milk. Tod and I will sleep on the sofa bed in the living room. From the bedroom come Lily's weak cries. I haven't slept the whole night with Tod since the period after I was called to his old school, and he refused to sleep on his own. He would squirrel between Marcus and me, thieving our pillows and sleep.

The story tape is still playing. I made Tod turn it down to a murmur so it wouldn't disturb Lily.

It's *Danny the Champion of the World* again, the bit where Danny and his dad fill raisins with sleeping medicine to drug the pheasants. Tod thought that pheasants were poor people with raggedy clothes until I explained that they're birds and that hunters shoot them. He found this disturbing, which I found odd, considering that he relishes the ancient Egyptians' more disturbing practices.

The powder won't harm the birds, just put them to sleep. It's not poison, not like the stuff that Carl has stashed in his hut behind the double garage. Lucille told me about it when she came to wax my legs, the final stage in the three-pronged approach to holiday beauty. She said, "He's borrowed a knapsack sprayer from a landscape gardener he met at a wedding. I don't want anything to do with it. I'm not even happy about having the stuff in the shed."

"He can't just kill someone's garden," I protested.

"Ro, he's obsessed with that damn grass. I told him it'll look even worse if he sprays it, all straggly and dying. But there's no stopping him, not now he's got the equipment."

I was so stunned I didn't even wince as she ripped the gauze from my shins.

Tod isn't being Salmon Man, but really trying to swim. Small waves lap around Dad's palm-printed trunks. Tod is horizontal on the water's surface with his neck jutting forward like a turtle's. All that's stopping him from plummeting under the water is Dad's hand, supporting his belly.

At first, Tod wouldn't follow Dad's instructions. He wanted a net and a bucket so he could catch hermit crabs like those other boys were doing. Sunscreen clung to Tod's pale back in thick swirls. Catching crabs looked much more fun than swimming. He said, "I'll never be able to swim in sea water. It moves about too much."

"The salt helps you to float," I explained, but he didn't be-lieve me.

I went to buy three strawberry ice creams from an elderly man with a freezer compartment attached to his pushbike, and when I came back, a small cluster of children was gawk-ing at the wild creature, with seemingly unconnected limbs, flailing through the sea toward my dad.

Tod swims a little farther each day. By day four, the fre-netic sploshing has been replaced by jerky strokes, which re-quire such mental and physical exertion that Tod needs at least half an hour's rest, shrouded in beach towel, after each five-minute swim.

"What's wrong with him?" asks a small child. She is wear-ing a crisp white dress patterned with embroidered poppies and is clutching the hand of a slightly larger, identically dressed girl.

"He's been swimming," I explain. "It's really hard work, when you're learning."

"We're not allowed to go swimming," the older girl says.

"Why not?" Tod asks from under the towel.

"We'd get wet," the little one says. They are sisters, named Margot and Darcey, after the ballerinas.

"You know what?" says the big one. "There's a special ma-chine near the pizza café. If you twist the handle really hard, a toy falls out and you don't have to put in any money."

The girls' mother is wearing tight, pale pink trousers and a pink T-shirt. She looks like a fondant. Tod has emerged from the towel and instructs Dad to help him make a sand maze, which must have its entrance close to the water so the channels fill up as the tide comes in. "Me and Dad did this," he explains, "on the Island of Wight."

Margot and Darcey want to help. "As long as you don't

sit on the sand," the fondant says. "They're your best dresses, remember."

We find Margot and Darcey each morning, gathering spoils from the free toy machine, and also Jacob, who is five and a half, yet insists on being transported by buggy, which makes me feel better about Dog and the spout cup. Jacob shows Tod how to climb the gnarled pine trees by fixing the toe of your sandal into the cracks of the bark. Tod shows him the pound coin from the old lady at Gatwick. He's made friends, simple as that. I haven't been forced to invite anyone for tea or damaged a kid's stomach with my spaghetti.

I buy postcards and write TOD CAN SWIM!!! in enormous letters on one depicting a flamenco dancer with real satin stuck onto her dress, like the one Dad once sent me. Jacob wants to see what's under the satin.

"It's just another dress," he retorts, awash with disappointment.

As I write our address, I wonder what's happening at that other house, where weed killer will be seeping into the roots of poppies and cornflowers, causing them to droop and finally keel over. Don't criminals often return to the scene of the crime? I picture Carl slowing down as he drives past Joe's house, checking that everything's poisoned. I asked Marcus, "Can't you talk to Carl, stop him doing this?"

"It's Carl's business, not ours," Marcus said.

On our last day, the rain comes. It hammers the spiral staircase like a downpour of nails and causes Dad and Freda to conclude that Lily shouldn't be taken out, as she might catch a chill. Dad is delighted to see rain because it will be worth opening the Happy House for once. He runs the soft play center by himself. I'm not sure if this is legal but he says his opening hours are too erratic to employ staff.

Dad takes the entrance fees, stacks kids' shoes in the pigeonholes, and sells plastic jugs of rank purple juice and spongy disks impregnated with raspberry gloop. At the end of each session, he cleans the play equipment, fishes half-nibbled cakes and the occasional abandoned nappy from the ball pool and mops down the toilets.

"I've never seen you looking so happy," I told him last night, over another tinned dinner.

"It's Freda and Lily," he said. "They've made me feel properly alive."

I felt a little twist in my stomach when he said that.

A boisterous family from Bradford arrives at the Happy House. They have brought their own ice creams, which is not allowed, but Dad is too busy dispensing drinks to notice. The ice creams are called Crazy Zoo. They come with a plastic animal whose head and limbs can be removed and attached to the body of another species, to make a composite creature. A girl wearing sunglasses—the frames are yellow and heart-shaped—yelps that she's lost a vital part of her Crazy Zoo animal. "I want my bull's head," she bellows.

"I've got one at home," Tod tells her. "It won me a prize."

"I want *mine,*" the girl mutters, peeling a fragment of sunburned skin from her shoulder.

He helps her to hunt for it, and when they come back, still minus the bull's head, they've lost her sunglasses, too.

Even Tod can't stomach Dad's jammy cakes, so we head out into the rain and share a pizza in the Italian café. It wasn't supposed to have spinach, and has to be entirely de-spinached before Tod will acquaint himself with it. I spot Margot and Darcey, eating daintily without requiring alterations to be made to their food. The fondant mother is wearing a plunging white top made from crinkly fabric, the kind that's meant to look un-ironed. The girls' dad is holding their mum's hand across the table and not eating at all, just looking at her. "Try this," she keeps saying, offering him forkfuls of food.

Then I get it: they haven't been together long enough to accumulate filing cabinets and a vat of horse manure. Darcey doesn't say Dad, she calls him Peter.

When we come out of the restaurant, the rain has stopped and Tod finds Jacob knee-deep in the sea. Tiny fish dance around his chunky legs. He's feeding them torn strips of bread. I plonk myself near his parents, who have come on holiday with another family. I once suggested to Marcus that we try a two-family holiday so Tod would have someone to play with. The only people we could think of with children of around Tod's age were Will, captain of Marcus's octopush team, whose trips to Africa and Thailand exceeded our budget, and Suzie, with whom Marcus is reluctant to engage in a five-minute telephone chat, let alone a two-week holiday.

Jacob stumbles out of the sea, announcing, "I want a Crazy Zoo."

"You don't even eat them," his father retorts. "You just want the bloody toy."

Jacob climbs into his buggy, beaming hatred.

"It's only an ice cream," his mother hisses. "Let him have it."

"He's had one already."

"It's his holiday, for God's sake."

Holidays are supposed to make everyone happy, so why are they so difficult? On the last holiday I had with my parents—camping in Scarborough, we always headed north to Dad's childhood haunts—it took us nearly three hours to put up the tent. He had forgotten to pack the poles, so we clambered over barbed wire and scoured the woods for sticks of the right length. When Mum opened the boot of the car, a gas bottle rolled out and clanged onto her foot. Her big toe

swelled up so badly she couldn't wear her favorite tan sandals, only Dad's wellies. She accused Dad of making the bottle fall out—at least not packing the car carefully—and threw
fruit at him. Strawberries or even a tangerine might not have
been so bad, but these were tinned mandarin segments.

As Tod coaxes Jacob out of his buggy, I wonder if divorce
can actually be a good thing. Since she met Perry, Mum has
swapped her faded dresses and put-upon hair for smart
trouser suits and a springy perm. And I can't imagine that
Dad would hide in the garage these days, nibbling cheese,
even if he had one.

We are leaving and Dad's car won't start. I had planned to
buy a small gift for Marcus at Palma airport and now we'll
be lucky to make the flight. The car rouses itself briefly, then
slides back into its nap. "Easy, girl," Dad murmurs with each
turn of the key.

Freda teeters at the top of the spiral staircase, clutching Lily
and chewing her bottom lip. "Call them a taxi, Ernest," she
insists.

"We'll just have to be patient," Dad says cheerfully. "She'll
go when she's ready."

Finally the engine growls into life and we're off, with Dad
driving so slowly I have to jam my teeth together to prevent
myself from nagging at him to slam his foot down.

"What will happen," Tod asks, "if we miss the plane?"

"We're not going to miss the plane."

"Will Dad be upset," he continues, "if we're stuck in Majorca forever?"

"Of course he'll be upset. He's dying to see us." As we
approach the airport I remember how keen he was for us to
come here without him. I had barely mooted a tentative plan
before he had applied for Tod's passport and booked our
flights, which I thought was unusually helpful.

Tod and I tip out of the car and I haul our case from the boot. I want to hug Dad but there isn't time. A gaggle of stringy brown girls tumble out of a taxi and leg it, their sandals slapping the tarmac. I grab the hand of my son who can swim and make friends and yank him toward the check-in desk.

We are Late Passengers. The zingy pink label slapped onto our suitcase announces our shoddy timekeeping. The girl at the desk makes a big show of checking her watch and phoning the departure gate to announce our late arrival. I can't understand what she says but suspect that it's something about an idiot mother and a boy with a chaotic eyebrow who is rapping a pound coin on the edge of her desk.

We are thundering across the concourse when Tod stops in his tracks. "Mum," he asks, "does something bad happen if you lick a tree?"

"Tod, we're going to miss the damn plane."

"*Damn* is a bad word, Miss Cruickshank says."

"We're going to make the plane late. Everyone will be really angry."

"Mum, does something—" he starts again.

I set down the case, which another late passenger knocks flat as he hurtles past us. "Why are you asking me this?"

"Jacob made me do it. We were climbing the big tree and he told me to lick it. When I'd done it he said something bad would happen to my insides."

I grip his hand and kiss the top of his sweaty head. "Nothing bad's ever going to happen to you," I say, and we run.

part four

The maze is a journey, a puzzle to be solved.

chapter 18

More Trouble With Tod's Hair

We bring home a carrier bag of Crazy Zoo animals, a pottery dolphin money box in which Tod will keep his pound coin and tiny, blood-sucking insects.

It's in the garden that I first notice Tod raking his scalp. Marcus and I are acting according to instructions on the leaflet slipped through our letterbox, urging Chetsley residents to ensure that borders and hanging baskets are well tended in preparation for Best-Kept Village judging day. I spot Tod clawing his head and conclude that his scalp is flaking from all that Majorcan sun. Or maybe I didn't wash his hair properly—Dad's place had only a dribbly shower, and no bath—and there's sand stuck to his scalp.

A flat-leafed plant, like ivy but meaner and faster growing, has snuck up our garden walls and spiraled itself around the lupins. If I tried to unwind it, I would be here for years.

Gardening is, according to the glossy magazine I found in the seat pouch on the plane, the new sex. The magazine also reported that navy is the new black and staying in is the new going out. Everything is the new something. But the magazine lied; there is nothing enticing about weeding, particularly when the other adult present flips the top off a beer and chats to the newsagent girl over the wall, while you fret that you're confusing weeds with proper plants.

Marcus has at least mown the lawn, with Carl's whizzy machine, and instructed Tod to collect the clippings. Tod is squeezing the fluted petals of foxgloves, trying to trap bees. "Can you *help?*" Marcus demands, when he's finished his garden-wall chat.

"I don't know where to put it," Tod says, stuffing handfuls of grass clippings into his jeans pockets.

"Use the wheelbarrow," Marcus suggests.

"Do I have to?"

"Yes, you do. This is a family thing. We all help each other."

By midday, Marcus has fetched a second cold beer, which he drinks while lying on a blanket on our front lawn. He has even brought out a cushion to use as a pillow. Tod has also given up on our gardening enterprise, having filled the collapsible wheelbarrow with grass clippings and knocked the thing over. I am the only one actually gardening. I thought this was supposed to be a family thing, with everyone helping each other.

By one-thirty, Marcus has consumed a third beer and is snoring softly in the faint sunshine. Despite our—mostly my—efforts, the garden still doesn't look right. The plants Marcus ordered from an advert in a Sunday supplement— enough to fill a ten-foot-long border, the ad said—turned out not to be proper adult plants, but wizened little things called plugs. I suspect that we should have nurtured them in some cozier place: the shed, maybe, rather than scaring them witless by thrusting them straight into the ground.

Marcus wakes up just after three, by which time Tod has added an annex to the 3-D maze and retired to his room to continue his What Joe Does dossier. I find him writing: *Joe is macing the treehows roof. It is pointy like a reel roof.* He stops writing to poke at his scalp with the blunt end of his pencil.

"I'm all itchy," he complains.

"Yes, me, too." Muck from the garden has impregnated our skin, like the plant extracts in those anti-cellulite tights.

Tod is too busy clawing his head to greet tea with any enthusiasm.

"Why are you scratching?" Marcus asks. There's a pale line over the bridge of his nose, where his shades blocked out the sun during his three-hour nap.

"Can't help it," Tod says.

"Do you think he's got nits?" Marcus asks.

"It's probably bugs from the garden." Aren't gardens swarming with wildlife? I remember Pest Controller and his warning about biting insects. This is our comeuppance for trapping a nest, probably housing several chicks, in the attic. I read an article in the *Gazette* about thieves raiding birds' nests and selling the eggs to collectors. The ornithological expert warned that it's against the law to interfere with wild nesting birds. We have shut out the adult birds, leaving underage chicks with no food or parents.

Marcus abandons his dinner and rakes his fingers through Tod's hair, but it's too matted to see anything. "Is the chemist open on Sundays?" he asks. "We need a nit comb."

"I don't have nits," Tod insists, using his fork to access a troublesome zone behind his right ear.

★ ★ ★

I am armed with a fine-tooth comb, a gloopy lotion that promises to kill head lice plus their eggs, and a leaflet that informs us that black specks are, in fact, nit dung, meaning that my son's head is being used as a toilet. Tod huddles on the sofa beside me, wincing at each stroke of the comb. I tap it onto a sheet of white paper. There are brown dots, which do not appear to be doing anything spectacular, or even moving. Tod's binoculars don't work close up, so we dig out the magnifying glass from his bug-collecting kit.

"They've got bodies," he announces, "and wriggly legs."

We find some in my hair, too, and place them next to their relatives so they can party together.

"Do they look like that?" I ask, studying an illustration on the leaflet of a head louse, magnified two thousand times.

"Much worse than that," Tod declares.

I could cope with a more photogenic species, like dragonflies or ladybirds. On the leaflet, this super-nit appears as a horrific, armor-plated beast with hairy, jointed limbs and a rabid appetite for small children. We learn that, after hatching, young lice are capable of reproducing within ten days. Now I feel really sick. They are doing it right now, copulating wildly on my head and Tod's head, but not on Marcus's head, as he has checked himself thoroughly and reported that he is entirely louse free.

Never mind reassurances that nits "prefer clean hair." That's put on the leaflet to make you feel better. We may not be obviously dirty but, as a family, the Skews appear to attract vermin. Look at the birds, the *Anobium punctatum*. I wonder if the nit lotion is a milder, heavily perfumed version of KillAll, which Mr. Leech sprayed on to our joists. We never required so many poisons in London.

"You could have picked them up in Majorca," Marcus suggests. "You said Tod played with lots of other kids."

"Only Jacob and those girls, Margot and Darcey."

"Even ballerinas get nits," Marcus retorts.

I notice that he has positioned himself at the far end of the table, at a safe distance from Tod and me, and says that it might be better if I, rather than he, slap the lotion onto our heads, save him being infected.

Then he trips off to join Carl's quiz team at the Poacher's.

Tod and I are sprawled across his unmade bed. I am trying to read to him but it's too distracting, having your head smelling of sick roses. The nit lotion must be left on overnight so that it penetrates the eggs. "You missed a bit," Tod keeps complaining—we're on the chapter about picture mazes, where a recognizable shape, like an eagle or dragon, can be seen from above—then grumbles, "I'm hungry. Can I have supper now?"

As I wait for his toast to pop up, I haul in our suitcase from the hall and open it. Why are pink sandals quite acceptable in Majorca, but not for the school run? Something good happened to us on that holiday. There are so many people in our pictures: Dad, Freda, Lily, Jacob, the chef from the restaurant across from Dad's flat, who let Tod watch chickens sizzle on their spits in the kitchen.

Even Jacob's parents, and the ballerinas' mother in her fondant ensemble, have snuck into our photos. We appear to have lashings of friends. Tod's toothy smile beams from a brown face, and my own face appears almost crack-free. I look like Ro who used to run a film archive and never encountered lice infestation.

My holiday clothes still smell of Dad's stew. I tap out his number, hoping that I won't interrupt a cozy Ernest-and-Freda moment, or an intense nappy-changing procedure.

"Hello?" It's Freda who answers. "Oh, Ro, it was wonderful to meet you both. The flat feels so quiet without you."

"Freda, I'm sorry to tell you this, but Tod and I have nits."

"Oh, don't worry," she tells me, "we've applied the lotion and we think they're all dead now." I start to ask if Lily caught them, then remember that she doesn't have hair.

I put down the phone and play a message that we haven't picked up. It's Will, captain of Marcus's octopush team. *"Marcus, Ro, haven't seen you in ages. We're planning a barbecue, week on Saturday, can we drag you back to the city for our famous lamb burgers? Speak soon, toodle-oo."*

I call him back.

"All settled in the middle of nowhere?" he asks.

"We're fine, how's the team?"

"Great, best season so far if we win next week's match. Pity Marcus has been out of action since you moved."

I go to speak but my voice doesn't work. Nothing happens. Tod is shouting from his room. It starts with a barked *Mum. Mum.*

"Ro? You still there?" Will asks.

"He's just been…very busy."

"I understand. You're doing up a derelict house. He has to put his family first."

Tod is yelling louder now: *Maaaam. Toahhhst.* "That's right, Will," I say, prodding my head to check whether the lotion is still sticky or has formed a meringue-like crust.

"So you'll come on the nineteenth? I'd hate to lose touch just because Marcus has jacked in octopush."

"Let me see what we're up to."

I put down the phone, snatch two slices from the toaster, and slap on hard slices of butter straight from the fridge. I half fill his milk cup, microwave it for twenty seconds, then dispatch supper by express delivery to His Supreme Highness upstairs.

"This toast's cold," he retorts.

★ ★ ★

Mum didn't snoop in cupboards, drawers or even the garage, after Dad had left her. I took a week off work to stay with her, when the martini was taking hold, and watched as she loaded everything he owned, and had not taken to Majorca, into black bin liners. Dad hadn't been one for hobbies or hoarding, and I was surprised that he actually owned so much stuff.

Mum got up at six-thirty on a Friday, the council's special collection day, and placed the sacks on the pavement. You could see his silver reading lamp, and his own breadboard that he had kept in the garage, poking though a hole in a sack. Mum seemed much cheerier as she made breakfast. If Natalie had been there, and not engulfed by chicken pox, she would have commented that the *chi* had started to swish through Mum's house more freely.

There was so much *chi* flying about that Mum had a nap after breakfast, although that also could have been due to the effort of lugging thirteen full bin liners into the street. I wondered why he hadn't taken these things with him, and what he'd have done if he'd seen them being driven away by a truck with a cage on the back, filled with rusting cookers and foul mattresses.

Like Mum, I don't rake through other people's private things. I'm just curious, and that's an admirable quality. Tod wants to know things, like what the inside of a stomach looks like, and how dead people turn into skeletons. I'm pleased about that. Like my son, I'm just *interested*.

Marcus's system is so finely honed that I can flick through his papers without removing anything from its file. Here are instructions, plus guarantees, for every appliance we own, even the baby listener we haven't used since Tod was a toddler. Does anyone read these things? We never learned to tape a program, even before the video broke. The microwave is used only to warm Tod's bedtime milk. How did we accumulate so many appliances? Those *Boxed Brainwaves* don't recommend shopping for white goods together. The juicer hasn't been switched on since my pre-holiday health kick. We used the bread-maker once, to make pizza dough, and it came out gloopy and glued to the sides of the tin. We would have had better results with the Corby trouser press.

I check Marcus's mobile account in the bills file. The only numbers I recognize are my mobile and our home phone. These are work-related people, so why should I know them? Sarah, of course, is too busy having her toe cuticles pushed back and massaged with sweet almond oil to rifle through anyone's personal things.

Upstairs, in Tod's room, the Dalmatian fish dart between fronds that could be plastic or real, living plants. Tod has kicked off his spaceman duvet and is lying with arms and legs splayed. Toast crusts litter the carpet. In our bedroom, one wardrobe door hangs from a single hinge and won't shut properly. It never recovered from the removal men's rough handling. Marcus has promised to fix it, but I know that he remembers the trauma of building the thing in the first place. The shop where we bought it offers a home-build service, but who bothers with that? It looks so easy, in the diagram. "Any idiot can do this," Marcus announced. He made me take Tod to the park by our old flat so he wouldn't be distracted. When we came back three hours later, with hailstones trapped in our hair, he was still surrounded by rectangular panels and crumpled instructions and said, "I didn't expect you back so soon."

The inside of his wardrobe is reasonably neat, apart from a jumble of old jackets and flippers at the bottom. Each shirt is on its own hanger. His ties are loosely rolled and stored in a shallow wicker tray on the top shelf. In his chest of drawers are folded sweaters and T-shirts in black, white, gray, navy. These are the only colors I've ever seen him wear.

A packet of condoms has been slipped down the side of his pants drawer. "How do you know you won't have any more babies?" Tod asked in front of my mother and Perry at Boxing Day dinner.

"We just know," I said quickly.

Marcus grunted as he tried to unscrew the lid from the piccalilli jar.

"But you said," Tod blundered on, "it just takes some kissing and the seed swimming along the woman's pipes."

"Anyone for some tongue?" Mum asked, waving a plate laden with purplish slices.

"Mums and dads only make a baby if they both want one," I muttered under my breath.

In the hall I find Marcus's briefcase. It contains details of flats, three of last week's papers, and a velvet giraffe stuffed with beans, which he must have bought for Tod and forgotten to give him. I find his address book in the briefcase's inside zip pocket. I am listed in the *H* section—Ro Hall—with work and home numbers. No mobile, then. No child, or jointly purchased white goods with instruction booklets carefully filed, back then. There are lots of names I don't know in his book, but no Sarah, not even an *S*.

Marcus shows up just after midnight with the excellent news that Carl's team won by twenty-two points, despite the dimwit who insisted that the Velvet Underground came from Stoke. I sit up in bed, watching him undress. He flings his jeans in the direction of the linen basket, but misses.

"What have you been doing?" he asks.

"Oh, this and that. I spoke to Will."

"Will? What did he want?" He tries for a smile but it's so unsteady he has to turn away from me.

"He asked us over for a barbecue, week on Saturday."

"Oh." His T-shirt lands in a soft hoop on the floor. He places his socks in the linen basket. Wearing just his pale blue and white striped boxers, he lowers himself to the edge of the bed. "Don't think I can make it," he says.

"Why not? I'd like to go. In fact I *want* to go. Is there a problem?"

"Did he invite all of us?" All of us, that sounds like a lot.

"Of course he did."

Marcus glances at me. He has drunk just enough to give his face a slight sheen. His cheeks are flushed, and I can smell beer.

"What?" he says.

"You're a bloody liar, Marcus."

"What are you talking about?" There's a little laugh, as if he thinks I'm hysterical—imagining things again, like bad smells in the house.

"*You* know."

"You're just weird these days. Sometimes I think I don't know you any—"

"It's always me," I yell, "who's weird or making stuff up."

"Well, it is," he says, tugging off his boxers and trying to slam them to the floor, but of course they don't make any noise, not even a soft *flump.* He slides into bed and curls up at its farthest edge.

And it's not me: it's you. You don't play octopush anymore. You say you're playing, every Thursday night, but that's not what you do. I wonder if Sarah has asked him to leave me, if she stomps around her flat in her spindly heels, with her hair flying, or if she's content with a part-time arrangement. *Let's keep it this way, darling. She'll never find out. She's hardly ever in London. Yes, she does pop in to see that dreadful friend of hers—the one who's addicted to fried food and producing children—but your paths won't cross . Why would they? When she's not at that book-*

shop, serving three customers a day, she's usually at home, socializing with damp-proofing contractors and pest controllers. She never used to be like this.

"Don't you dare pretend to be asleep."

"I'm not pretending anything," he says.

"Marcus, I know you don't play octopush. You haven't played for months."

He sits up, and is laughing now, chuckling softly like he's just cottoned on to the joke: oh, I get it. "Not in Will's team," he says. "I switched, remember, just before we moved? I've been coaching Hackney Under 21s. I told you, Ro."

"You've gone to a youth team?"

"It's great coaching experience. They've been in the top three of the junior ladder since—"

"You told Will you'd stopped playing?"

"I didn't want to hurt his feelings."

"Won't he find out?"

"I'll speak to him," he says, then his lips are all over my face, and he's no longer tired: can't I see how much he still wants me? I close my eyes, and we're back in my old flat, on one of those workday afternoons when we'd meet in the park and sneak home to bed, where we'd lie until lilac-tinged shadows crept into my room.

If you want to know something, just ask. And I can't.

chapter 19

Bad Tarts

Perry had planned to celebrate his sixtieth birthday in the garden, enabling guests to mingle on the lawn and admire the koi carp. But what started as a promising day has, by lunchtime, slumped beneath pewter clouds. We are now jammed into Mum and Perry's low-ceilinged, white-with-a-hint-of-green living room, surrounded by crystal rose bowls and bone china plates bearing Mum's tarts.

"More nibbles?" she asks.

"I've had enough, thanks," I say, as she waves the plate in my face. Everywhere I look, there's barely touched pastry. No one seems to know what to do with themselves. Perry's old workmates from the electrical appliance shop are bunched up at the back door, smoking Embassy cigarettes. Mum's friends from her flower-arranging group are lined up on the sofa like quiz show panelists.

"Anyone for Trivial Pursuit?" Perry suggests, petting his moustache with a forefinger.

Marcus is pulling his let's-go-home face. I am experiencing an overwhelming desire to be out of here, away from Trivial Pursuit, which Perry is setting out on the dining table, and Mum's fishy mayonnaise.

"It's been lovely," I tell her, "but I'm seeing a friend while I'm in town, and Marcus has business to sort out."

"Here," she insists, "we'll never get through all these." She fills a Tupperware carton with tarts, hands me my birthday present—a swan-shaped parcel with red ribbon tied flamboyantly around its neck—and hurriedly kisses my cheek.

Tod and I tumble from Marcus's car at the park gates. I turn to wave the carton of surplus tarts and mouth to Marcus that I want to leave them in the car, but he has already driven away.

"Ro!" Suzie shouts. Tod grins and pelts toward her.

Suzie's kid, Barney, plummets headfirst into my stomach. He looks up at me, grinning, and says, "What's in that box?"

"You really don't want to know, Barney."

"Good party?" Suzie asks, smirking. I pull a face. "Come on," she says, tugging my arm, "let's see if we can knacker these two out."

In our old park, a bunch of adults are playing noncompetitive football. I recognize a few of the regular players from our street. It's noncompetitive because caring about winning is deemed a Bad Thing. One Sunday morning someone buzzed at our door, asking if we'd like to join in. The man had flaccid pink thighs, and curly black hairs sprouting over the neck of his T-shirt. "We're busy today, maybe next Sunday," Marcus explained, a pattern that continued until the man gave up and left us alone. We had to avoid walking past the park on Sundays.

Noncompetitive football appears to consist of jogging daintily on the grass, and occasionally shouting, "Well done, Libby!" although today I spot one of the women delivering a pretty competitive kick on the ankle.

I drink insipid tea, and Suzie has water, in the park café where all the food is deep fried, even the bacon for sandwiches. Tod and Barney are crouching on the path outside, studying ants. They are trying to make the ants carry things: fragments of leaves, cigarette butts.

"Ro, I have something to tell you," Suzie says. Her hair is secured in a fuzzy bun, and her lipstick has worn away, leaving a wonky brown outline like chocolate.

"No, you're not."

She nods.

I watch Barney through the open café door; he's three but still a baby really. His shorts are padded with nappy, his dummy attached to his Fat Controller T-shirt by a red plastic clip.

"I've already stuck a notice in the newsagent's window, trying to sell his cot, stage-one car seat, all that baby guff," she says flatly.

"What does Peter think?"

"He can't understand why I'm so worried. Says that one more won't make any difference."

I place my hand over hers and squeeze it.

"And we've used up all our favorite names," she adds.

"We've got some baby name books in the shop. I'll start racking my brain."

"I don't want it, Ro," she says quietly.

The smell of frying fills the café like thick breath. Sarah doesn't come to deep-fried bacon cafés. There's no need— she doesn't have children.

"Ro, are you okay?" Suzie asks. "You look kind of peaky."

I want to tell her, but Tod and Barney have buffeted back into the café and want one of those ice-cream lollies that shock your teeth with a hard toffee center. I open the plastic carton and waft Mum's fish tarts in their faces.

"Ew," says Barney.

"Put the lid back on," instructs Tod.

As we leave, the waitress hurries over to wipe toffee lolly remains from the table.

"You sure everything's all right?" Suzie says. "You don't look very well." Barney's arms are wrapped around her knees, causing her to shuffle, as if trapped in a sack.

"It's just the fish tarts," I tell her, opening the carton and flinging Mum's offerings to the ducks.

My birthday falls on a Monday, the day after Perry's sixtieth. I am thirty-six, and therefore no longer in my early thirties. To celebrate this monumental event, I am spewing up peach-colored fluid in the vague direction of our green glass Habitat bowl, a wedding present from Anna intended to contain elegant salads, and not my stomach lining. Marcus is holding the bowl under my chin. Forget Valentine's Day, and flowers delivered to a loved one's workplace. True love, I figure, while wiping my jaw with a damp tea towel, is demonstrated by a willingness to catch someone's sick. *Boxed Brainwaves* should mention this.

As Tod and Marcus consumed only maize snacks shaped like maggots, they are both bristling with health. "What's wrong?" Tod demands.

"Mum's got food poisoning," Marcus mutters.

"Will she die?" he asks brightly.

"Of course not," I snap, spitting into the bowl. Tod once informed me that, if Marcus and I were both to drop dead, he would choose to live with Suzie because they have pizza and cola bottle sweets. He looked quite excited at the prospect of being orphaned, as long as it involved daily consumption of Four Seasons with Cheesy Crust and unlimited refined sugar. I wouldn't have been surprised if he had a pre-packed suitcase stashed under his bed.

I give my face a proper wash and brush my teeth, gums and tongue.

"You going to be okay?" Marcus asks, checking his watch.

"I'll be fine," I tell him. Now I just feel weak and mildly dizzy, as if most of my blood has been siphoned off.

In the shop, Julia administers peppermint tea and deals with customers, so all I have to do is alternate between my chair at the till, where I gaze at the computer, and the toilet. Tod is sprawled on the floor in the shop's darkest corner with his felt tips and paper. As he rejected the Summer Kids' Club in Lexley, and even arts and craft sessions at school, he has been spending my working days in the shop. "But the Summer Club sounds great," I insisted, forcing him to study the leaflet. Its itinerary included nature walks, fancy dress contests and a wide range of sporting activities.

"I'm not going," he insisted. His "What I Did During the Holidays" diary will read only: "I sat in the bookshop." Today he is designing an underground maze, its passages snaking deep into the earth, perilously close to its fiery red core. He demands that I try it out, see if I can negotiate the pathways without being horribly burned.

"Please go home, Ro," Julia says at lunchtime. "I can manage fine on my own today."

"Thanks," I say. "You could watch that dinosaur video, Tod." I suspect that Julia doesn't want me fouling the shop with my breath, which is still laced with Mum's fishy fillings.

A birthday present arrives in the afternoon post, and I let Tod rip it open. It's a snug-fitting, pale gray tracksuit from Natalie. I must have over-egged my enthusiasm for running. Mum and Perry's present is a wicker basket shaped like a swan, with a cracked neck, and nothing inside it. Marcus's parents have sent a card, with a note saying that they weren't sure what to get me but have a velvet ottoman which is surplus to requirements, and they'll bring it next time they visit.

There is a card from Anna, a black-and-white picture of a woman wearing a beaded fifties-style gown, holding a cocktail. The woman is grinning and she has her party lips on. The caption reads: *Muriel was devastated when her children left home.* Tod's card, to which he has stuck tinfoil hearts, reads: You Are a Fantustic Mum. Marcus hasn't given me anything yet.

Despite my bad stomach, I start lugging as many of our possessions as possible upstairs, in preparation for floor sanding. Sandy is starting work tomorrow. Sandy the sander will exfoliate our floors. I stack chairs, bookcases and the TV around our bed, figuring that Marcus can deal with the table and filing cabinets. This isn't what a person with rotting tarts in her gut should be doing. I should be lying down, with someone stroking my head.

I'm still upstairs, heaving furniture about, when Marcus arrives, early for once, and shouts, "Ro? Stay up there. Don't come down till I'm ready."

"When what's ready?" Tod yells from his bath. He scrambles out, and runs naked and dripping to greet Marcus, but is sent back upstairs, out of the way. Marcus doesn't want Tod hopping around him, barking questions.

Finally, Marcus shouts, "Ready."

As most of our belongings are now crammed into our bedroom, there are few places where he could have hidden my presents. In the kitchen I delve into the cupboard where we keep the fish gravel sieve. I check under the sink, and behind all doors and curtains.

"Cold," reports Marcus.

Tod has pulled on a belt-less dressing gown and is teetering on the edge of the bath to access the top of the old-fashioned cistern. I hope that Marcus hasn't hidden my exquisite underwear in such an unhygienic location.

"Garden?" I ask.

"Warmer," he says, smirking.

Although it's not quite dark, a yellowish light, maybe a candle, glows from the tree-house window. A fire hazard, Carl would say. Joe is sitting there, swinging his legs over the edge of the platform. Tod waves and Joe waves back. I study the strip of soil Marcus refers to as a herbaceous border, and note that the plug plants have yet to burst into life.

"Keep looking," Marcus says.

Round the back of the house I'm getting warmer, warmer, hotter now—*boiling* hot. A balloon on a string drifts limply from the shed door handle. In the collapsible wheelbarrow are two parcels. One is a thickly knitted sweater, the kind Anna warned me that previously stylish women start wearing once they move beyond the M25. There's a chrome shelf to span the bath and hold flannels and soap, the sort of bathroom accessory that would get in the way should you be seized by a desire to hold your very own foam party.

"There's something else," Marcus adds, and his mischievous look tells me, *This is your special thing. You're going to love this.*

Tod has found it, propped against the oil tank, and hands it to me, quivering with anticipation. The parcel is long and thin with a flat end. It's very crowded, with three us squashed into the shed. I rip off the paper.

"Well?" Marcus says.

"What the hell is it?"

"It's a hoe, Ro."

"That rhymes," sniggers Tod, pulling his dressing gown tight across his stomach.

"I know what it is, Marcus."

He steps backward, out of the shed. "It's a joke, darling. Of course it's not for you. I just thought we'd better have our own garden tools. We can't keep borrowing Carl's."

"A hoe," I repeat.

"The other things are your real presents." He strides back to the house, with Tod scampering ahead.

I stand at the open shed door.

Marcus looks back, checks my face. "What?" he says.

Tod has clattered into the house. It's just me and Marcus out here, and I'm still clutching the hoe. "I have something for you, too," I say.

"What did I do," he says, laughing, "to deserve a present?"

"I'm pregnant, Marcus."

He tries to smile. His jaw trembles with the effort. To stop it shaking, he presses a hand over his mouth. "Are you sure?" he asks through his fingers. "How did that happen?"

"There was one night—"

"You *can't* be. We're so careful…"

"Well, I just am." He hadn't been careful Marcus then; he hadn't even been properly awake, or he would have taken steps to ensure that this would never have happened.

The hoe falls from my hand as he throws his arms around me, and clangs heavily on to the side of the oil tank. He's holding me, but it feels like hugging a fridge.

"Marcus," I whisper, "I know we didn't plan this, but I can't tell you how happy I am." My face is wet, and the tears feel sticky between my face and his. Then I realize that they're not just my tears.

"I'm going to have it," I tell him, thinking, *no matter what you say.*

"Of course you are, darling, of course you are."

Ridiculously, I am more worried about how the mysterious fillings of Mum's party fancies, rather than Sarah, might affect our unborn child.

chapter 20

Sarah

Sandy arrives with his throbbing machine with which he will blast a hundred years' worth of gunk from our floorboards. We have already slung out Gordon and Betty's autumnal carpets. They looked even worse, hanging out of a skip, than they did in our house. A century's worth of split milky tea had clogged up their pile, and I had started to wear slippers to avoid skin-on-carpet contact. When she passed our house, Tina the hairdresser gave Harry a sharp tug on the arm and snapped, "For God's sake, don't touch that."

By day four of sanding procedures, the three of us are living and sleeping in our bedroom, surrounded by most of our furniture. I am unused to seeing my family so close up. Marcus is spending as much time as possible in London, and escaping to the Poacher's with Carl most other evenings. I am too worn down by the screeching of Sandy's machine to muster up any anger.

Tod views the ordeal as great fun. Children are remarkable in their ability to embrace chaos and filth. "It's like camping," he says, writhing delightedly between Marcus and me in bed.

"Don't have enough space," Marcus mumbles into his pillow. "I feel like I'm going to fall out."

"No one has enough space," I remind him. But he's right. We will fall out in the most awful, gut-wrenching way, when he's not at work or the Poacher's and Tod isn't around. When will that be?

Suzie told me that, when the new baby arrives, she doesn't know how she'll find time to go to the toilet. Marcus hasn't mentioned our baby since Hoe Day. I'm already sneaking quick looks through that baby name book. I suspect that he has managed to convince himself that he dreamed up our brief conversation, and that everything's normal.

And it's not like camping. At least when you're installed under canvas or nylon, you have actually chosen to bundle your family into one ridiculously small space. Yes, we chose to invite Sandy into our home, but how could we have known what to expect? I had anticipated some noise, slightly louder than the whir of a hair dryer. I hadn't expected relentless screeching, or that I would be wearing the same socks for days on end, and find thick yellow dust in my knicker drawer. We weren't warned that Sandy would strew Gorby Cottage with toolboxes spewing wood filler and treacherous power tools, and that huge portions of our home would be sealed off by clear plastic sheeting.

Sandy left hours ago but the air still tastes of wood because, in fact, it is wood. Marcus and Tod are asleep now, but I'm lying here, wondering how so much dust might affect a six-year-old's lungs. He is a passive dust-breather. By the time he wakes up, he'll have inhaled the equivalent of a six-foot plank.

And what about school? Autumn term starts next week. School doesn't care that you're dirty and can't find your purse, or that your offspring's good shoes are lost, probably crushed under a bookcase. Tod will start a new term, on September the tenth, whether or not Sandy has finished his business in Gorby Cottage.

"It's an awful upheaval, isn't it, having your floors sanded?" Lucille sympathized. "But I suppose it'll look great when you've laid new carpets." She had brought me a tincture called agnus castus to soothe my hormonal mood swings. The small print on the label read: *Not to be taken by pregnant or lactating women.* "Promise you'll start taking it?" she asked.

"I'll start tomorrow," I told her.

Joe's garden didn't die. When we came back from Majorca there were so many wildflowers, forming great swaths of color, like when you sprinkle dry powder paint onto wet paper.

Now Joe points out the poppies that burst in splashy oranges through the grass or, rather, he is showing Tod, and I just happen to be *with* Tod. We are only here because Sandy's machine is still roaring, and ninety percent of our home is inaccessible.

"It's a *wilderness*," Tod declares.

"That's what I wanted," Joe says, crouching beside him. "I wanted to see what would happen if I let it go its own way, and didn't interfere at all."

I sit on the grass behind Tod and wrap my arms around his shoulders. "Our garden doesn't feel like this," I say. "We bought these plug plants and they've done nothing, and I can't keep up with the bindweed."

"What I did," Joe says, "is throw wildflower seeds from the

tree house, and the flowers have grown where the seeds landed."

"I don't think Marcus would go for that."

He catches my eye, and I start laughing.

"What is it?" Tod asks, swinging round to face me.

"Nothing, honey, I'm just imagining Dad's face, if I threw seeds all over the place."

In fact I'm warming to Joe's low-maintenance approach. Everything is alive and growing; his garden didn't even get sick. "Carl messed up," Lucille told me. "Must have got the dilution quantities wrong." He had crept out with the knapsack spray, checked that Joe's truck wasn't parked in the drive, and that the house was in darkness. Then he sprayed the whole garden, working as quickly as possible. That must have been around two a.m.

Carl was exhausted after a terrible day spent photographing a wedding at Summerlea House. No one would cooperate. The bridesmaid had grass stains on her frock. The bride and groom didn't want traditional shots, they demanded reportage, but what did that mean? Carl has been in wedding photography for seventeen years. This wasn't his style at all.

Joe brings me tea in a glass mug. Tod is scaling the rope ladder to the tree house, shouting, "Mum, come up and see." The tree house has a pitched roof, you can see that from the road, and an ancient window I assume Joe found in a skip. When I look in skips, there are only mounds of wet plasterboard and cracked toilets. Inside the tree house, propped against a wall, is a white canvas marked with loose, penciled lines. A tarnished lantern hangs from a hook.

Joe climbs in. This tree house is too small for three of us— more cramped, even, than our shed. I can smell myself, stale wood from the sanding. I need a bath, or at least industrial strength deodorant, and Sandy out of my life.

"What do you do in here?" I ask.

"I look out. It's a great view, don't you think?"

Tod jabs the canvas and asks, "Are you an artist?"

"I paint, but being a joiner is my real job. Do you know what a joiner is?"

"You make things in wood," Tod says. "Could you make me a tree house?"

"Do you have a strong enough tree, one that's broad enough to take the weight?"

"No," Tod huffs, picking at flaking green paint on the door.

"And I'm not sure people would like it," Joe continues. "Someone came round, a man from the council, said he'd had a call from a neighbor concerned about it being…just *being* here."

"What happened?" I ask.

"He looked at it from the road and agreed that it was just a shed in a tree, and you don't need permission for sheds. He also asked if I could build him a house in his sycamore because it would keep his kids out of his hair."

Tod climbs down the ladder so there's just Joe and me in the tree house. I sit on the platform and watch Tod letting himself tumble backward into cushions of grass. "I built this," Joe tells me, "so I could see the garden from above, like a bird would. If you paint it from here, and take the grass right to the edges, so your picture's *all* grass, it doesn't look like a garden at all, just colors."

I'm about to tell him that I draw and paint, at least I used to, but worry that he'll ask to see my work and not know what to say if he doesn't like it. I don't want to spoil anything, even though there's nothing, really, to spoil.

He's just a neighbor. We're sitting very close, on the platform. Tod is lifting stones close to Joe's house, looking for bugs.

"Do woodlice bite?" he shouts up.

"No, I don't think so," I say. Joe's hip is touching mine. I should move away from him, climb down and help Tod to identify insects. Joe lights a cigarette and offers me the open packet. "No, thanks. I gave up years ago."

"So you're never tempted," he says.

"God, yes, all the time, with the sanding, and the way things are." Ridiculously, my eyes fill with tears. Some mothers blub at anything. I am *not* one of those women.

Joe puts his hand over mine. "What I like about you is—" he begins.

Tod has found something—I hope it's not a something that bites—which he holds in cupped hands.

What he likes about me is the way I let Tod be himself. "You think that's good?" I cut in. "His teacher said he's not all there, like he's got some disorder. Marcus calls him Wonderboy because he lives in Tod World."

Joe's hand is still covering mine. I must not feel bad, because the grass didn't die, and we're just talking: isn't that what you do with neighbors in places like Chetsley? You pass the time of day. Whenever I ask Marcus how he can bear to be around Carl so much, he says, "I'm just being neighborly." *We'll never settle in if we don't make friends.*

"Joe," I say, "I'm pregnant."

"Well, that's wonderful."

"It should be, but we're not right, me and Marcus. Having a baby is the last thing we should be doing."

He pushes my straggly, growing-out hair from my face and says, "It's going to be fine, Ro, whatever happens."

"Mum!" Tod yells from below.

I spring away from Joe as he scrambles up the ladder and

onto the platform. Tod has mud up one nostril and a trembling beast, not unlike a nit magnified two thousand times, in his palm.

An entire bottle of agnus castus could not rescue Lucille's day. She showed up with her hair not secured in an elegant coil or French plait, but flapping about her shoulders, not knowing how to behave without fine silver clips or the tortoiseshell gripper.

I invited her in, and she stomped into our kitchen, but refused to take off her jacket.

"We're going for a walk," she announced. "I have to talk to someone, Ro, or my head will explode."

Now we are pounding across Chetsley Common in the drizzle, on our day off. Tod is at Harry's birthday party, a football party, at the Leisure Centre in Lexley. He didn't want to go. I tried to explain that it's rude not to show up at a party unless you're very, very sick. "My throat hurts," he whined unconvincingly.

Lucille is dressed for a serious walk, probably involving paths that aren't properly tarmacked, judging by her boots. We set off and arrive at a gap in the fence that looks as if it leads to someone's garden, but turns out to be the start of a proper footpath.

"This came this morning," Lucille announces. From her jacket pocket she pulls out what looks like a bill. "Twenty-one calls," she retorts, "to Chile. Who the hell do we know in Chile?" She stops dead and jabs a finger at the amount.

"That's a lot," I agree. "Do the children have penpals or something?"

"Of course not. No one has penpals anymore. It's all chat rooms." She stomps on, brushing past brambles.

I wonder if this path leads to somewhere interesting, like a café, serving warm brownies.

"And that couple," she rants on, "it wasn't his fault. Carl knows how to cover a wedding. There's your bride and groom shots, bride with her parents, groom with *his* parents—all together if they prefer, that works out cheaper—and no one stood where they were supposed to. The best man told Carl to leave, said they could have done a better job themselves."

She pulls a mangled page of the *Lexley Gazette* from the pocket where the bill came from. I wonder why she is showing me these things. We stop, and I read:

Photographer Wrecked Our Wedding

When they booked a local photographer to capture their dream day, Adam and Jennifer Richards, of Cedar Manor, Newton Meadows, had no idea that their celebrations would end in tears. "Adam and I hoped that the pictures would reflect our informal wedding and give a feeling of fun and happiness," Jennifer, 29, told the *Gazette*. "The photographer tried to force everyone into groups, and shouted at my seven-year-old niece for getting grass stains on her dress, then disappeared to the bar until he was, quite clearly, under the influence."

Nothing could have prepared Adam and Jennifer for the shock of seeing their prints. "It was a beautiful, sunny day, but everything looked so bleak. My niece's eyes were red from crying and my mother wasn't in any of the pictures. The tragic thing is, we can't do a rerun, and will have to rely on memories of our special day."

The Richards are seeking compensation. Carl Gilbert, of Gilbert Wedding and Portrait Photography, Black Street, Lexley, declined to comment.

"The trouble with weddings," Lucille says, "is they plan them for years and spend thousands, then complain that the pictures aren't sunny enough, like Carl can control the weather."

"Can they actually sue?"

"They can refuse to pay. Then Carl's only option is to take them to Small Claims, which isn't worth the hassle. Come on," she sighs. "Let's find raspberries."

Lucille has brought a Tupperware carton to transport the fruit. The raspberries taste ridiculously intense, not like shop fruit at all. I must bring Tod here and show him real food, bursting from nature's larder. He should grow a little less fond of jam doughnuts and learn to appreciate fresh produce. He still insists that fish is made in a factory, shrink-wrapped and bar coded, bearing no relation to real creatures with gills, like the Dalmatians in his bedroom. When I cooked trout, he glowered at its mouth, which hung slightly ajar, and said, "I don't eat *that* sort of fish."

Lucille drops berries into the carton. As I stuff my face, she says, "What should I do about this bill? I've called to check. It's definitely ours."

"Have you tried phoning the Chile number?"

"I'd feel stupid, like I was checking up on him."

"You think Carl's been calling Chile?"

"Who else could it be? *Someone's* done it. But I'm not a snoop, Ro. I wouldn't stoop so low."

The path takes us up and away from Chetsley and eventually—miraculously—back to the end of Lucille's road and pleasingly close to her coffee machine and chocolate shaker. In the show home, damp laundry is draped over every radiator and even the peach-colored leather suite.

"Why don't you phone that number?" I suggest.

She glares at the phone and then, consulting the bill, taps out the number. She takes the phone to the hall, the walls of which are festooned with photos of Adele in so much hobby-related attire—ballet, tap, majorettes—that I wonder whether the child ever wears ordinary clothes.

Lucille stalks back into the living room.

"Who was it?" I ask.

"It wasn't a person, Ro. Just a recorded message." She is wincing, as if her tongue is coated with oil.

"What sort of message?"

Lucille pops a raspberry into her mouth. "Oh, baby," she breathes, "you've got me *so* horny tonight…"

"What, like a sex line thing?"

She nods, and spits the raspberry out on her hand.

"It must be a mistake," I say firmly. "They can't be based in Chile. I've always imagined them being recorded by some woman in Croydon, in a rancid old dressing gown, sawing at her toenails with an emery board and—"

Lucille is blinking rapidly. She hands me the carton of fruit. "Actually," she says, "I don't like raspberries."

"They'll only get sawdusty in our house."

"I suppose," she mutters, "I could make raspberry fucking muffins."

I wonder how such delicacies might go down at Carl's next PTA cakes and candies stall.

By the time I'm home, Sandy is loading his equipment into his van. Despite the dust that coats every surface—the roof of my mouth and, I suspect, all of our internal organs—I'm sorry to see him go. It's been quite novel, coming home from work to find a responsive adult to talk to.

He slams the van door shut and says, "You're the first person who's had their whole house sanded at once and not moaned. Most places, the owners are off on holiday."

"I'll remember that for next time."

"I hope you don't mind me breaking that lock on the cupboard in your son's room," he adds. "The boards go right to the wall and I wanted to treat them properly, in case you want open space under the window."

"That's fine. We've never had a key for that cupboard."

"I can fix another lock if you want one."

"No, just leave it."

I fish out my checkbook from my bag and write his check.

"I found an old tin in that cupboard," he adds. "Maybe the other owners left it. I put it on the windowsill in your son's room."

I thank him, and watch his van rattle away, then call Marcus to inform him that our home is now a vision of loveliness.

His voice is drowned out by an announcement over the tannoy at Charing Cross. "Train's cancelled," he says irritably.

"Why doesn't that surprise me?"

"I'm not in charge of trains, Ro, just stayed late to finish some—"

I bang the phone down.

Tod's floor is still sticky so I put him to bed in our room. At nine-thirty, Marcus still hasn't shown up. I can see that tin on Tod's windowsill, and could tiptoe *ever so quickly* across the floor, but don't want to wreck Sandy's varnish. I could borrow Carl's extendable ladder, open Tod's window and access the tin from the outside, but that sort of behavior really would warrant a front-page story in the *Gazette*.

Ten-seventeen. Tod is mumbling, dreaming. I hear him say, "Jipshuns." I creep to his doorway and test the vanish with a finger. It's not quite dry, but I step quickly to the windowsill and snatch the tin. Its tarnished, slightly rusting lid depicts a thatched cottage smothered thickly with roses.

I sit on the stairs, aware of Tod's faint murmurings, and

open the tin. There are photographs, still in their paper wallet from the developers. They are all of the same girl. Her fair hair falls in chaotic waves, which someone has tried to tame with a rainbow clasp. She is wearing a purple T-shirt with a hippo on the front, and gazing at the candles on a birthday cake.

There's a woman behind the girl. You can only see her mouth and chin. Her gray top looks stained, and she's not wearing makeup. Her hands rest on the child's shoulders, as if prompting her: *go on, blow.* Maybe the girl has too many wishes to choose just one or doesn't want to extinguish the flames. Her lips have formed a soft, expectant shape, not a pursed, about-to-blow shape.

I wonder if the candles are the re-lighting kind, giving other children the chance to blow and make wishes, but when I flip through the rest of the photos it doesn't look as if there were any other children at the party. Just the girl, with a smear of cake on her cheek and a stuffed rabbit in her hand.

The cake has yolk-yellow icing, and four candles. It's been decorated with one of those icing pens, the kind I once let Tod use to draw on biscuits. He sucked on the tubes and went crazy, punching my leg and slamming doors with such force that the upstairs girl banged on our ceiling. As the icing wore off, he retreated to his room, crying because I'd confiscated *Mazes and Labyrinths* for hitting me.

I wonder if this girl ended up like Tod after the icing pens, in tears because it was all too much. After our night at Millington Park, Marcus's parents reported that Tod had hardly spoken in the Leeds Castle maze. "He seemed overwhelmed," Maureen said.

In one photo, if the woman had turned slightly to the camera, you'd be able to see her face, in profile at least. I don't know her, but I do know the girl. She has a chin dimple just like her dad's. She has his full mouth and nearly black, mischievous eyes.

Sarah is the name on the cake.

chapter 21

Acting Normal

"We could move back to London," Marcus says.

"What, move again after all the work we've had done? We can't do that." I stare at him, wondering if he's joking, testing my reaction.

"If it would make things better—" he begins.

"I thought you liked Chetsley."

"I do like it. I'm just not sure that *you* do."

We are occupying a circular table beneath a blackboard listing the Poacher's award-winning fare. It's Monday night. There's only Marcus, me, the humbug man and Bandit, the humbug man's dog, in the lounge. The man is clutching his half pint and brown paper bag of sweets. Lucille bullied us into going out, after I let slip that today is our wedding anniversary. I think she wanted to get out of the house and avoid conversations about Chile.

We have been married for eight years. In early photos of us together, like in Paris, there's always a bit of touching going on—hand holding or my arm pressed around his waist. We stood on Pont Neuf, and in Jardins de Luxembourg, and handed our camera to strangers. The camera was our first jointly owned purchase; we didn't own a microwave then. These passersby always took the trouble to size up the picture properly, and wish us a wonderful holiday.

"I'm just fine," I tell Marcus. "And we're not moving." He looks at me, knowing, of course, that anyone who insists that they're fine is extremely *un*-fine.

In fact, I am having trouble speaking. My voice is too high, like I've gulped helium. In my trouser pocket I have a photograph. Its sharp corner pricks my thumb. My horribly childish intention is to quietly place it in front of him on the table, and walk out of the pub.

"I just think we should be open-minded," he says.

"That's what you said when we looked at the house. Tod's not changing schools again. There's been no bullying here. He's doing okay."

"That's it," Marcus snaps. "You bring everything back to Tod and what Tod needs, not what's good for us."

From the bar, the humbug man is tuning in to our conversation with rapt interest. This is what happens when couples don't go out enough: we store up gripes, like the small change that weighs down our pockets. At the first sip of alcohol, they tumble out and scatter noisily onto pub floors.

The landlord throws a handful of crisps over the bar, which Bandit snaps at eagerly. Marcus nudges my hand away from a blob of wax on the table, which I've been madly picking at.

"I shouldn't be away so much," Marcus says. "Tod needs me around."

Now who's bringing everything back to Tod.

I sip my lager. I'll only have one, and I'll drink it slowly; that can't cause any damage. "Actually," I tell him, "Miss Glass says he's doing really well. She's pleased with the way he joins in with class discussions."

"Who's Miss Glass?"

"His new teacher. She's lovely, just in her first year of—"

"He's only been back for a week, Ro."

"It's been a good week. We haven't even been late."

Marcus asks for more beers at the bar, clearly forgetting that I shouldn't be drinking at all. "Terrible shame about the Best-Kept Village award," the man mutters. "Losing to Newton Meadows, of all places. Shouldn't have happened, *wouldn't* have happened if certain individuals—we know who we're talking about, Mr. Skews—had done their bit."

"Such a pity," Marcus agrees.

I wish that we hadn't come to the Poacher's tonight. All weekend, I have managed to act normally. It's easier to be normal at home than in a pub with only three customers, one landlord and a dog. I painted the hallway and even let Tod help, to ensure that the procedure was chaotic enough to avoid anything else being discussed. Marcus didn't ask why the permanently locked cupboard in Tod's room was now open and empty.

During our normal weekend, I even produced meals to coincide with mealtimes, as if operated by remote control. These offerings were devoid of color: fish, rice, mashed potato. Food for ill people. At the second white meal, Marcus laughed and said, "It's like living in a hospital." I stared at my anemic dinner, and would have welcomed Dad's stew from a tin, if I'd had no involvement in its preparation.

Marcus returns now from the bar with our drinks. "I asked for water," I remind him. "I shouldn't be drinking."

"Sorry, I'll—"

"Why won't you talk about the baby? You're acting like it's not happening."

"That's not true," Marcus insists.

"You don't want it."

"How can you say that? It's happened, and we'll manage. Now please stop shouting."

The humbug man nods from his bar stool. He picks up his drink, and Bandit's lead, and walks unsteadily to our table. The dog rests its wet mouth on my thigh. "Poor Bandit had an accident," the humbug man says. "Jumped into the stream on the common, cut his leg." He makes us examine the blackened wound where the vet mended him with nine stitches.

I run my fingers over the photo in my pocket: its shiny surface, then the blank side, the matte side. I want to slam it on the table, but the man's staring at me, blinking moistly, and his dog's still resting its chin on my leg. There's a small patch of drool on my trousers.

"Let's go home," I say under my breath.

"Oh, don't be so down, folks," the man says. "Chetsley will win again next year, you'll see."

Lucille is surprised to see us home so early. I want her to leave immediately, and yawn dramatically.

"Isn't it amazing," she says, "how your fish have bred?"

"Bread? They're only supposed to have fish food. Has Tod been dropping crumbs in the tank?"

"I mean *babies*," she says. "Tod hadn't even noticed. There are at least seven little ones, though it's hard to be sure, because they won't stay still and be counted. Anyway, you have a whole family in there. Isn't that wonderful?"

★ ★ ★

Our shower is housed in a freestanding plastic box, the kind of construction which, minus its creepy plastic curtain patterned with crustaceans, might have featured in a 1960s sci-fi TV program. You would step in as your normal self. Some noises would happen, the box would judder and you would emerge, swathed in tinfoil, with superpowers.

I usually avoid our shower and I am only enduring its luke-warm trickle before bed in the hope that I might step out not as Ro Skews, assembler of lunchboxes and obliging sales assistant at Coffee & Books, but a woman capable of removing Marcus's hair from his scalp with one swipe.

The shower has dwindled to a splutter. It's like standing under a leaky gutter. I don't understand why the plumber couldn't do anything to increase the water pressure—"your tank," he said, "it's the position of your tank"—and how Marcus has managed to exist for three days without mentioning the cupboard or missing tin.

He's downstairs now, tapping away on his laptop in the kitchen. He's being busy. Too busy to talk to his ill-humored wife. What I am planning to do is climb out of this shower and make some kind of scene. Stamping on our newly sanded floors, that would cause quite a ruckus, but I'd have to be wearing the right kind of shoes and my pink sandals have been missing since we moved our furniture for Sandy. All I can find are my fat country boots, and suede slippers. I will not attempt to stamp while wearing slippers.

If I start shouting, I'll wake Tod. What I did, when my parents were rowing downstairs, was shut off my ears and get out my pens and my drawing books. It didn't harm me one bit. Kids can do that, cut off everything beyond their immediate world. You just focus so hard on what you're doing, wondering whether light brown or ginger is the right color for the boy's hair in your drawing, that you're barely aware of the crash of a solid but breakable thing—the phone, maybe—hitting a wall.

Children know how to be mad. They don't consider which shoes to wear to create maximum impact when foot stomping. When I was pregnant with Tod, and witnessed a girl throwing herself onto the floor in Knickerbox because she wasn't allowed to remove all the lace briefs from their hangers, I vowed that my own child would never exhibit such unsociable behavior. Motherhood, I figured, would consist mainly of pleasurable activities, like sponge painting and reading *Where the Wild Things Are.* I actually believed that, as my child's incubator for forty weeks, I might have some control over how he or she would turn out.

Then I discovered that all children have tantrums. Tod had an outburst so wild and furious—worse, even, than the kite incident on Chetsley Common—that the salesgirl in the Early Learning Center let her boiled sweet fall out of her mouth. Marcus and I were trying to remove him from a push-along car. It took both of us to prize his grasp from the steering wheel. I worried that we had damaged his fingers and that the woman on her mobile—whose neatly plaited daughter was playing quietly with a doll's house patio set—was actually calling the police.

In the shower, cold water is now dribbling on to my head. I pull on my dressing gown, still thick with wood dust despite being washed at ninety degrees, and use the milk-and-honey body lotion, which I filched from Millington Park, on my face.

Marcus has been dozing on the sofa. "I thought you hated that shower," he murmurs.

My dressing gown feels clammy, and I'm shivering. What I had planned to say was: *Could you tell me, please, when Sarah's fourth birthday was?* My inner toddler would rise in my throat.

I would be as scary and beyond reason as Tod in the Early Learning Center.

Marcus opens his eyes and says, "You haven't dried yourself properly. You're making a puddle."

What I do is snatch Tod's school sweatshirt from the arm of the sofa and fling it at him. It flops against the side of his head, and drops silently onto his shoulder. Calmly, he picks it off and folds it neatly. Then he stands up, turns off the TV and leaves the room.

That showed him.

chapter 22

A Little Mistake

When I ran away to Blackpool, I lost Scooter Phil on the Pleasure Beach. He'd been looking after my money. I pushed between queues for the rides, and ran out of the fairground, past B and Bs with vases of sun-bleached plastic flowers on their windowsills. Most of the houses had cracked concrete forecourts instead of proper gardens. A boy of around my age was fixing a bike on a gravelled square in front of a pebble-dashed house called Seaview, which didn't have a sea view at all.

"Are you lost?" the boy asked.

I dropped my bag at my feet and told him about Phil, my money and not knowing what to do.

"Come back later," the boy said. "We've got a caravan in our back garden—I'll make sure it's unlocked. You can sleep in there if you promise not to mess anything up."

His face was so kind, I wanted to cry.

"My dad'll go mental if he finds out," the boy added.

I came back when it was dark and my legs ached from walking. The inside of the caravan smelled of damp swimming things trapped in a plastic bag for several decades. I tried to sleep but was worried about being discovered by the boy's dad. Just before six, I crept out and stood at the side of the road that runs along the seafront. A Mini pulled up beside me. The driver, a woman of around my mum's age, said she was going to London. As she drove, she forked coleslaw into her mouth from a plastic tub wedged between her thighs.

The woman gave me money for the tube and a lecture about letting Phil look after my money. She said, "I hope, after this, you'll learn to take responsibility yourself."

"If it's not a school day," Tod protests, "so why do I have to get up?"

"We're going on a day trip," I announce. The baby fish flick lazily around the tank. Some are mainly black, like one of the adults; the others are silver, like the other parent, but don't have its spots.

"Don't want to go out," Tod grumbles. "Want to stay home and draw."

I have decided that we are taking a trip on a riverboat. It will be excellent fun, and may even encourage Tod to appreciate nature. We have lived in Chetsley for nine months. It's about time he took an interest in wildlife—ducks, for instance.

I tell Marcus my plan in a robotic voice: "We-are-going-on-a-boat."

"Aren't you coming, Dad?" Tod asks at breakfast, with a pained look.

"I think your mum just wants to go with you."

"Why?" Tod asks. He is still wearing pajamas and has failed to respond to my several thousand requests to get dressed. Each time I place his clothes beside him—thick, polo-necked sweater and jeans, suitable for a boat trip—he wanders out of the room. "I want Dad to come," Tod insists.

"I'll take you out another day," Marcus says.

A small trough has appeared between his eyebrows. I wonder if it has been caused by the strain of acting normal or our colorless meals.

The boat leaves from Newton Meadows, a ten-minute drive from Lexley. It seats around thirty but, by the time we arrive, is only a quarter full. As the engine starts, Tod exhibits more interest in a bobbing Fanta can than a family of mallard ducks. "When does it speed up?" he asks.

"It doesn't, sweetheart. It's not a speedboat. We're on a river cruise and you should be enjoying yourself."

Everyone else seems content with the boat's steady pace. I start to tell Tod how to distinguish the male mallard from the female, but he's not listening. He hasn't even brought his yellow binoculars. It appears that they are to be used for spying only on Joe, not on wildlife.

A harassed young couple keeps passing their baby to each other, in the hope that the partner will take responsibility for the child for more than two minutes. At each change of holder, the child's cries grow louder and I begin to wish that we'd reach the wide bit of river where the boat will turn round and head back.

I want to offer to hold their child, to remind myself what a person so small and new feels like in your arms, but worry that they'll think I'm some crackpot. I'd be so embarrassed if they refused. The other passengers would stare and we'd all become horribly aware of the engine's low rumble.

"Are we nearly there yet?" Tod asks.

"There isn't a *there,* Tod. We'll just go back to where we started." I realize now that this excursion has been a mistake. Don't I know the first thing about children? They want to *go* somewhere. A destination, preferably with gift shop and café attached, should feature on any day trip. The young mother announces that baby's nappy's dirty, that's why she's upset, and totters past the small counter where hot drinks and cheese rolls are served, and into the toilet.

"What are boat toilets like?" Tod enquires.

"They're usually very cramped and smelly from the chemicals."

"What chemicals?"

"Formaldehyde, I think. It's really stinky. You can use it to preserve things, like animals."

"Why?" he asks.

"So they don't go—you know—all rotten."

Tod smiles at this. He watches the woman emerging from the loo with her now silent baby. "I want to see," he demands.

"See what?"

"The toilet."

"Tod, we didn't come to look at the toilet. Why don't you see which birds you can identify? Look, I think that's a pigeon."

He is still staring at the loo door, waiting for someone to go in so he can glimpse the wonders within. "I want to go," he announces.

"We can't go, Tod, the boat's only just turned round. We're stuck on here for at least another half hour."

"I need to pee," he insists.

I accompany him into the toilet where he nags me to demonstrate the pedal flusher several times and explain where the stuff goes and what happens when that tank thing is full up. Where does it go then? It's only when someone raps firmly on the door that Tod will remove himself from the toilet zone.

He fires questions about formaldehyde all the way back to Newton Meadows. I can't face going home yet, so we drive to the Coach and Horses, a pub with a beer garden and fenced-off play area to keep children away from their parents. The play area's gate is too hefty for small children to open.

Tod shuns the play area, and the bright orange, sinister-looking pellets on his Bob the Builder plate—whom he regards as the antichrist—which were advertised on the children's menu as chicken nuggets. He nudges the plate to the farthest edge of the table, as if fearing contamination from Bob in his yellow hard hat, and announces, "You're cross with Dad."

"What makes you think that?" A woman wearing a frightful wide-brimmed yellow hat, the kind that should be banned from areas in which small children are playing, gives me a sharp look.

"Why are you mad?" Tod asks.

"Everyone gets angry sometimes. It's normal."

He flicks a nugget off the table. It hits the stone flags with a *clack*. "It's not right," he mutters.

"It's just life, Tod. No one can be happy all the time."

"Why?" he asks.

The yellow-hatted woman glances at him pitifully. Who is she to be so judgmental? Her son, who's been crying for at least twenty minutes to be liberated from the play area, has mooched away to pluck crisp packets from the litterbin.

"Why what?"

Tod jabs at his lower teeth. "Why's it wobbly?"

I have blundered through sperm-meeting-egg scenarios and forgotten to tell him that his milk teeth will fall out. "It's wobbly," I say, pulling him on to my knee, "because you're growing up."

★ ★ ★

We must be back in Chetsley by three because Julia is holding a special event at the bookshop and needs me to help. Muriel Hope, a renowned children's author and illustrator, will read from her new book. By the time we arrive, the shop is already milling with customers, and Julia is darting from group to group, flushed a delicate pink from the effort of mingling.

Muriel is a long, skinny woman with a mischievous face, perfectly designed for spying through gaps in fences. We have forty copies of her new book, plus her range for younger children, *What's Inside a Snail?, Where Does the Sun Go at Night?* and the bestselling *What Do Babies Keep in Their Pockets?* Julia has set out juice for the children, wine for the adults, and pinned up posters depicting the covers of Muriel's books.

When no more customers can fit into the shop, Julia dispenses thank-you-for-comings and says, "Could the children please sit at the front, as Muriel Hope, my favorite children's author, will read from her delightful new book, *Alfie's Dream.*"

Muriel tucks speckled hair behind her ears—her coloring reminds me of Bandit, the humbug man's dog—and extracts rectangular-framed glasses from a crocodile case. She begins: "Alfie loved dreaming. He dreamt every night, and every day, when he wasn't even asleep. This is how Alfie's troubles began."

Tod sits cross-legged on the floor, inches from Muriel's pointed-toe boots. He seems to be enjoying this even more than the chemical toilet demonstration.

"Alfie's dreams made grown-ups cross. Whenever Alfie's mum told him to put his shoes on, or they would be late for school, Alfie would dream about being a bat. Imagine, he thought, having a furry mouse body and wings. Those wings were such a cool shape, Alfie thought."

Tod's eyes are fixed on Muriel's hands. She has long, elegant fingers, like tapered candles, and wears several twisted-silver rings.

"At school, Miss Woods noticed that Alfie was not doing his work. He was watching a bird hopping along the tops of the railings. I wish I could do that, Alfie thought."

I spot Joe, lurking at the back of the shop. I haven't seen him since that afternoon in his tree house, when nothing happened. Why is he here? It's all parents and children. I recognize most faces from the school gate. They are the women I greet with bright, hopeful smiles, willing them to ask Tod for tea. I can't understand why Joe would be interested in a children's author.

"Although Alfie was in trouble with his mum and his teacher, he didn't get into bother at weekends because that's when he was with his dad. Alfie's dad took him out at night, on bat hunts. His dad explained that bats have high-pitched squeals for voices. People can't hear them, Alfie's dad said. But Alfie was different. He could hear bat noises."

Muriel sets the book down, and a queue forms at the table where she is poised to sign copies. Harry shoves his way to the front, filches a Biro from the beehive-shaped pot at the till, and uses it to poke his rear end. "Itchy bum," he mutters angrily.

I wonder if this is another symptom of the wheat allergy.

Lucille is here, and gives me an I-need-to-talk look, but I'm too busy at the till to speak to her now. When the books have been sold and most of the customers have gone, I find Joe and Tod discussing Alfie and whether he might actually turn into a bat—not like Batman, but a real animal with a mouse body, that hangs upside down as it sleeps.

"My son never went for Batman," Joe says. "He preferred the Joker, the Riddler, Catwoman—the baddies. They were more exciting."

"I didn't know you had a son," I say, which comes out sounding like, *Why didn't you tell me you have a son?*

"He lives in Dorset, with his mother," Joe says.

Lucille plonks a hand on my shoulder and smiles richly at Joe. "You're the one with the garden," she says. There is wine on her breath as she guides me away from Joe and Tod and hisses, "The phone mystery's solved."

"Who was it?"

"Leo, who spends all his time in his room with that bloody astronomy book, only that's not what he does really."

"What does he do?"

"I found a stash of girlie mags wrapped up in his basket-ball kit at the bottom of his wardrobe. That's normal boy stuff, I can handle that. At the back of the mags are small ads for phonelines. I confronted him, knew he was lying when he insisted on washing up, drying *and* putting the dishes away. He's so sorry—thought it would be the same price as a local call. The ad didn't say that this woman, this Lisa-Ann, is in Chile."

"What are you going to do?"

"Thrash him?" She shrugs. "We worked out that, if we cancel his pocket money for twenty weeks, that should just about cover the calls." Lucille snorts. "No wonder he's so tired all the time."

As Joe and Lucille leave the shop, I hear her saying that it's great, how he's let his garden grow wild and doesn't give a stuff what anyone thinks.

Muriel Hope thanks Julia for attracting such a crowd.

"Before you go, would you mind looking at Ro's work?" Julia says. "She's a wonderful illustrator. I've told her she shouldn't be working here, but illustrating her own—"

"We're in a hurry," I say, snatching Tod's hand.

"No, we're not," Tod says. "You're not talking to Dad. You don't *want* to go home."

I wish now that Julia hadn't badgered me into bringing my drawings. Muriel's mouth has set firm, and she looks rather desperate around the eyebrows.

"Show her, Ro," Julia says brightly.

I pull out my folder from under the counter and hand Muriel the drawings.

Muriel flips through so quickly she couldn't possibly see anything, and thrusts them back into my hands. "Very good," she says, ramming her glasses case into her bag.

"They're meant to hang together, as a sort of story."

Tod is grinning at Muriel. "I've got a wobbly tooth," he announces, peeling back his lower gum to reveal the trembling incisor.

"That's lovely," Muriel says, "but I really have to dash."

If you want to know something, just ask. Marcus is in bed, trapped beneath the new duvet I bought to reward us for enduring the sanding. I am blocking the bedroom door, so he can't escape.

"Marcus," I say, "I need to talk to you."

He sits up and rests his chin on his hands. The walls look plum-colored in the streetlight that ekes into the room, but are really marshmallow pink. We haven't painted it yet. It's still Gordon and Betty's bedroom.

"Ro," he says, "please come here."

I sit on the corner of the bed and wait.

"It happened a long time ago."

"How long ago?"

"She was born just after Tod's first birthday."

I am incapable of performing basic mental arithmetic. Was she conceived when I was pregnant or after Tod's birth? Tod was one. Add nine months. No, *subtract* nine months. "What I need to know is, when did she—when did you—" I need to know when it happened, precisely when, but feel like I'm biting on foam, the kind that's inside the seats on buses. "You were having an affair," I say finally, "when Tod was a baby. It's gone on all these years."

"No, not all these years." Neither of us is shouting. We don't do that, we wouldn't want to upset Tod.

"You had someone else."

He rubs his face, making a papery sound. "I know we planned Tod, but who knows how it will really feel, being somebody's parent? And I met Babs—"

"So that's her name." It doesn't suggest Agent Provocateur underwear but large, faded knickers. My voice is steady, and I'm not even crying. I'm not doing anything, just perching on the bed's soft corner. We could be having our new-kitchen-or-paint-the-old-one debate.

"It just happened, Ro. I showed her a flat and—"

"It just *happened*. You were freaked out by having a baby, so you decided to make another."

"I didn't want her to have it."

"Why not?"

"It wasn't an affair, not a relationship. It was just a thing."

That word—*thing*—triggers something inside me. My inner toddler. "What kind of thing?" I yell at him.

"A little mistake," Marcus whispers.

"Was I supposed to find the photos? I have to say, Marcus, it was more challenging than your usual treasure hunts."

"You must think I'm really twisted to do something like that."

"I think you're worse than twisted."

I want to know where the flat was, and he tells me: two streets away from Tod's school. Not just Tod's school, Tod and *Sarah's* school. She started reception class four months before we left London. Tod might even have played with her. Did he know her? What does Marcus give Sarah for her birthdays? What kind of presents does he give Babs—underwear? A chrome bridge for the bath, or a hoe?

"That was just a joke," he says into his hands. Does he give them money? Yes, he gives them money when he sees them, at least once a week. He won't say how much, it's irrelevant.

Did he give Sarah that rabbit for her fourth birthday?

Yes.

Does he love her?

Yes, she's his daughter.

Does he love Tod?

He won't even answer that. I must be out of my mind to ask that question.

Does he love her, this Babs, with whom he had a *thing?*

"I feel nothing for her. We're just Sarah's parents."

Oh, is that all. The nearest throwable object is Tod's lighthouse snow dome, which he left on my bedside table, and which doesn't hit Marcus but the marshmallow wall behind him, bouncing back and skidding across the bedroom floor, its snow blizzarding madly. It doesn't even crack.

I feel a tug on my dressing gown sleeve.

"You woke me up," Tod whispers. He is naked and shivering.

Marcus looks up and says, "Put your pajamas on, Tod. Go back to bed."

Tod picks up the lighthouse snow dome. "Mum," he says, "please stop."

chapter 23

Tooth Fairy

Marcus has his usual hurried toast and coffee and attacks his nostrils with the nasal hair clipper. He looks very clean, very handsome. He has barely aged since we met. The only real difference is that small trough now in the space between his eyebrows. If you saw him, speed-walking to his Covent Garden office, you would stop him to ask directions without worrying that he would send you in the wrong direction, or turn out to be crazy.

I can hear Tod in his room, protesting, "It's not even *morning.*"

"Just wanted to say goodbye," Marcus says.

"Are you going to work?"

"Yes, of course."

It's the start of an ordinary day. I will have a quick bath before Tod is properly awake—can't face the superpower shower first thing—and boil two eggs. While Tod's having breakfast I'll pack his lunchbox and gym kit—jobs that mothers like Tina do the night before—and wet the back of his head, try to squash his disobedient hair. Then I'll jam my mouth shut to stop myself from nagging as he teases a shoe with his toe.

Everything will be normal. The only difference is, Marcus isn't coming back.

Tod waggles the trembling enamel the whole way home from school. He doesn't want the tooth anymore, he wants money. Hard cash. The tooth fairy loot will be dropped into the dolphin moneybox, along with the pound from the Gatwick lady. "I can't wait," he says, "for all that money."

At bedtime I read from *Mazes and Labyrinths,* tuck Tod in, take his spout cup and locate Dog on the bathroom floor. Then I pack his schoolbag for tomorrow and make his lunch. I trim each sandwich with scissors to neaten its edges. I lay out a clean school uniform, plus pants and inside-out socks, and even remember to feed the fish. I am *managing*.

"Is Dad back yet?" Tod calls down from his room.

"He's staying in London. You should be asleep, darling." I didn't say "tonight" so, technically, I haven't lied.

When he's finally asleep, I pull out my drawings from their folder and spread them all over the living room floor. They are all of the same boy. I'd try to draw different characters but every child would always turn out the same, even if I changed his hair color or turned him into a girl, which indicated that my lecturer was probably right in doubting that I would ever make it as an illustrator. This boy didn't have a gang. He just had lots of other boys who looked exactly like him. That became the idea of my story.

I turn on the computer in the room we've always referred to as the study, although no one's ever done any studying in here, and start typing. I had a name for the boy but can't remember what it was. I should write things down, like my sister does. Make lists, own clipboards. The only names I can think of are Sarah and Babs. If Marcus had gone to the right flat, gone to Cedric Street instead of Cecil Street, we'd never have met. I wouldn't have hunted for his damn Easter eggs. There wouldn't have been a tin in the cupboard, or a Tod.

I stab the off button and slap the keyboard for not helping me. Marcus's things are all over the house. He hasn't even taken his toothbrush. Most of his books are still packed in a box with the removal company's name—Smart Moves—stamped on the side. We've lived here for nearly a year and not even properly moved in.

My drawing things are in a dented cardboard box, beneath another box, containing the casserole dishes from Marcus's parents. Some of the inks have dried up but there's enough to have a play about. I drag the box into the living room and remember my old thing of drawing the boy carefully, then placing another sheet over the first, using the drawing as a guide, and making him freer.

I only notice that it's gone three a.m. when there are no more sheets in my pad.

Something smacks on to the bed, something heavy and shouting and out of control. There's a scream, I think it's my scream, and Tod, crying and flinging his arms around my neck. "What is it? Calm down, sweetheart—tell me what's happened."

Marcus was wrong, that night at the Poacher's, when he accused me of bringing everything back to Tod. I haven't considered him at all. I try to convince myself that I'm head-

ing for some Fabulous Mummy award by trimming his sandwiches with scissors.

"Tod," I say, "please tell me why you're crying."

He jabs at his gum. "The tooth fairy didn't come."

"Did it fall out? Take your finger away. Show me."

He's still making *ur-ur* noises as he stretches his lips.

"It's still there," I tell him, "it hasn't come out yet."

"In my dream it did," he rages.

Over breakfast I tell Tod that sometimes, the tooth fairy
sets a treasure hunt when a child is *about* to lose a tooth, as a
trial run for the main event. "So maybe you should start looking, in the smallest room we have that isn't the study."

He flings down his spoon, zooms into the bathroom and
emerges with the pound that the almost-lost tooth fairy had
cleverly concealed beneath the apple soap.

"Shall we go to Lexley after school," I suggest, "and spend
all this money?"

Retail therapy is, I feel, fair compensation for an absent dad.

"I could tell something was wrong, that day on the common," Natalie says. "What's happened, Ro?"

"There's someone else, or there was someone else. He says
it's all over."

"I'll come and stay for the weekend, leave the kids
with Hugh."

"No, please don't do that. I don't want any dramas
around Tod."

"I'm not dramas," she says, her voice cracking, "I'm your
bloody sister."

As far as I'm aware, this is as close as Natalie has ever come
to proper swearing.

Tod and I are driving back from Lexley where he prowled
around the toyshop, examining boxed puzzles. He made the

shop girl explain how bar codes work, and show him her bleeping gadget, before selecting a construction kit consisting of magnetic straight bits and silver balls. He has fashioned these into a bracelet. He wanted to spend only the nearly-gone tooth pound, the soapy coin, but not the Gatwick lady's pound.

We are passing the golf course road when Tod asks, "Is Dad on holiday?"

"Of course not. He wouldn't go on holiday without you."

He tweaks his bracelet. He knows that something is different, probably because I stumped up the extra nine quid required to buy the magnetic construction kit.

"Will he still be my dad?" Tod asks, gazing out of the passenger window.

"Yes, he'll always be your dad." I am finding it hard to see through the windscreen, and switch on the wipers and demister, but of course it's just my eyes. I grope for Tod's hand but he tugs it away. "You'll still see Dad," I explain. "It might be a while, until we talk and see what we're going to do." I glance at Tod, trying to figure out if what I've said is enough, like the seed–egg explanation, or has just confused him even more.

He runs the magnetic bracelet back and forth along his wrist and says, "What I like about this is, when you put the wrong bits together they push away, and when you get it right, they just stick."

The aching starts in the early hours. I can't remember if it's okay to take paracetamol when you're pregnant so I squirm in bed, trying to shrug off the pain.

By morning there are flecks of blood and I know what is happening. I walk Tod to school, and every few minutes that cramping comes again, and Tod tugs at my hand, saying,

"Mum, we're going to miss the bell. Miss Glass started giving late marks and if you're really late, you're marked absent."

On my way home I call the shop on my mobile, leaving a message: "Julia, Ro. Sick again. I'm so sorry." My plan is to drive to Lexley General—assuming they have an A&E department—and hope I'm not kept waiting for hours. No, that only happens in London. We're in the country now. I'll be dealt with quickly, efficiently, and be home in plenty of time to pick up Tod.

I sit on the loo, the pain constant now. When there's a lull I'll find our Lexley street map, and the hospital, and drive myself there. There isn't a lull, it just gets worse, and there's nothing I can do to stop it.

Through the living room window I can see Joe, throwing lengths of wood from his truck on to the drive. My plan is to pull on my coat, calmly cross the road, and ask if he could possibly drive me to Lexley.

What I do, as he holds me tight, is say, "Please, Joe, I need you to help me."

There's no heartbeat. "I'm very sorry," the doctor says. "I know this doesn't make it easier, but it's extremely common."

He has silvery hair and the soft, pink hands of a younger person. I feel blank inside. All I can do is study his immaculate nails and say, "Thank you."

"There's no reason," he adds, glancing at me, then at Joe, "why you shouldn't go on to have a healthy pregnancy in future."

Joe is holding my hand. Each wall is painted a different shade of cream, like various cheeses. There are flowers, still in their patterned cellophane wrapper, which have been jammed into a jug with its handle snapped off.

"I'm very sorry for both of you," the doctor says.

As I must stay in for a D&C, Joe will pick up Tod from school, then leave him with Lucille, and collect me later from hospital.

How easily things can be organized. I was pregnant, and now I'm not. Babs and Sarah are real, my baby doesn't exist. Everything seems eerily simple.

Monday morning. "Sure you want to wear that to school, honey?" I ask.

"Why shouldn't I?" Tod demands.

"The other children might make fun of you, wearing a bracelet."

"It's not a bracelet," Tod insists, "it's magnets."

"And you're going to wear your magnets all day."

"They'll be jealous."

"Who'll be jealous?"

"Joely, Adam and Claudia Turnpike."

"Who are they?"

"My friends, of course," Tod retorts.

I'm heading home, passing the bookshop, when Julia runs out and calls after me, "Here's a letter for you."

It's addressed to Ro (illustrator) c/o Coffee & Books. Inside the envelope is a postcard depicting Muriel Hope's Alfie in a bat outfit. She has written:

Dear Ro,
So sorry I had to rush off after the reading. I have two-year-old twins who refuse to settle to bed if I'm not there. Bad mum was late home! Just wanted to let you know that I loved your illustrations. They're so full of humor and life. Pls send a selection to my agent, Anto-

nia Devine, at Devine Associates, 42 Eden Terrace, Chiswick, London W12. Best of luck, you deserve it. Muriel Hope

"Good news?" Julia asks.

I thrust her the card. She reads it, grabs me, and we scream and jump up and down. It's not the kind of behavior you'd expect in Chetsley High Street.

"Marcus hasn't been here all week," Nettie blusters down the phone, "not since he popped in on Tuesday morning, took a client out—then nothing. It's ridiculous, Ro."

"Could he be at the new office?" I suggest.

"Don't you think I haven't been there, done my utmost to track him down? He could at least call. Has something happened?"

"I think Marcus should tell you."

She puffs on a cigarette. There's a popping noise, then a savage exhalation. Marcus would never tolerate smoking in the office.

"Maureen is worried senseless," Nettie adds.

I know this. Marcus's mother has also left several messages. "I think," I say carefully, "that Marcus needs some time on his own."

"Don't we all?" barks Nettie, as if all this is my fault, like I should know or care where he is.

Joe is spending next weekend in Dorset with Ed, his son. They are going camping. Joe wanted to wait until next summer, but Ed insisted, so Joe has bought a two-man tent. He is putting it up in the garden to make sure everything fits together.

"Let me help," Tod demands. It's blustery, kite-flying weather, not putting-up-tent weather.

"Okay," Joe says, "but you'll have to really help and listen to me, okay?"

Joe's outsized sweater is peppered with sawdust, his jeans streaked with green paint. As I watch them, battling with billowing nylon, I realize that I have been put off camping not only by my mother's foot being damaged by a gas canister, but by the fact that you have to practice erecting a tent. You don't have to *practice* lying in hotel beds or ordering room service.

"Look, Tod," Joe says, "let's fit the poles together, then see if we can feed them through these channels in the tent."

Remarkably, it does turn out to be tent-shaped. We leave Tod zipping and unzipping its entrance, and climb up to the tree house.

"Can I ask you," I say, "when you and Ed's mother broke up?"

"When Ed was a bit older than Tod."

"Was it awful?"

"No," Joe says, pushing unkempt hair from his face, "it wasn't awful. It was the only thing we could have done."

"That's what I'm trying to tell myself. That we're not damaging him, screwing him up." Tod dives headfirst out of the tent and lies facedown, flapping hands and feet, being Salmon Man.

"What about you?" Joe asks. "How are you feeling since—"

"There are so many reasons why I shouldn't have been having a baby. So really, it's a good thing it happened."

He looks at me. "You don't really think that."

"Of course I don't."

He strokes my hair, then puts an arm around my shoulders, like any friend would.

★ ★ ★

I spend each evening of the following week writing the story and producing more drawings to match the bits where it spirals off, as if writing itself, and I'm just putting words in the right order. Tod works steadily on the 3-D maze, which is now the size of a coffee table with sticky-out bits, like jetties, made from planks left over from Joe's tree house. Tod has made a WAY IN sign and attached it to the entrance on a Sellotape hill. We are both very busy, which prevents us from mentioning Marcus.

I have explained, "Me and Dad just can't live together anymore. We'll still see him, I'm just not sure when." Tod accepted this with a small nod, as if I had told him that his bike was in the cycle shop in Lexley, having its chain fixed. Later I found a crayoned self-portrait. It had angry black eyes and a downturned slash of a mouth.

At least the livestock nightmares have stopped, and he wolfs entire dinners without having to be nagged or bribed with a doughnut if he clears his plate. It could be a growth spurt—his school trousers now finish at his ankles and new shoes are an urgent requirement—or maybe it's due to the fact that some color has crept back into our meals.

It's just after midnight when I hear the siren. I switch off the PC, and run to Tod's window, which overlooks the street. The ambulance has pulled up at Joe's gate. Lucille, Carl and Adele are crouching around another person, who is half sitting, half lying on the pavement. Adele is wearing what look like pajamas, with a coat on top, and some kind of enormous footwear.

Two ambulance men pull out a stretcher and load the person onto it. Lucille wipes her face on her coat sleeve and climbs into the ambulance. Carl and Adele march across the road and bang on our door.

"So sorry to burst in on you like this," Carl says.

"That's okay, what's happened?"

"That tree house. It's coming down, if I have to do it with my bare hands. He shouldn't have been up there—but that's boys for you. Next thing he's fallen off, and his friends, his so-called friends—"

"Who fell off?" I ask, as they follow me into the house.

"Leo," Adele announces, with a dramatic shiver. Her eyes gleam excitedly. "His friends ran off and left him."

"Thank God he had his phone," Carl says. "I'd only just given it back to him. Confiscated it after that Chile business."

I offer Carl a drink, but he asks for Marcus instead. "We're going to go over, as soon as that weirdo shows up."

"Marcus isn't here."

"Where is he?" Carl has plonked himself on the sofa.

Adele, I realize, is wearing bunny slippers, their whiskers smattered with mud.

"He's in London," I tell Carl.

"Then I'll see him myself, first thing tomorrow."

"Joe's away," I tell him. "He's camping in Dorset with his son."

"You know him?" Carl snaps.

"Yes," I say, "I know Joe."

When they've gone, I switch the PC back on and try to write, but only garbage spurts out, which I delete. As I'm undressing, I notice that there's something in my trouser pocket, that has been through the wash. Sarah, her mother and the yellow birthday cake have survived a forty-degree spin cycle.

"Can I come in?" he asks.

"What are you doing here? You should have warned—"

"Dad!" Tod roars, haring downstairs and careering head-first into Marcus's stomach. "Dad, Dad," he pants, "Leo fell off the tree house and broke his leg. It's in a big plaster like a mummy's leg."

"Poor Leo," Marcus says, glancing at me. There are dark smudges under his eyes. He hasn't been clipping his nasal hairs.

"What do you want?" I whisper, when Tod has scampered to the living room to drag through the 3-D maze.

"I just wanted to see you."

We take Tod to the common, so he can show Marcus how amazingly fast he can ride his bike. This was Marcus's idea. He thinks that this way, we'll be able to talk. I rant on about school, and Tod's collection of "I'm a Good Helper" stickers, which he carefully sticks to his window frame.

"It was one little mistake," Marcus says.

"And he got five house points on Friday. Tod's house is in the lead now."

"I don't want to be away from you."

"Tod!" I shout. "Use your brakes, not your feet. You'll wreck your new trainers."

"I can't stay at Will's any longer. I'll need to get a flat. I don't want to do that, Ro."

"You think I care what you want to do?"

"Yes, we're having a baby," he hisses.

"I had a miscarriage, Marcus."

Tod pedals like crazy toward us, yelling that something terrible's happened. His magnetic bracelet has fallen off, by the stream, he thinks. We help him look for it and keep pouncing on scraps of foil wrapper, thinking they're silver balls. We finally spy it, still in one piece, glinting in the grass.

Tod slides it onto his wrist.

"I'm so sorry," Marcus says.

"Why don't you take Tod out somewhere? He'd love to spend some time with you."

"Let's do something together, the three of us."

He has forgotten that it will never be just the three of us.

1:25 a.m. I am trying to finish the story but have hit a dead end.

One little mistake. It was a mistake to take Tod to that puppet show in Lexley Town Hall last weekend. I thought he'd enjoy it, but it turned out to be way too babyish, about a flying panda. Tod leapt up, relieved, when the curtains closed and everyone clapped. He looked so disappointed when I explained that that was only the interval.

That's what I'd call a little mistake. It didn't matter; we sneaked out before it was over and discovered a jumble sale at the church. We bought a board game called Labyrinth. You use handles to tilt the wooden board, coaxing the ball to follow the right pathway.

Sarah isn't a little mistake. My baby wasn't a mistake. I wanted it to happen that night. It wasn't an accident.

A pregnant woman came into the bookshop today. Julia was creating an autumnal window display. She'd pulled out handicraft books—embroidery, quilting, appliqué—which our customers want to keep them occupied during the longer nights—and arranged fir cones and leaves to create a forest floor effect.

The customer's belly was round and tight as a pumpkin. The effort of carrying it had flushed her cheeks, and she sank heavily onto a chair.

Julia dumped an armful of twigs and said, "Like a coffee?"

"Fruit tea?" the woman asked, hopefully.

I went into the tiny back room to make it. As the water turned faintly purple I heard Julia say, "Not long to go now."

"Three weeks," the woman told her. "That's assuming she's not late."

"Oh, you know you're having a girl?"

"Yes, we found out. Wanted to get everything ready, have someone real to focus on. We've waited a long time for this baby."

I brought the woman her tea, but I couldn't look at her face.

There's a noise now, coming from outside. I'm not sure how long it's been going on, but the banging and crashing have wrecked any hope of finishing this story tonight.

I watch through the window. A pointed structure—the roof—hits the ground. Then the window is gone, and slowly—like a film of a tree house being built, but being played backward—the walls tumble down, and finally the wooden platform, until all that's left is an ordinary tree.

chapter 24

Kite Flying Made Easy

Suzie's children are engaged in a heated dispute over who gets to operate the remote control of a silver convertible car. Whoever manages to take possession of the joystick ensures that the car smacks into my ankles. Even Tod, who has no interest in vehicles, wants a turn.

Barney is four now and has shot-putter arms, but is still attached to his dummy and keeps pulling down his trousers to show me his new *Dexter's Laboratory* pants.

"Barney," Suzie says wearily, "no one's interested." This pregnancy isn't agreeing with her. She retches at the sight of an unwashed frying pan, and craves damp cellar smells, which are hard to come by in a second-floor flat. Peter brings home used dishcloths from the department store restaurant where he works as a porter.

Charts and rotas are pinned haphazardly around the

kitchen. There's a star chart for the efficient cleaning of teeth, and a stern-looking timetable entitled Who Gets to Sit Next to Dad. "You wouldn't believe the scenes we have over who sits next to Peter for tea," Suzie says. "I try to remember who sat next to him yesterday, and the day before that, but they're convinced I'm giving someone special treatment."

Peter emerges from the bedroom, having enjoyed a lie in, bringing with him an odor of duvet. It's twelve-thirty p.m. Suzie can't think what to make for lunch.

Barney's trousers and pants are off now, and he's twanging his thing and shouting, "Auntie Ro, I fell off the toilet and hurt my willy. Mum thought it had snapped."

"Let's go out," Suzie announces.

"Where are we going?" Barney asks, excitedly.

"You're not going anywhere. Auntie Ro and I are off for lunch. Goodbye."

"Aww," Barney moans, collapsing backward on the carpet.

"Wait!" Peter says. "What shall I give them to eat?"

"Dishcloths," she snaps.

"Yum yum," Tod sniggers, sending the car careering into Barney's naked backside.

In the café I tell her about Joe coming home to find the tree house no longer wedged firmly between the oak's branches, but shattered all over the garden. I tell her that Tod wrote What Joe Does on a fresh sheet of paper and drew a series of pictures, like comic-strip frames, of Joe fixing the tree house until it was just like before. He refused to believe that it could never be mended.

Suzie is spooning in rice pudding, her comfort food of choice. She clears the bowl and stomps up to the counter to ask for a refill, then returns. "And he's a friend of Marcus, this Carl guy?" she asks.

"Kind of."

"How *is* Gorgeous these days?"

I watch as she stirs the thick, gloopy pudding. It looks like something you'd slap on to a wall to create a textured plaster effect. "He's fine," I say.

She looks up at me. "Ro, has something happened?"

"Well, I assume he's fine. We've split up."

"God, why didn't you say?"

"He had an affair, around the time Tod was born…" I want to blurt out every detail—Sarah, the birthday cake, his overnight stays—but the café's too public, with its dazzling strip-lights, and the woman behind the counter doesn't look like she'd tolerate an emotional display. She prods the jacket potatoes in the oven and bangs the door shut.

We take the slow route home, through the park where we used to push Tod and Sam in their buggies, when I really thought Suzie knew everything. We stop at the pond, and I wonder if those ducks are still choking on Mum's fishy tarts, and I hear myself saying, "I had a miscarriage, Suzie. I keep thinking the baby knew what was happening to us, and didn't want to be born."

I can feel her firm bump as she hugs me—her fourth child, the one she's scared she won't be able to manage.

"Sweetheart," she says, "the baby didn't know anything."

Tod doesn't want to leave Suzie's. Peter allowed the children to pile up the sofa cushions and pillows from all of the beds, and make a den in which the four of them huddled together and feasted on fluoro-pink and -blue popcorn, which was, Tod reports, "much nicer than the boring stuff you make, Mum."

However, for practical reasons—space, sanity—Tod and I are spending his half-term break at Anna's. Her three-story town house, inherited from her parents, is far too big for one person.

"Love your bracelet, Tod," she says, kissing his head and pulling me into the house by a hand. "And your binoculars, too. You'll be able to see the canal from your room."

Anna has bought a narrowboat, which she has christened *Beatrice,* in honor of Beatrice Dalle, her heartthrob. She has promised to take us for a cruise, and Tod is delighted to learn that this will incorporate a stop-off at the King's Cross sanitary station to empty the chemical loo. We also plan to visit the British Museum and Parliament Hill, where Tod can fly the kite he has packed in his bag. This will be such a fun trip.

Anna shows Tod the room at the top of the house. On the sequined bedspread she has laid out children's books she picked up from junk shops. In these stories the mums wear aprons, the dads wear ties, and they are greeted by excited children when they come home from work. There is often a large, bounding dog—a red setter or collie—and everyone's always delighted to see one another.

"Where are you sleeping?" Tod asks me.

"In the little room downstairs."

"Can't you sleep here?"

"Do you mind?" I ask Anna. "I think he'd be happier with me."

"Of course," she says, "you do whatever feels best."

Tod unpacks slowly, carefully placing his clothes and kite on the double bed. He places Dog on the pillow, to guard *Mazes and Labyrinths,* and his pens, drawing books and dolphin moneybox on the dresser.

"How has he been?" Anna whispers on the landing.

"He's been okay. Actually, he's been more than okay."

"I'm *fine,*" Tod shouts from his holiday bedroom.

He doesn't want me to read to him tonight; he wants Anna to do it.

"I tried to skip a bit," she tells me later, "because I thought it was too grown up for him. He gave me such a telling off."

She pours me a drink and I'm relieved that it's not mescal but lukewarm white wine, which she forgot to put in the fridge.

"So, darling," she says, "is this really it?"

"Yes, this is it." I have never known her to have a relationship that progressed beyond a few, nervy dates. She told me once that she couldn't possibly live with another person; she's too selfish and set in her ways.

"How do you feel?" she asks.

"Starving. What do you have?"

"More wine," she says, laughing.

In the British Museum, Anna swoons over gilded Egyptian masks. Tod gazes at a fragment of filthy linen from a burial tomb. It is three thousand years old and reminds him, I suspect, of our bed linen at home. "Mum, it's one of those spikes," he yelps. In his loudest voice he tells Anna that it would have been poked up a dead person's nose to pull out the brain.

"Ugh," she says, "why did they do that?"

"The Egyptians thought that brains weren't important," Tod informs her. "The heart, that was the special bit."

A group of children are examining a dead man, called Ginger, who lies in an oval-shaped hollow with his knees pulled up to his chest. The sand in which he was buried sucked the water from his body, preserving him.

I worry that there's too much death here: bones, bandages, the ochre remains of what used to be skin. "Maybe we should have gone to the zoo," I whisper to Anna.

"No," Tod says, "this is great. Look—that's a mummified bull."

"Can't we look at the jewelry?" Anna says with a sigh.

It's taken us nearly an hour to find the right spot on Parliament Hill where Tod will agree to try to fly his kite. "It's too steep here," my kite master kept protesting, "and too close to those other people. We'll get tangled up." Now Tod is clutching the kite, ready for takeoff. Anna has the string. "We're so high," he announces, "I can see everything. Where's Dad's office?"

"Let's concentrate on the kite," Anna says.

"Can we go and see Dad?" he asks, stamping his foot impatiently.

On the sole occasion that Tod visited the premises of Skews Property Letting, he spun on Marcus's swivel chair, fell off and cracked his forehead on the edge of Nettie's desk, requiring a speedy trip to A&E at University College Hospital.

"Tod, are we going to fly this thing?" Anna shouts into the wind. "Hold it up high, higher…that's it—let it go, here's the string, now *run*."

Up, up, up it goes.

Anna has a plan. I will sell Gorby Cottage, move in with her until I find a place for me and Tod, buy decent shoes that at least make a *noise* when I walk, and run the Archives again. She might even pluck up the courage to sack Stanley, and let me choose my own assistant. Someone who doesn't flinch when the phone rings.

Tod will go back to his old school. It will be as if Chetsley never happened.

"So that's the plan," she says.

"It's a great idea, but we're not moving, Anna."

"Don't tell me," she says, "you actually like living out there in the sticks?"

"*I* do," announces Tod.

"So it's true," Mum says, "that you're in London, with no plans to see me?"

"Mum, I'm in a hurry."

"I'd have thought you'd want to talk to me. Natalie said that Marcus has moved out. I could have told you, the moment I met him. *A-ha,* I thought, here's someone who thinks he's so charming—"

"You liked him, Mum," I remind her.

I am tugging Tod along Frith Street by a clammy hand. He keeps pulling back, trying to peer into restaurant windows.

"Did I?" Mum says. "Well, I've never had the best taste in men. Look at your father."

"I'm sorry, Mum, but we'll have to talk another time. I'm meeting someone for lunch."

"Oh, who?"

"An agent. I've never met her before—"

"You're having lunch with someone you've never met, but can't see your own mother? Natalie wouldn't do this."

"Wouldn't do what, Mum?"

"Get herself into this terrible mess."

In a blond wood Soho café, Antonia Devine leans forward to examine Tod's wobbly tooth. "It's really loose," she says. "Looks like it'll fall out any minute. You should eat something hard—why don't we order the crudités?"

Antonia called me on my mobile, saying that she had left several messages on my answering machine at home. She had received the illustrations and story and wanted to meet me. I had expected frightening poshness, even minor aristocracy, but Antonia has a rowdy laugh and doesn't even seem to mind Tod being here.

"What I think we should do," she tells me, "is start by sending it off to an editor I know who likes this kind of style."

"What happens then?"

"If she likes it, you have an excellent publisher for your book. Of course, there are no guarantees."

"What does 'no guarantees' mean?" Tod asks.

"It means that no one knows what will happen," Antonia says.

We are upstairs on a double-decker bus. Here is the park, where I would push Tod's pram, looking for people to talk to. I'd be pleased when Tod had a doctor's appointment, and would babble to strangers in the waiting room until they buried their faces in ratty copies of *Woman's Own*.

Until I met Suzie, I hadn't figured out that what a new mother must do is install herself on a park bench. If she waits long enough, another mother with child, who frequents the same doctor's waiting room, will park herself a respectable distance away on the bench. The women will glance at each other and ask their babies' ages. It's a sizing-up process. That's how Suzie and I became friends.

Here is the playground with the helter-skelter Tod was always too scared to go on. This is where we get off the bus. "We're *going*," a dad announces, holding open the playground gate, as if that will encourage his son to walk through it. The boy has pouched up the front of his T-shirt in order to carry the maximum quantity of bark from the ground. The playground used to be tarmacked, but recent improvements include the bark, and the removal of the squeaking roundabout. "Don't you care," the dad shouts, "that Robert will be standing at school with no one to meet him? What will he do then?" The boy runs up the helter-skelter and sends down a shower of bark. "Robert will *cry*," his dad shouts up.

We follow the dad, who is hauling along the screaming boy by the cuff of his coat. Here is Laurel Road Primary, Tod's old school.

"Where are we going?" Tod asks.

"We're just going for a walk."

"Why?" he keeps asking. "Why are we at my old school? I want to go back to Anna's."

The mothers I knew, when our children were approaching school age, obsessed over league tables and extracurricular facilities. Some parents changed religion, or pretended to change, so their children could go to the school of their choice. Others lied about their addresses. We chose Laurel Road because it was close to Tod's child minder, who would look after him until I came home from work.

The bell sounds and children flood into the playground. Robert's dad made it in time, although the younger boy is still demanding to go back to the playground to gather more bark. Kids are kicking footballs, trading cards and pleading to go to each other's houses for more play.

I spot Jill, the head teacher at the main entrance. She has a pale, round face, like an uncooked pie. She nods at me, but looks confused, like she can't understand why I'm here. Hadn't we moved to the country where Tod wouldn't be bullied anymore?

Children are being taken home by mums and the occasional dad. The yard empties quickly. Pigeons peck at dropped crisps on the pavement. "Let's go now," Tod says, tugging my arm.

Jill is holding a small girl's hand and glancing around anxiously. The girl's chaotic hair is secured away from her serious forehead with a clasp. She is holding a soft toy and has dumped her lunchbox and schoolbag at her feet. All the other children have gone home.

From the direction of the park, a woman is running. She flies past me and grabs the girl's hand.

"I'm sorry," she's saying, "couldn't get out of the office on time. Stuck on a call. Shall we go to the park now, or do you want to get sweets from the shop?"

The girl gathers her belongings, but doesn't answer. She's freezing her mother out.

"We could rent a video," the woman says.

"I'm cold," Tod complains. "I want to go on Anna's boat to that toilet place."

"I told you, she can't get the engine started."

"I want to go *home*."

"Come on," I say, "let's go."

We follow the mother and daughter, who has dropped her toy. They're walking faster now. Tod has to trot to keep up.

"My legs hurt," he whines.

We're so close now that I can see that the girl's hair is matted at the back, as if she's just rolled out of bed. Her schoolbag is covered with peeling-off stickers.

"You could watch the rest of *Snow White*," the woman says.

"Okay," the girl says. "Did you remember chocolate spread?"

"I forgot. I'll get it tomorrow."

I could reach out and touch her, the girl who's forgiven her mother, despite the lateness and no chocolate spread. "Excuse me," I say.

The woman turns round. She has a soft, likable face. Milky gray eyes, pale lips. "Yes?" she says, smiling.

I hold out the soft toy—the rabbit. "I think your daughter dropped this."

chapter 25

Home

I don't know what the fish have been eating since we've been away—gravel, maybe, and hopefully not each other—but there appear to have been no casualties. Before we left for London I bought a chalky pyramid, called a Nutri-Block, which can keep fish fed for up to a week, but forgot to drop it into the tank.

In his bedroom Tod surveys his mummy pictures. "Do you think they're related to Ginger in that museum?" he asks.

"You never know. They could have been his mates." I'm glad that it's Ginger who has lodged himself in Tod's head, and not the mummified bull. I don't want the livestock nightmares rearing up again.

In Joe's garden, the tree house parts have been stacked against the garden wall. At least Carl can rest assured that the grass won't grow anymore, not until spring.

"Why did Carl break the tree house?" Tod asks from the window. Beneath it, where there was once a locked cupboard, are shelves for his special things.

"Carl was mad because Leo fell out of it and broke his leg."

"That wasn't Joe's fault. That was Leo's fault."

"It's not that simple, Tod."

"It's not *fair,*" he blusters.

On the new shelves Tod has placed his binoculars, moneybox and the lighthouse snow dome. He keeps prodding the loose tooth, craving hard cash. This is my fault for buying him the magnetic kit. He thinks that a pound can be exchanged for a gizmo worth ten times its value.

"Try to forget about your tooth," I tell him.

"I want it out. It's so *annoying.*"

"Let's do it quickly, then. We could tie a piece of cotton round it, and the other end to…"

"A car," Tod says. "A fast car, like Dad's."

"Good idea. Your tooth pings out, and it's on the end of the string, burning a groove in the road…"

"Or a plane," Tod chirps. "We tie a silver thread to my tooth, and the other end to the tail of a plane."

"And the tooth doesn't come out. You're carried away to…"

"Majorca!" Tod shouts, and we're laughing now.

Occasionally, when he's not refusing to put on his shoes or making puddles of pee on the bathroom floor, he makes me feel that everything else is just *stuff.*

Dear Ro,

It was lovely to meet you and to talk about your book. I have sent the manuscript, and copies of the illustrations, to the editor we discussed over lunch, and would hope to hear from her in the next month or so. I think the book's lovely. I wish you every success with *The Boy in the Maze.*

With very best wishes,

Antonia Devine

"You wrote a story?" Marcus says. "How?"

He is calling from Will's. I can hear Will's son Max—I assume it's Max—blasting the same note over and over on something like a tin whistle.

"I didn't really plan it. It just sort of happened."

There's a pause, and the tin whistle stops. "That's incredible," he says.

"No it's not. I just wanted something to take my mind off…"

"We need to talk, Ro."

"What about? What do you need to tell me? That we moved here to get away from Babs and Sarah? That you wanted us out of the way?"

A pause. *Just a little mistake, she's nothing to me.*

"Please, Ro," he says, his voice cracking.

I replace the receiver and walk steadily to the filing cabinet. His papers fly from their files: House & Car, Finances, Hobbies, everything muddled and falling around me like leaves.

It's not me, this sort of behavior. My inner toddler must have done it.

Tuesday teatime, and Tod and I are painting his bedroom. He wanted white. There were so many whites to choose from that I ended up shutting my eyes and buying the can where my finger landed. It turned out to be just white.

We have covered his bed, chest of drawers and most of the floor with clear polythene left by Sandy. Tod's drawings have been removed carefully from the walls and stashed in a drawer. We have a roller each.

"Don't want to help anymore," Tod reports, after a few weedy strokes.

He shuffles away to the window to observe the inhabitants of Chetsley through his binoculars. "Mum, it's Lucille," Tod reports.

"Are you busy?" she calls up.

"Painting," I tell her. "Okay if we come round tomorrow for Halloween?"

"Of course it's okay." Halloween is a major production at Lucille's house. I'd have thought that Adele would have outgrown the concept of fancy dress, but she's had her mother create an authentic Grim Reaper ensemble. She will wear a black cloak, and Tod's mask from his age-three-to-four skeleton outfit. God knows how she'll stretch it over her walloping head. For a scythe, she will carry the hoe Marcus bought for my birthday, to which Adele has already attached an impressive tinfoil-covered blade.

Tod flops down on to his bed. "Mum," he says, "why doesn't Anna have any children?"

"Maybe she hasn't met the right person."

"How does the sperm know it's going into the right person?"

"Well, it doesn't know. It can make mistakes." I climb on a chair to access the area where the wall meets the ceiling.

"What do people do then," he rants on, "if it's a mistake?"

"Look, Tod, this is your room. You wanted it white. Are you going to help me or what?"

"I said, what do—"

"Just *paint*."

Wednesday. Antonia Devine calls me at work. She says: "Ro? I have very good news. You have an offer from Bookworm. They want to publish *The Boy in the Maze*."

Sian is pouring coffee for the humbug man, who has taken to coming in and asking for books we can't find on the computer, no matter how many searches we run. I think he comes in here for company and just invents authors' names.

"They'd like to meet you," Antonia continues. "Shall we set up a meeting? When is your day off?"

"Friday," I tell her.

"Ro, are you still there? Isn't this fantastic?"

When I've put down the phone, I yell so loudly that the shoebox-head dog shoots out from under the table and howls.

A pleasing aspect of Halloween is that a parent can get away with cobbling together an outfit with virtually no talent in the needlecraft arena. I have everything to hand: moon-printed fabric, donated by Marcus's parents. I'll cut a square, fold over one edge and thread through something to gather the neck—the cord from Marcus's dressing gown will do nicely—and Tod will be the proud owner of one extremely spooky cape.

Tod doesn't want a cape. He wants to be a bat, not as in Batman, but as in Muriel Hope's book, *Alfie's Dream*. A *real* bat. "It can't be that difficult," he retorts.

Marcus has made one visit, carefully timed so I'd be at work, to collect essential possessions. But most of his things are still here: his octopush kit, nearly all of his clothes, the trashed filing system. In the hall I find his umbrella. If I pull the nylon from its spokes and cut it in half, we'll have two floppy bat wings. I'll attach these wings to garden canes to keep them rigid. In his black sweater, gray school trousers, wings and an old Batman mask—previously unworn, and too small, but we manage to jam it on—Tod is ready for takeoff.

The less pleasing aspect is that trick-or-treating requires a parent to accompany their young offspring as they bang on the doors of strangers, demanding money and sweets. In most of these strangers' windows are artfully carved pumpkins, with glowing mouths and eyes, not like our botched creation with one letterbox slit, because I cut the eyeholes too close together and the middle section caved in.

We stop at Lucille's, where there's an ocean of sweets and a pissed-off Grim Reaper who's not allowed out trick-or-treating because she's contracted a virus called slapped-face syndrome. I'm curious to see how red Adele's face really is, if it really looks slapped—but she's hunched on the sofa, wearing the skeleton mask and stabbing the carpet with the blunt end of my hoe. Carl looks up from the *Lexley Gazette.*

"Haven't seen Marcus for a while. Does he still want to be in the team? The quiz final's next week—tell him we need him." He turns back to the front page story: "Professor Tickles Charged with Drunk Driving."

"Tod," I say, "why don't you sing your Halloween song, the one you learned at school? You're meant to do something to earn your sweets."

He stands up, adjusts the right bat wing, opens his mouth and announces, "I've forgot it."

We leave Lucille's laden with confectionery and bang on Harry's door. No answer. He'll be out trick-or-treating in some spectacular creation, with a wheelbarrow to carry home all his sweets and cash. It has started to rain and we have run out of people to visit.

"Let's go home," I tell Tod. "I'm freezing and it's school tomorrow."

"No, let's go and see Joe."

"It's so late, Tod. I'm sure he won't have anything for you."

"Please, I want to."

"We're not staying long, okay?"

He charges up the path and hammers Joe's door with his fist.

"No one's in," I say quickly.

The door opens. "Ro, bat, do come in," Joe says.

It's the first time I've been in this house. Joe's paintings are propped against walls, with tools and planks lying against them, as if he doesn't think of them as anything special. There are overgrown plants bursting from pots, and books heaped up unsteadily on an old, gnarled table.

"Got any treats?" Tod demands.

"I'm glad you came," Joe says, "because I do have something for you. Tod, would you wait down here for a moment? I want to show Ro something first."

"Okay," Tod says warily.

"Come upstairs," Joe whispers.

"What for?"

"Please come up. Tod's fine here—aren't you, Tod? Look, there's charcoal and paper on the table. You can draw."

Tod pulls off the Batman mask and rolls a stick of charcoal between his palms. I follow Joe upstairs to a small room, a bedroom, which overlooks the garden. There is only an unmade single bed, and a lamp on a small circular table. He turns off the lamp.

We are the ghosts of Halloween
The spookiest spooks you've ever seen

Downstairs, Tod is singing the song that Miss Glass taught him at school.

Joe stands at the window and says, "Come here."

We sleep all day and we spook all night

So you'd better watch out, 'cause you're in for a fright. Whoo!

"What is it?" I ask.

"There's something I want you to see."

I stand beside him and peer through the window. Even with the outside light on, I can't see what he means. There is grass down there. Sixteen-inch grass, Carl reported, by the end of summer. "I know the tree house has gone," I say.

"Yes, but there's something else."

"You're building another one?"

"Look down," Joe says, "down at the grass."

And then I see it. Coiled pathways loop back on each other, swirling across the whole garden. Where the path starts, close to the house, is a white sign on which he has painted: START. I can't see where the end is, the goal. Maybe it doesn't have an end.

"Do you think Tod will like this?" Joe asks.

"Tod!" I yell. "Come up here." He clatters up, with blackened fingers from the charcoal, which adds to his battish look. "Look out of the window," I tell him.

He is quicker than I am, sees it immediately, and tears back downstairs and out into the garden where he charges into the maze.

A trio of rubber-faced ghouls pause at Joe's fence, wondering, perhaps, why a four-foot-high bat is running in circles and spirals. As they hurry away, I look over at our house, mine and Tod's house, with the varnished oval sign now gone. It's no longer Gorby Cottage. It's just plain Number Nine.

At the center of the maze, Tod is holding up something, some kind of prize he's found. It's only when we're out in the garden, and he runs toward us with his palm outstretched, that I can see his treasure.

Tod is holding his tooth.

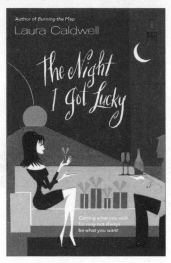